PRAISE FOR WILLIAM G. ...
AND HIS BRADY COYNE MYSTERY SERIES

"William G. Tapply belongs to the growing school of Massachusetts-based writers who threaten to make Boston the new capital of the whodunit. . . . Tapply's novel, crisp and clean and muscular, won't hurt Beantown's chances in the slightest."
—*San Diego Union*

"Coyne, with his wry, understated narration, is one of the most likable sleuths to appear on the crime scene."
—*The Washington Post Book World*

"Boston has probably supplanted Los Angeles as the home for hard-boiled writers . . . and William G. Tapply admirably represents the genre."
—*Time*

"This series is a model of superbly written thrillers with a nice touch of mellow humor."
—*St. Louis Post-Dispatch*

"William G. Tapply [is] a major-league mystery novelist. His stories are lean, his characters textured and convincing."
—*The Boston Globe*

Also by William G. Tapply

TIGHT LINES

A Brady Coyne Mystery

WILLIAM G. TAPPLY

A Dell Book

Published by
Dell Publishing
a division of
Bantam Doubleday Dell Publishing Group, Inc.
1540 Broadway
New York, New York 10036

If you purchased this book without a cover you should be aware that this book
is stolen property. It was reported as "unsold and destroyed" to the publisher
and neither the author nor the publisher has received any payment for this
"stripped book."

Copyright © 1992 by William G. Tapply

All rights reserved. No part of this book may be reproduced or transmitted in
any form or by any means, electronic or mechanical, including photocopy-
ing, recording, or by any information storage and retrieval system, without
the written permission of the Publisher, except where permitted by law. For
information address: Delacorte Press, New York, New York.

The trademark Dell® is registered in the U.S. Patent
and Trademark Office.

ISBN: 0-440-21410-6

Reprinted by arrangement with Delacorte Press

Printed in the United States of America

Published simultaneously in Canada

May 1993

10   9   8   7   6   5   4   3   2   1

OPM

For Melissa

"No one who, like me, conjures up the most evil of those half-tamed demons that inhabit the human breast, and seeks to wrestle with them, can expect to come through the struggle unscathed."

SIGMUND FREUD,
Complete Psychological Works

I EXITED OFF the eight-lane highway in Lexington so I could follow the cultural route to Concord, which traces the meandering trails where the Minutemen skulked on the morning of April 19, 1775, as they took potshots at the British lobsterbacks from behind stone walls and oak trees. On this particular September morning I saw only scattered farm stands with their mountains of pumpkins and hand-painted signs advertising late corn and early apples. In the boggy places beside the road the swamp maples reflected crimson in the water.

Autumn in New England. It always depresses me. Dressed in its desperately spectacular colors, fall is the time of death, not to mention the end of the trout season.

I steered past the old homes of the Alcotts and Hawthorne and Emerson, past the places where Melville holed up for a while and Thoreau mooched off his friends, and into the village of Concord. Cars with out-of-state plates lined the streets and retired folks from Iowa with cameras around their necks prowled the sidewalks. On this particular day, still summerlike, the men favored short-sleeved shirts and the women wore Bermuda shorts. Fall is high tourist season for historic New England places.

Up on the hill most of the old literary boys were resting

in the Sleepy Hollow Cemetery, another favorite tourist attraction.

I took a right at the Colonial Inn and followed Monument Street past the rude bridge—actually the third or fourth incarnation of the original bridge—that, as Emerson immortalized it in his poem, "arched the flood" on the April morning that marked Concord on the map before he and his fellow transcendentalists were even born.

I started to turn into the pea-stone driveway beside the old Ames house. I had to jam on my brakes as a shiny black Jaguar backed out past me. The driver either didn't see me or had chosen to ignore me. I glimpsed his profile through the window—bony hairless head, beak-shaped nose, aggressive chin. A man obviously so important and busy that other vehicles were supposed to move aside for him. His Jag had several antennae sticking out of it. Cellular phone, CB, probably a stock market ticker.

At the end of the driveway he shifted, spewed pea-stones at me, and glided away in the direction of Concord center. Then I pulled into the driveway. Susan Ames's Mercedes was parked there. Beside it crouched a pockmarked old yellow Volkswagen Beetle. I tucked my BMW behind the Mercedes, climbed onto the front porch, and banged the brass knocker.

She wore a short black skirt, black stockings, and a white blouse. She was slim and pretty and thirtyish, with chocolate-colored eyes and black hair cut short and parted at the side like a boy's. She wore neither jewelry nor makeup. She didn't need it.

"You," she said, eyeing my gray pinstripe and attaché case, "must be the lawyer."

"Bull's-eye. And you?"

"I'm sort of a secretary, maid, handyman, nurse, cook,

confidante. Your basic all-round Friday-type person. General factotum."

"Well, General, sir, I'm Brady Coyne." I held my hand out to her.

She grasped it and smiled. "Terri Fiori. Come on in. Susan is out on the terrace."

I followed her into the foyer and through the broad passageway that bisected the big old colonial. The Ames house had stood there since 1748. Minutemen had drunk rum and plotted in it with Colonel Buttrick and Captain Eben Ames in the cold winter of 1775. A few generations later the Concord writers used to gather there to argue transcendentalism and Unitarianism and drink more rum with Francis Ames, a very minor poet and failed philosopher himself. The big dwelling had nine fireplaces, six bedrooms, two parlors, a library, two studies, a birthing room, and a mud room to go along with the dining room, the kitchen, the two pantries, and the assorted bathrooms. The servants' quarters were upstairs in back.

Susan Ames lived there alone.

Terri Fiori paused inside the glass doors that overlooked the fieldstone terrace and beyond it the lawn that swept down to the river. Warm morning sunlight filtered through the big maples and willows. She put her hand on my arm. "She's been looking forward to seeing you."

"How is she doing?"

She shrugged. "She's dying."

"Yes, I know. But—"

"You'll see."

I hesitated.

She gave me a gentle push. "Go ahead," she said. She smiled. "Hard, huh?"

"I knew her when . . ."

"I know." She gave my arm a quick squeeze.

I took a deep breath and pushed open the glass door. Susan was sitting at the patio table. Her glasses were perched low on her long aristocratic nose. She was studying a stack of papers. She wore a bulky sweatshirt and baggy blue jeans. Her white hair hung in a long pigtail over her shoulder. Aside from a few more creases in her craggy face, she looked the same as ever to me.

"Susan," I said.

She raised her eyes over her glasses without lifting her head. "Well, Brady Coyne. Come sit."

I went over and sat across from her. She held her hand out to me and I took it. It felt weak and bony to me, but that could have been my imagination.

"You've been avoiding me," she said.

"Nonsense," I lied.

"You should be used to dealing with half-dead old people by now."

"You never get used to it."

She smiled. "That's what we love about you."

"Tell me how you are."

"Well, I survived my three-day sojourn at Mass General."

"Yes. You told me you'd been in when you called. And?"

She took off her glasses and put them on top of the papers in front of her. She pinched the bridge of her nose. "I have been given three choices," she said, gazing past my shoulder toward the river where the morning sun glinted off its surface. "There is an operation. There is chemotherapy. Either one, they tell me, will buy me maybe six months."

I waited for a moment, then said, "And the third choice?"

"Nothing. Do nothing. Wait." She turned her head and looked evenly at me. "I have selected number three."

"And that . . . ?"

"Could give me six months, too. Or maybe only one. Modern medicine, Brady, is about as precise a science as your law. I shall take my chances and let nature follow its inevitable course. I die regardless."

"Aw, Susan."

"Enough," she said. "This is a morbid subject. I forbid it. We must discuss the future."

"You mean your will."

"The disposition of my estate. Yes."

I shrugged. "It's a simple will, Susan. Everything goes to your daughter. Should she predecease you—"

"An unlikely instance, it would now seem," she said.

I nodded. "Well, if she should, then the house and its contents and all your liquid assets as well all go to the Concord Historic Places Commission. Is there something you'd like to change?"

"Mary Ellen is the problem."

I nodded. I had heard it from Susan many times before. Charles and Susan Ames's only heir had always been a problem. "We can still alter your will, you know," I said.

"Frankly," said Susan, "I'd like to. I don't mind her getting the money. But I'm worried that she'll turn the house into a communal shelter for foreign revolutionaries, or free-loving potheads, or motorcycle gangs. There are absolutely priceless things in here. You know that. First edition Emersons and Alcotts. Furniture that Eben Ames himself sat upon and slept in. Copleys and Singers and Doolittle engravings on the walls. I doubt if my wayward daughter has any conception of the significance of any of this."

"We'll bequeath it all directly to the commission, if you want. It'll take me about two days to redo it."

Susan hugged herself. She stared up into the sky for a

moment. Then she looked at me and shook her head. "No. It's not how Charles would have wanted it. I'm just a temporary trustee here, Brady. It came through his family, and now it's mine only because Charles happened to marry me and then died before I did. He left it to me with no strings attached. He trusted me to care for it as he would have, and when the time came, to pass it on to Mary Ellen. And she to her heirs, and so on."

"Except . . . ?"

"Except, as far as I know, Mary Ellen has no children." She smiled. "As far as I know, she has never married and never will. Of course, part of the problem is, I don't know what she's done. Anyway, it appears that, after two and a half centuries of Ameses, Mary Ellen will be the end of the Ames lineage. In which likelihood, Brady, I want her assurance that she will do the right thing."

"The right thing."

"Yes. Give the place to history. It's a simple request. Take care of it as long as she lives, and bequeath it to the commission when she dies. If she doesn't want it, she can turn it over to the commission directly. Willard Ellington," she added, "is very eager to acquire it."

"Who?"

"Willard Ellington. The current director of the commission. His family wanders back to the Minutemen in a murky sort of way. Willard owns a bank in town. He was, at first, quite gleeful to hear that my days were severely numbered. I believe that he would consider it a major feather in his cap if he negotiated the acquisition of the Ames House. Then when he realized that Mary Ellen would get the place, he sobered up fast. He was just here, in fact. You just missed him."

"Actually," I said, "he just missed me. He drives a Jaguar?"

"That was Willard. I asked him to wait for you to arrive, but he fancies himself a very important man who has no time to wait for anyone else. Everything must follow his schedule. That's Willard."

I nodded. "He was in a big hurry. He seemed distracted."

"We conferred, and I think it was the first time he realized that when I die he'll be at the whim of Mary Ellen, and that she's likely to outlive him, and that the commission will not get this place during his lifetime. He is unhappy that I will not bequeath the place directly to them. But," she said with a twirl of her hand, "I won't. Charles wouldn't have wanted it."

"Well," I said, "the hell with Willard Ellington. We'll do exactly what you want."

"Good."

I paused. "Which is what?"

"Pardon?"

"What exactly *is* it that you want, Susan?"

"Oh. Simple. I want to talk with Mary Ellen. Get her assurances."

"You need me for an interlocutor?"

She smiled. "I have never needed an interlocutor for anything, Brady Coyne."

"Then pardon my ignorance, Susan, but why don't you call her yourself?"

"Alas. I haven't spoken with her in eleven years. Since the day she inherited a significant amount of money from her father. You know what happened."

"Not really. It's a subject we haven't discussed. I believe you told me that she quit college and did some traveling."

Susan laughed. "Traveling. That is probably what I said. How euphemistic of me. She ran off with that—that Arab, is what she did. And for some reason that remains obscure to me even today, she has neither spoken nor written to me since."

"What happened, Susan?"

"I honestly don't know. She and Charles were very close. She and I less so. But we weren't enemies. We got along, if distantly. I suppose I wasn't the warmest or the most nurturing mother. I believed a young woman should learn independence and self-sufficiency, and I placed little emphasis on teaching her traditional female skills such as tatting and cooking. Which was probably just as well, since she was more interested in fast automobiles and fast company. But I loved her and tried to care for her. Charles doted on her. Her reaction when Charles died so suddenly was—it was strange."

"Strange?"

"She didn't react at all. She was at Tufts. She came home, of course, when she heard. She stayed here through all the morbid business of corpse viewing and church ceremonies and burial. Then she brought that Arab with her to the reading of the will. Afterwards she said good-bye to me and drove off, and I haven't seen her since. I still don't understand."

"Have you tried to contact her?"

"No. It's not up to me." She hesitated. "That sounds strange, I know. Understand, Brady. She was nineteen. A young woman, not a child. Her father's death clearly affected her. She and I, as I said, had never been close. So after the business of Charles's death, the fact that I didn't hear from her for a few weeks did not seem unusual. After a while I tried to call her at school. I learned she had not returned. So I tried to call the—Professor Rahmanan. I learned he had taken a leave. I inquired further and deduced that he and she had run off. Okay. Young women do such things. Mary Ellen was brought up to be independent. Weeks turned into months.

And months into a year, and then more years." Susan smiled softly and shrugged.

"And no word whatsoever?"

She shook her head. "None. You—you get used to it. That may not speak well for me, but it's true. I'd think of her now and then. But she was not a part of my life. Truthfully, it would be inaccurate to say I've missed her." She looked down at her hands. "Until this. Until now."

"You haven't tried to track her down?"

"No. She has made her choice. I always assumed one day I'd hear from her. I guess I still assume that. Except now . . ."

"And you don't know where she is?"

"I haven't the foggiest."

"So . . ."

"So I want you to find her, talk to her. Persuade her to communicate with me. Reassure her that I—I still love her."

I stared at the old woman. I thought I understood. It was simple, and it had little to do with wills and estates. She just wanted to hug her daughter before she died. She was too proud to say so directly.

I reached across the table and grasped one of her hands in both of mine. "Susan," I said gently, "I'll hire a private investigator to track her down. It shouldn't be difficult."

"You will do absolutely no such thing, Brady Coyne. The Ameses do not hire sleazy private investigators."

"They're not all sleazy."

"Of course they are. There are better ways."

"Meaning me."

"Of course."

I smiled and nodded. "Yes, I expected you had something like that in mind."

"You've always been kind to me," she said.

Susan was too genteel to mention the hefty retainer she paid me for what she called my kindness. "I'll see what I can do," I said. "But you've got to help me."

"I can't help much. I do know this. The Arab's name was—or still is, I imagine—Sherif Rahmanan. He was a professor of international relations at the Fletcher School at Tufts, a man in his forties then, with, I believe, an Arab wife and a clutch of Arab children, whom he eagerly abandoned for my amoral—and quite suddenly wealthy—daughter, who was a child of nineteen. He was very swarthy and spoke with an accent. Mary Ellen seemed quite proud of him. She tugged him about on her arm like a trophy. I was convinced at the time that this was some attempt to embarrass me, or hurt me, though for the life of me I still can't understand why. Nineteen! She'll be thirty in two months. That's one third of her life that I have missed. I wonder what she's like now." She shrugged. "Anyway, that's all I know."

I took my notebook from my jacket pocket and wrote "Sherif Rahmanan, Fletcher School" into it. "Do you have a photo of Mary Ellen?" I asked.

"Her high school graduation picture is the most recent. It's twelve years old. Will it help?"

"Maybe."

"Sit tight. I'll get it."

She got up and went into the house. I leaned back and gazed over the backyard. Yellow warblers flitted among the shrubbery that bordered the sweeping lawn. From the river beyond I could hear ducks quacking at each other. I closed my eyes and lifted my face to the warm morning sun.

"Are we catnapping?" she said.

I opened my eyes. She was back in her seat across from me. Beside my arm sat a mug of coffee. She was holding one for herself against her chest, warming both of her hands with it. "No," I said. "We are savoring the sunshine. Winter's coming."

"Don't I know it." She smiled and handed me a framed photograph. "Mary Ellen Ames as she looked her senior year at Concord Academy."

The teenaged Mary Ellen Ames had a long thin face with prominent cheekbones, a delicately pointed chin, and Susan's narrow aristocratic nose and silvery eyes. In the picture Mary Ellen was not smiling. She was quite beautiful. She had the kind of face that would continue to be beautiful throughout her life. "A lovely young lady," I said.

"She was. Oh, she was wild and unpredictable and difficult. Headstrong and brilliant. But, yes. She was lovely in many ways. Until . . ."

"Yes." I touched the picture. "May I keep it?"

"Of course. If it will help."

"Everything will help." I slid the photograph from its frame and put it into my attaché case. Then I lit a cigarette and sipped my coffee.

"I can't think of anything else," she said.

"Call me if you do."

"I will." She stood up. "Come see my flower beds."

She held her hand out to me. I took it and rose. She led me down the two wide stone steps from the patio onto the lawn. The grass was long and soft and damp and impossibly green underfoot. We walked hand in hand along the edges of the mulched gardens. "I've planted lots of bulbs," Susan said. "Daffs and croci and snowdrops and narcissi and tulips. Tell me why."

I turned to her. "Huh?"

"Tell me why I've done this. They won't bloom until spring."

"Oh." Susan expected to be dead by then. "You can give me a tour when they've come up," I said to her.

"Don't try to bullshit me, Brady Coyne."

"I try not to bullshit anybody, Susan."

"Try harder."

"Yes, ma'am."

We finished our tour of the backyard and returned to the house. Terri Fiori was seated at the kitchen table with a stack of papers in front of her. I poked my head in and said, "Take care, General."

She looked up and winked at me.

Susan led me to the front door. "I don't know what I'd do without her," she said.

"She seems very competent."

Susan jabbed my side with her elbow. "Competent? You are an incorrigible bullshitter, Brady Coyne. Terri's beautiful, is what she is."

I shrugged. "I hadn't really noticed."

Susan chuckled.

I opened the door, then turned and hugged her and kissed her wrinkled cheek. "Be well, Susan. We'll keep in touch."

"Can you do it?" she said. "Can you find her?"

"I don't know," I said. "I'll try."

I STOPPED at the Walden Sandwich Shop in West Concord for Italian subs for me and Julie. I thought of dropping in on Doc Adams at his Concord office. It was likely that Doc would be performing surgery at Emerson Hospital, but maybe his unbearably delicious assistant Susan Petri would be in, and I could ogle her.

Somehow, my morning with Susan Ames had deflated my enthusiasm for that. Even Susan Petri. A temporary condition, I trusted.

So I took the back roads through Concord and Sudbury and Lincoln, out past the farm stand at Nine Acre Corner where I bought a pumpkin for Julie's daughter, past all the harvested corn fields where murders of crows and gaggles of Canada geese gluttonized, past the Sudbury River, past Walden Pond, and finally back onto the highway. Autumn was everywhere, the annual and inevitable maturing that presaged the death of the earth, and it reminded me of the cycle of all things. Turn, turn, turn. Susan's impending death found its place, as, one day, would my own.

I recalled the way Terri Fiori had smiled and winked at me. It made me feel better.

I got back to my office in Copley Square a little after noontime. Julie was on the phone. I plunked the pumpkin down on top of her desk, gave her a sniff of the bag with the subs in it, and went into my office. I thumbed through my telephone directories. No listing for Mary Ellen Ames anywhere.

A few minutes later Julie joined me.

"Hey, thanks for the pumpkin," she said.

"It's for Megan, not you."

"We'll carve a jack-o'-lantern and name it Brady."

"I'd be flattered."

"Let's eat," she said.

We spread waxed paper over the top of my desk and dug into the thick sandwiches. We drank Pepsi from cans and chomped on giant dill pickles and barbecued potato chips. I told her about my morning with Susan Ames.

"Boy," she mumbled around a large mouthful. "That sucks."

"Death generally does," I said.

"About her daughter and her, I mean."

Megan, Julie's daughter, was five. I knew what she was thinking. I have two boys of my own.

"So how do you plan to find Mary Ellen?" she said.

I reached over with a napkin and wiped a dab of olive oil off her chin. "I guess I'll start with this Rahmanan and see where it leads me."

She nodded. "And when you find her?"

"I'll tell her her mother wants to set things right before she dies."

"And if she refuses?"

I shrugged. "That's between Susan and her."

"What can I do?"

"Just keep the world at bay for a while so I can make some calls."

We swept the detritus from our lunch into the wastebasket and Julie went back to her desk. I looked up the number for the Fletcher School and pecked it out. I didn't know if Professor Sherif Rahmanan still taught there, but it was the logical place to start.

When the woman answered the phone, I asked for him.

"I'll ring his office," she said.

So he was still there.

Another woman answered the phone. Again I asked for Professor Rahmanan.

"He has no classes today," she said. "May I take a message?"

"Is he home?"

"I have no idea where he is, sir."

"Thank you. I'll try again. No message."

The big Boston directory listed a Rahmanan, Sherif at a Bailey Street address in Medford. I tried the number. After a couple of rings a woman picked up the phone and said, "Hello?" Even from just those two syllables, the thick accent was obvious.

"Professor Rahmanan, please."

"And who is this?"

"My name is Coyne. I'm an attorney."

"One moment, please."

A minute later a man's voice, also accented, but cultured and precise, said, "How may I help you?"

"My name is Brady Coyne. I'm Susan Ames's lawyer, and I was hoping—"

I stopped. He had hung up.

I waited the length of time it took me to smoke a Winston, then rang the Rahmanan number again. This time the man answered.

"Now look," I said quickly. "You are going to talk to me. One way or the other. Do not hang up on me."

"Please. Just leave me alone."

"No."

"What do you want?" he said softly.

"I don't want to embarrass you. I need information. About Mary Ellen Ames."

"I cannot talk. I cannot help you."

"Listen, Professor," I said. "I will give you one hour to call me. If I don't hear from you, I will get into my car and come to your house. Surely I will find somebody there who can help me."

There was a long hesitation. I expected him to hang up again. Finally he said, "Give me your number."

I gave it to him.

"I will get back to you."

I fooled around with some paperwork Julie had left for me. Three quarters of an hour later my console buzzed. I picked up my phone and Julie said, "You got your man, Dick Tracy. Professor Rahmanan on line two."

"I think it was Sergeant Preston of the Yukon who said that."

"No. He always said, 'King, this case is closed.' "

"Elliot Ness, then," I said.

"Oh, boy," muttered Julie.

I pressed the blinking button and said, "Professor."

"Please," he said. "Quickly. What is it that you want?"

"I want to talk to Mary Ellen Ames. That's all. I have no interest in delving into your past. Do you know where she is?"

"No."

"Oh, come on. You and she—"

"Please, sir. Just leave me alone. I cannot help you. I have returned your call, as you insisted. Now I have answered your question."

"I have some other questions."

"This is awkward. I cannot talk."

"Meet me, then."

"I cannot do that."

"One way or the other, Professor, we will talk."

He hesitated a long moment. "Where?"

"Do you know Hung Moon's? It's in Somerville. Must be near you."

"Yes. All right. I know it."

"How's eight?"

"Tonight?"

"Yes."

"Eight is not good. The evening is not good for me." He paused. "I will be there at five. I can give you an hour."

"Fine. Five."

"How will I recognize you, Mr. Coyne?"

"I'll be wearing a lawyer's costume, complete with attaché case. You?"

"I have a beard, sir. I look like an Arab."

HUNG MOON'S is on Highland Avenue in West Somerville, just over the line from Cambridge. It was a favorite spot of Les Katz, a private detective friend of mine. Hung Moon's, Les always said, had the best monosodium glutamate in Boston. Les liked the Cambodian waitresses, who shuffled around in their soft sandals and tightly wrapped saronglike dresses and, according to Les, offered services beyond the delivery of food and drink. The last time I was at Hung Moon's was the last time I saw Les Katz alive. That was a couple of years earlier.

I arrived a few minutes before five. The large dining room was empty. I smiled at the hostess and ducked into the bar to the left of the foyer. Two beautiful Asian women wearing business suits were seated there drinking white wine. The bartender was a young Asian man with a smooth face and a wispy Ho Chi Minh beard and a classically inscrutable expression.

I climbed up on a barstool at the end opposite the two women. The bartender came over and emptied the ashtray in front of me. "Sir?" he said.

"Jack Daniel's. Rocks."

He nodded. In a minute he slid my drink in front of me. I lit a cigarette and took a sip of the drink and Sherif

Rahmanan appeared in the doorway. He looked at me and frowned. I reached down beside me and held up my attaché case. Rahmanan came over and sat beside me.

He was wearing chino pants and a green crewneck sweater. He had a dark beard, liberally flecked with white. The fringe of hair that half-circled his head was mostly white. I guessed he was close to sixty years old. When Mary Ellen was nineteen, this man would have been approaching fifty.

I held my hand out to him. "Professor. Thank you for coming."

He hesitated, then took my hand briefly. He didn't bother to grip it or shake it. "You threatened me," he said. "I had to come."

"You know what I want," I said.

"And I already told you. I cannot help you."

The bartender presented himself in front of Rahmanan. He asked for a glass of soda water.

"You know Mary Ellen," I said. "I need to talk to her."

"I do not know her any longer. I once did. It was many years ago. It is over. I am deeply ashamed."

The bartender placed a glass in front of Rahmanan, who nodded absently and did not pick it up. "Look, sir," he said to me. "My wife is, how do you say it, Americanized. Women from my country traditionally do not question the behavior of their husbands. Husbands do as they please. Women are taught to accept and serve. It is our culture. It is my culture. My wife, she is not a traditional woman. She does not think that way. I have learned that I no longer think that way, either. According to my culture, I should feel no guilt, no shame. But I felt deep shame, vast guilt. I begged her forgiveness, and she reluctantly granted it to me. We have not been the same since then. I will not subject her to any of that again."

"I don't want to screw up your marriage. I just want to talk to Mary Ellen."

He paused for a long time. "This has nothing to do with me?"

"Nothing."

"You mentioned her mother."

"She is dying. She wants to reconcile with her daughter."

"She has forgiven her, then? And me?"

"I don't think forgiveness is the issue. Susan Ames couldn't care less about you."

"I must trust you on this."

"You can."

There was another hesitation. "Very well, sir. I will trust you." He took a deep breath and let it out slowly. "I have not spoken to or seen Mary Ellen in many years. Our—our relationship—it lasted only a few months. Directly after her father died. Then she tired of me. It was easy for her, difficult for me. I had left my wife. I had three children at home then. I did not care. When Mary Ellen abandoned me, I returned to my family. It was—painful. I continued to love Mary Ellen. I tried to see her. I kept track of her, called her, watched her, followed her. She would have nothing to do with me. She threatened me."

"Threatened?"

"She threatened to have me taken to court. For harassing her. It didn't matter. Her threats only served to intensify my obsession." He had been talking in a monotone, staring straight ahead. Now he swiveled on his stool and faced me. "I behaved without pride, Mr. Coyne. She was very young, very beautiful, very American. I could not believe that this young woman could be attracted to me. I was teaching an introductory international relations course at Tufts, a large lecture class, and one day this young woman came to my office, and—"

I waved my hand quickly. "Spare me," I said. "I don't care about this."

He blinked at me, then nodded. "Of course," he said. "In any case, when—when her attraction died, I could not bear it. You see, my wife and I—our marriage was arranged by our parents. I had never known love. Having never known it, I did not miss it. But when I had it, after Mary Ellen Ames seduced me, and then I lost her love, I was very depressed. I did not know how to behave. It took me many years, sir."

"She seduced you, huh?"

"I see that you do not believe me." He shrugged. "It does not matter. That is how it was."

I sipped my drink. "You're right," I said. "It doesn't matter."

"I behaved badly," he said.

I shrugged.

"I left long messages on her answering machine. I sat in my automobile in front of her building, waiting to see her come and go. I watched the place where she worked. I did this for several years after she left me."

"Where did she live?"

"She was living in Cambridge."

"Was?"

"As I told you, it has been many years now. She moved. I could not find her again. It was a relief. After a while I stopped trying."

"You have neither seen nor spoken with her recently, then?"

"No. Many years."

"How many?"

He scratched at his beard. "Seven or eight."

"And you don't know where she's living?"

"No, sir. The last time I tried to reach her, she had moved, no forwarding address, no phone number listed."

"What was she doing, the last time you were in touch with her?"

He chuckled softly. "She was a salesperson in a bookstore."

"Why is that funny?"

"Because Mary Ellen has great wealth. She has no need to work."

"Where is the store?"

"On Massachusetts Avenue between Harvard and Central Square. It specializes in literature of the counterculture. It is called Head Start Books. She no longer works there." He shrugged.

"What about friends? Do you know any of her friends?"

He shook his head. "No. I never knew her friends."

"And since she moved . . . ?"

"I have not seen her. Seven or eight years. I have returned to my family. Mary Ellen Ames is no longer a part of my life."

"There must be something else," I said.

"No, sir. That is all. I have told you everything. I hope you will leave us alone now. I can help you no more."

"I may need to get back to you."

"Sir," he said, "if you must do that, please call me at the school. I promise you I will return your call. Do not call my home."

"Fair enough," I said.

"Now I must leave," he said.

And leave he did, without shaking my hand. I watched

him go, a small, dark, slumped figure. From behind, Professor
Sherif Rahmanan was a hunched old man.

I turned back to the bar and picked up my drink. The
professor had not touched his glass of soda water.

4

WHEN I GOT to my office the next morning I rechecked the Boston telephone book for Ames, Mary Ellen, and after that I pored through the various suburban directories. She was listed in none of them, which could have meant several things. She might have married and been using another name. She might not have been living in the Boston area, married or not. Or she might have an unlisted phone or have taken a new number since my directories were published.

I dialed 555-1212.

"What city, please?"

"Cambridge, Boston, I'm not sure," I said. "Last name Ames, A-m-e-s. First name Mary Ellen."

"Do you have an address?"

"No."

"Just a moment." A moment. "I have an Ames, M. E. It's an unpublished number."

"That's probably her. What was the address?"

"I can't tell you, sir."

"Sure. Okay. Thanks."

I hung up. Easier than I had expected. It was a simple job for Charlie McDevitt, my old Yale Law School chum and currently a prosecutor for the United States Department of

Justice, Boston office. Charlie knew how to wheedle unlisted phone numbers from NYNEX. I dialed him at his place at Government Center on the other side of town.

Shirley answered. "Mr. McDevitt's office."

"Come away with me," I said. "Just you and I on a tropic isle. We'll eat papayas by day and make love by moonlight."

She laughed. "Ah, and it's you, Mr. Coyne." Charlie's secretary is a widow with seven grown and fecund children, a grandmother many times over, plump and white haired. She resembles remarkably the famous portrait of George Washington that hangs in every third-grade classroom in the country.

"How are you, sweetheart?"

"I am wonderful, Mr. Coyne. How are you?"

"I am well, dear. The grandbabies?"

"Well, Ronnie's wife is waiting on twins."

"And that will make—?"

"Nineteen, God love 'em all."

"Well, congratulations," I said. "Is Simon Legree in?"

"He told me to say no. But for you, Mr. Coyne, he is in. Sit tight."

A minute later Charlie came onto the line. "Let's see," he said. "Today's Wednesday. Not today. And not tomorrow or the next day. Maybe Saturday."

"I wasn't thinking of fishing," I said. "But Saturday sounds good."

"The Farmington?"

"I'll pick you up at seven."

"You got it." He hesitated. "That wasn't why you called?"

"I can't account for my subconscious, God knows. But what I thought I had in mind was more mundane."

"A favor, right?"

"Yep."

He heaved a big phony sigh. "What this time?"

"An address and phone number."

"You try the phone book?"

"Well, shit, Charlie."

"Sorry. Let's have it."

"Mary Ellen Ames. That's A-m-e-s. Somewhere in the 617 area code. She has an unlisted telephone, so I know she's there."

"This'll cost you, pal."

"I'll buy you a ham and cheese sandwich Saturday. That's it. This is a piece of cake for you."

"I'm gonna hold out for dinner on the way home at that Mexican place in West Hartford."

"You're a tough guy."

"Damn right. I'll get back to you."

"When?"

"You in a hurry?"

"Yes. I've got a client who's dying."

"Give me an hour."

He actually called me back in twenty minutes. Mary Ellen Ames had a Beacon Street address, a low number that meant an expensive town house overlooking the Common. I dialed the phone number Charlie gave me.

It rang three times. Then a machine answered the phone. "This is Mary Ellen," came a breathless voice. "I'm not here now, or maybe I just can't come to the phone or something. But if you'll leave me some kind of intriguing message, I'll call you back. Wait for the old beep. Ready? Here it comes."

The old beep was a long one. It suggested that her tape was full of messages. When it finally ended, I said, "This is Brady Coyne calling. I'm your mother's attorney. It's very important that we talk. Please call me as soon as you can." I left both my office and my home number. I hoped my message was sufficiently intriguing.

I spent the rest of the morning doing the essentially sad things that keep lawyers in business—working out problems for people who don't trust each other enough to work them out themselves, preparing them for the inevitable tragedies that befall us all sooner or later, protecting them against an untrustworthy world, negotiating bureaucracies for them, interceding with the state on their behalf.

An honest and honorable world wouldn't need lawyers.

Susan Ames, I kept thinking, didn't need a lawyer. But she needed a friend. I'd rather be a good friend than a good lawyer, anyway. I hoped I could persuade Mary Ellen, when I found her, to be a good daughter.

I wondered about Susan's relationship with Terri Fiori. I guessed that Susan regarded her more as a daughter than a general factotum.

I remembered how Terri had winked at me. Susan had said she was beautiful, and I agreed. I'm a sucker for olive skin that needs no makeup and black hair and big brown eyes.

I lit a cigarette and dialed Susan's number in Concord. Terri answered.

"General," I said. "It's Brady Coyne."

"Oh. Hi, Mr. Coyne."

"You better call me Brady."

"Why?"

"Because I'm about to ask you out to dinner."

She hesitated. She hesitated too long.

"Look," I said. "I'm sorry. You weren't wearing a ring . . ."

"I'm not married."

"Yeah. A guy, though, huh?"

"No guy."

"Well, then, how about Friday night?"

Another hesitation. Then, "I don't think so, Brady. But thank you."

"Well, I'm sorry."

"Don't be sorry. It's flattering." A pause. "Did you want to speak to Susan?"

"No," I said. "I called to talk to you."

"Oh. Well, I hope you understand."

"I don't. But it's okay."

I hung up, stubbed out my cigarette, and tried to get back to my desk work. My mind kept wandering. I hate getting shot down.

Around noon Julie buzzed me. "There's someone here to see you," she said.

"Send him on in."

"You better come out," she said.

"Whatever you say, boss."

I got up and went out to the reception area. He was sitting on the corner of Julie's desk. In spite of his hair, which was a little longer than I remembered it, and in spite of the little gold earring that sparkled in his left earlobe, which hadn't been there the last time I saw him, I recognized him instantly.

"Hey, Pop," he said.

I went over to him. He hopped off the desk. We shook hands, hesitated, then hugged each other. "How are you, son?" I said.

"Great," said Billy. "Awesome."

I stood back and looked at him. My older son stood about six-two. A solid one-ninety. A handsome kid. No. A man. Twenty years old, and a man. About the age Mary Ellen Ames had been the last time Susan saw her. It gave me a pang when I made that connection.

"Want some linguini?" I said to him.

He grinned. God, I thought, he must devastate the girls at UMass. "That's what I'm here for. Marie's linguini with clam sauce."

Julie was smiling at us. Julie's big on family. So am I, actually, even though mine has been fractured for ten years. She waved her hand at us. "Go. Everything's under control here."

We walked to Marie's at Kenmore Square. Billy, who was brought up properly, mostly by Gloria, knew enough to inquire about my fishing adventures. I asked how his classes were going. We both gave upbeat answers.

I didn't bother observing that he was in Boston rather than Amherst, where the university is located, at noontime on a Wednesday.

He explained between the salad and the pasta. "I'm trying to get an internship at the Aquarium," he told me. "Got an interview at two. I'm really into marine biology."

"I thought you were majoring in government."

"Shit, no careers there. I switched."

"Well," I said, "marine biology is good."

He grinned. "You never told me what to do. You never gave me advice except when I asked. I appreciate that."

"It's not that I haven't had to bite my tongue," I said.

"I know that. I've seen the blood dribbling off your chin plenty of times."

We chatted about the perennial plight of the Red Sox bullpen, the price of gasoline, Billy's girlfriends. When the coffee arrived, my son leaned across the table and said to me, "Mom was up to school on Sunday."

"Nice," I said. "How is she?"

"She had a guy with her."

I shrugged. "Nice guy?"

He rolled his eyes. "Oh, yeah. Nice as pie." He grinned. "A lawyer, actually."

"Couldn't have been a nice guy, a lawyer."

"Well, there are exceptions." He frowned. "Dad, this guy, he's like closer to my age than Mom's, honest to God."

"Your mother's a young-looking woman. Don't blame him. Good for her."

Billy stared at me for a minute, then shrugged. "She never did that before."

"Did what?"

"Brought a guy with her."

"She's serious, then."

"She told me she was gonna marry him. This Richard."

"People do things like that."

He nodded. "Yeah, I guess. Funny. When you and Mom split, I always figured it was temporary. It was like you belonged together, and the fact that you didn't live together and had gone to court and everything didn't really change anything. I guess I still think that way. You know? I mean, you two are my parents. To me, you're a pair. It was weird, seeing her and Richard walking around the campus holding hands."

I smiled. "I can understand that." I understood his feelings perfectly, in fact. Picturing it in my mind, it felt weird to me, too.

We finished up and strolled back to Copley Square. We stopped outside my office. "I'm gonna hop a cab over to the Aquarium," said Billy.

I clapped him on the shoulder. "Good luck with the interview."

"Thanks. I can use it."

"One question?" I said.

"Sure."

"Um, what's with the earring?"

He grinned. "That's what Mom said. Only difference, it was the very first thing she said. Before she even kissed me. She goes, 'My God, William. There's something sticking in your ear.' "

"How did you answer her?"

"I told her it happened when I was drunk."

"Ah," I said. "So that explains it."

"Anyway," he said, "I guess that helps me understand why you two didn't make it."

"What does?"

"It's the first thing she mentioned." He spotted a taxi and waved at it. "But it's the last thing you mentioned."

"That," I told him as the cab swerved to the curb, "is exactly the difference between us."

We shook hands. Billy opened the back door of the taxi. "He's a wuss, Dad."

"A what?"

"A wuss. A dweeb. You know."

"Who's a wuss?"

"Richard."

"He's a lawyer," I said. "What'd you expect?"

F OR THE NEXT FEW DAYS I coddled clients, conferred
with other lawyers, negotiated out-of-court settle-
ments, composed wills, created codicils, and signed all
the letters that Julie wrote for me. I even made a court appearance.

Mary Ellen Ames did not return my call.

On Friday I called her again. I left the same message as
the previous one. This time I used the word "urgent."

Charlie and I drove down to the Farmington River in
Connecticut on Saturday. Each of us caught a few brown
trout on small flies. They were spooky and picky and hard to
catch, the way we like them. The fish had already begun to
take on their autumn spawning colors. Golden bellies, spots
as red as drops of fresh blood. The males were starting to
grow their bellicose underslung jaws, the better to frighten off
sexual competitors. The water was low and clear as Beefeat-
er's. The golds and crimsons of the foliage, the same shades as
the trout, reflected on the Farmington's smooth currents. On
the way home we stopped at Pablo's in West Hartford. We
washed down our burritos with a couple bottles of Dos Equis,
on me.

We got back late. No messages on my machine, from
Mary Ellen or anybody else. I slept late. Sunday afternoon I

watched the Sox, who were still miraculously in the pennant hunt, do battle with the Blue Jays on my old black-and-white television. Actually, I didn't watch the pictures. I read the Sunday *Globe* and listened to Ned Martin, that most literate of all sports announcers, use words such as "penultimate" and "modicum" and "quintessential" to explain the action at Fenway. I wished Ned still worked radio, where he belonged. Then I wouldn't need to turn on the tube to hear him.

The day passed with no reply from Mary Ellen.

I tried her number on Sunday night just before bed, and again Monday morning before leaving for work. No answer. I didn't bother leaving another message. It was apparent that she had no intention of calling me back. I figured I'd made a tactical error mentioning Susan. I supposed I didn't comprehend the magnitude of their estrangement.

So Monday after lunch I went to pay her a visit. I decided to walk to her place on Beacon Street from my office in Copley Square. It was one of those unnaturally warm early autumn days in New England. Indian summer. Normal folks love such days. They shuffle through the crispy leaves on the sidewalks. They spread blankets on the banks of the Charles and stare at its reflections, or they take strolls through parks and forests spying on migrating birds. They paddle canoes over the placid surfaces of woodland ponds.

Not me. The fall is for sweaters. Frost on the pumpkin. Skim ice on the ponds. Indian summer days make me worry about holes in the ozone layer, the greenhouse effect, global warming. They remind me that one day the polar ice cap will melt and the sea will rise to inundate Cape Cod and Back Bay, that plants and trees, deprived of their winter dormancy, will wear themselves out trying to procreate year round, that trout rivers will become too hot to nurture the fish I love the most.

Fall means death, yes. But it's supposed to, even though it does tend to depress me. Death and renewal. That's what autumn's for.

By the time I was standing in front of Mary Ellen's building I had my jacket slung over my shoulder and my tie loosened. My slender attaché case felt like it was loaded with bricks. My shirt was sticking to my back.

It was one of those elegant old brick edifices just down the street from the golden dome of the State House and overlooking, as I had suspected, the Boston Common. A hundred years ago a single old Boston Brahmin family—maybe even a Cabot or a Lodge or a Saltonstall or a Lowell—had lived there with a houseful of servants. Eventually a developer got hold of it and chopped it up into apartments. Then, with the condominium craze of the seventies, it was converted into expensive town houses. That's what had happened to all but a handful of those classic old buildings.

Mary Ellen Ames was living at one of the best addresses in the city.

Behind a shoulder-high black wrought-iron fence lay two immaculately manicured square patches of grass. Rhododendrons and azaleas grew against the front of the building, and at their feet pink and white impatiens bloomed bravely, awaiting the fall's first killing frost.

I unlatched the gate and walked up the brick path. I opened the tall front door and found myself in a high-ceilinged foyer with gleaming white marble floors. A mural depicting the Boston Tea Party adorned one of the walls. The Boston Massacre was on the other. I glanced around, looking for rows of mailboxes and buzzers or a telephone. There were none.

I mounted the two marble steps that led up to an inside door. I peered through the glass into a spacious lobby. A glittering crystal chandelier hung from the ceiling. These floors were also white marble. The walls were hung with dark portraits in clunky gold frames.

On the far side of the lobby a chocolate-skinned man with snow-white hair sat at a desk. He was bent over a book. I waved, but he didn't see me.

I noticed a bell beside the door. I depressed it and saw the man look toward me over the tops of the half glasses that were perched low on his nose. I waved again at him.

"What can I do for you?" came a disembodied voice from somewhere over my head.

I looked around, then at the man. I shrugged.

"Just speak, sir" came his voice. "I can hear you."

"I'm looking for Mary Ellen Ames," I said.

"Who should I say is here?"

"Brady Coyne. I'm her mother's attorney."

Usually I call myself a lawyer. The word "attorney" always sounds affected to my ear. But lay people, I have learned, seem to be more responsive to the word "attorney" than they are to the word "lawyer." Ever since Nixon, "lawyer" hás been a dirty word.

I watched as the man picked up a telephone on his desk and punched some buttons on a console. He stared at the ceiling for a few moments, then replaced the receiver. "She's not answering" his voice said. "Sorry. Want to leave a message?"

"Can I talk to you?" I said.

"Sure. Go ahead."

"This," I said, gesturing toward the ceiling where the speaker was hiding, "is a little weird."

I saw him smile. He got up and came to the door. He put his face close to it and said, "You got any identification?"

I held up my attaché case for him.

He grinned and shook his head.

I removed one of my business cards from the inside pocket of my jacket and pressed it against the glass. He bent to examine it, then looked up. "Anything else?"

I opened the attaché case and removed the photograph of Mary Ellen that Susan had given me. I showed it to him. He looked at it, then opened the door. "Come on in."

I stepped inside. I held out my hand to him. "Brady Coyne," I said.

We shook. "Harold Wainwright," he said. "Sorry about all that. They're very particular about security."

"I understand."

"That's a pretty old picture of her."

"Eleven or twelve years. It's her high school graduation portrait. You know Mary Ellen, then."

"Sure. I know everyone here. There's only sixteen units. So what can I do for you?"

"It's very important that I talk with Miz Ames. See, I'm her mother's lawyer, as I said. Susan Ames is dying of cancer. They give her maybe a month. I've got to talk to Mary Ellen about the estate. More to the point, I guess, the mother and daughter haven't spoken for eleven years. Susan wants to reconcile. Before . . ."

Harold Wainwright nodded. "Sure. But I don't know how I can help you."

"Well, what time does she usually leave in the morning? When does she get back? I've tried calling her, but she doesn't call me back, so I guess I'm going to have to catch her."

He stared at the chandelier for a moment. "I'm on seven to seven, sir. Days. Can't say Miss Ames keeps any regular schedule. In, out, whenever. Nice gal, though. Always has something friendly to say. Not like some of 'em, they'll look right through you like you're a piece of furniture, if you know what I mean. Not Miss Ames. Always got a smile for Harold, a kind word."

"Did you see her today?"

"Nope."

"What about yesterday?"

He shook his head. "I'm not on weekends, so I can't help you there."

"Well," I said, "when *was* the last time you saw her?"

He frowned. His eyebrows were as white as the hair on top of his head. "Boy, now that I think of it, it's been a while. Lemme think." He scratched his chin and peered up at the ceiling. "Hm," he said. "Couple weeks, I'll bet. Never really noticed. They come and go. Most of 'em have other places to live, too. You know, Florida or Killington in the winter, Nantucket, Chatham in the summer. I don't keep track of them."

"Does Mary Ellen Ames have a vacation place?"

He shrugged. "Seems to me she does. Couldn't tell you where."

"A couple weeks, huh?"

"Now, that just means I haven't seen her. I'm off at seven, back again seven in the morning. She could be comin' in and goin' out when I'm not here."

I handed him one of my cards. "Do me a favor," I said. "When you see her, give me a call?"

He took the card. "I guess I could do that. I mean, if her mother's dying . . ."

"Something else," I said. "Will you deliver a note to her for me?"

"I can leave it in her mailbox, sure."

I took a sheet of my business stationery from my attaché case. I wrote on it: "Ms. Ames, Your mother is dying of cancer. She hasn't much time left. She wants to see you. I need to discuss her estate with you. Please call me at your earliest convenience. Yours truly, Brady L. Coyne, Esq."

I folded it, slipped it into an envelope, wrote "Mary Ellen Ames" on the outside, and handed it to Harold Wainwright. He took it over to a row of slots on the wall beside the desk and shoved it through one of them.

"Is there a regular night man on duty here?" I said to him.

He nodded. "Young fella named Donald. He comes on at seven."

"One more favor, then," I said. "Tell him I plan to stop by tonight. See if you can persuade him to cooperate with me."

He nodded. "I can do that, sure. Can't guarantee he will cooperate, you understand. But I'll tell him."

"Thank you, sir."

We shook hands and I left.

As I was descending the path, a mailman pushed open the gate and walked past me. I turned around. "Excuse me," I said.

He stopped and looked at me. "Meaning me?"

"Yes. Do you have any mail for Ames?"

He didn't bother to check. "Nope," he said.

"You sure?"

"Positive, friend. It's being held at the post office."

"When did she request that?"

"She didn't."

"Has she moved or something?"

"Nope. Takes about two magazines to fill up one of them little boxes. Can't cram anything else into it."

"She hasn't been picking up her mail, then?"

"Nossir. Not for two or three weeks. I'm holding it for her. Left her a memo telling her we got it when she wants it."

I nodded. "Well, thank you."

He shrugged. "You betcha."

I SAUNTERED back toward Copley Square, dangling my jacket on my forefinger over my shoulder. By the time I got to Clarendon Street I'd worked up another sweat. But I wasn't pondering environmental disasters. I was trying to figure out how I was going to reach Mary Ellen Ames.

She hadn't been home in about two weeks. Nobody seemed to know where she was.

It had been nearly a week since I had talked with Susan. That meant she was a week closer to death.

When I got back to the office I called Susan's house in Concord. Terri Fiori answered. "Susan Ames's residence," she said.

"Good day, General. It's Brady Coyne."

"Oh, hi, Mr. Coyne. How are you?"

"Brady."

"Yes. Brady."

"I'm fine. How's Susan?"

"Oh, about the same. She tires quickly. She's napping now."

"Well, don't bother her. If you don't mind, just tell her that I've found that Mary Ellen is living on Beacon Street, but I haven't been able to catch up with her yet."

"I'll tell her," she said. "She's been talking about her daughter a lot lately. Since you were here."

"I understand. I'm doing my best."

"Look, Brady," she said.

"Yes?"

"When we talked before?"

"You mean when you shot me down?"

She chuckled. "Yes. When I shot you down. I feel bad."

"Don't worry about it."

"Oh, I don't feel bad on your account."

"No?"

"No. I feel bad on my account."

"You mean . . . ?"

"Sure. How's this coming Friday?"

"Boy, I don't know. I don't bounce back well when I've been shot down."

"Oh, shit," she muttered.

"I'm just kidding. Friday would be great. Where?"

"You mind driving out here? I get off around five-thirty, I'll need to get cleaned up, and frankly I hate to drive into the city. There's a neat Italian place near me. Want to meet there?"

"I love Italian," I said. And I love Italian women, I thought.

She told me how to find a little place in Acton called Ciao. Seven-thirty, Friday.

I fooled around with paperwork for the rest of the afternoon. I found myself humming tunes from *My Fair Lady* and remembering Terri Fiori's wicked wink.

But my thoughts kept swinging back to Mary Ellen. I found myself wanting very much to bring her together with Susan. I didn't know if she was avoiding me.

That evening, after a microwaved Salisbury steak, green

beans, and mashed potato and gravy dinner, I walked from
my apartment on the harbor back to Beacon Street. With the
sun down the air had quickly chilled. I wore jeans and a
sweatshirt and my running shoes. Not that I ran. I don't run.
Ever. As Mel Brooks's 2000-year-old man advised, never run
for a bus. There'll always be another.

I didn't work up a sweat at all. So much for global warming.

I climbed the steps and for the second time that day
entered Mary Ellen Ames's Beacon Street building. I peered
through the glass door. A young guy was sitting where Harold Wainwright had sat earlier. Donald, I presumed. He was
thumbing through a magazine and drumming his fingers on
the desktop. I rang the bell. He looked up and saw me.

"Yeah?" came his voice from above me.

"Brady Coyne. To see Mary Ellen Ames."

"Just a sec." Like Harold, Donald picked up the telephone and pecked at the buttons of his console. Like Harold,
he waited a moment and then replaced the receiver. "Nope.
No answer."

"You're Donald?"

"Yup."

"I was here earlier. I asked Mr. Wainwright to tell
you . . ."

He nodded. "Oh, yeah. Right. Hang on."

He got up and sauntered over. He opened the door.
"Come on in."

I went in and followed him across the lobby. He resumed
his seat behind the desk. A transistor radio sat on the corner.
It was playing a rap song, if "song" is the right word. He
switched it off. "So what's up?" he said. "Old Harold said you
were trying to get ahold of Ames. She ain't in now."

"It's really important," I said. "I'm her mother's lawyer. She's dying of cancer and I have to talk to Mary Ellen."

"Yeah. That's a bitch." He shrugged. "Don't know what I can tell you."

"When was the last time you saw her, can you remember?"

He was in his early twenties. He had a pasty complexion and a scrawny neck and a fuzzy adolescent mustache. I suspected he was holding at that moment the most important job he'd ever have in his life. He closed his eyes for a moment, pretending, at least, to concentrate. Then he opened them and shrugged. "I dunno," he said.

"I mean, recently? Tonight? Last week?"

"Not tonight, not last week. I'd notice. Nice-looking broad. Most of 'em here, they're old. I mean, really old, you know? They piss and moan and hobble around. The Ames chick, she's somethin' else." He gave me the sort of grin that invites an answering leer. I didn't give it to him.

"Try to remember," I said. "It's important."

He shook his head slowly. "Week before last, maybe. I don't know."

"What about friends? Has anybody been around looking for her? Besides me, I mean?"

"Nope." He paused. "Wait a minute. Harold said somebody came by this afternoon. After you were here. He told me to tell you that."

"Did he get a name?"

"Nah. I guess he didn't leave it, or Harold didn't ask. Harold said it was one of her guys."

"One of her guys?"

"Hey, she's got friends. This was one of 'em. I know who it was by Harold's description. I mean, not his name or anything. But I seen him."

"What's he look like?"

"Old guy. Older than you, even. Busted-up face. Like he was a boxer or something? Crooked nose, scar tissue around his eyes, pockmarks on his cheeks. Big guy. Not tall, but thick. Got these big shoulders." He shrugged his own narrow shoulders.

"No name, occupation, anything?"

"No. I seen this guy come and go with her a lot. That's it."

"And he was here today?"

"So says Harold. The way he described him, must be the same guy."

"This is the only man you've seen her with, then?"

He grinned. "Hell, no. Like I said, she's got plenty of friends. There's this other guy comes around a lot. Shit, he's nearly as old as Harold, I bet. This old hippie. Bald, earring, big long gray ponytail hanging down his back. Weird old dude."

"No name for him, either."

"Nope. And there are others. I don't remember any of them. I mean, none of the others spend the night, dig?"

"But these two do? The boxer and the hippie?"

He grinned. "Wouldn't you?"

I let that one pass. "Is there a superintendent in the building?"

"Sure. That'd be Jill. Speaking of bitches."

"I'd like to talk to her."

"That's what you think."

"Would you mind buzzing her for me?"

"Hey, it's your funeral, mister."

He picked up the phone, poked a few buttons, and said, "Hey, Jill. A guy's here wants to talk to you." He paused, listening. Then he said, "I dunno. Some lawyer."

He frowned at the receiver for a minute, then lifted his eyebrows to me. "She wants to know if you're her husband's lawyer."

"No."

"Nope," he said into the telephone. "He says no." He hesitated. "Yeah, all right."

He hung up. "She said she'd be up."

"Thanks."

He looked down at his magazine. *Sports Illustrated.* After a minute he snapped his radio back on.

"God*damn* it, Donald," came a voice from behind me. "You are *not* supposed to let people into the lobby and you are *not* supposed to be playing a radio."

I turned around. She was short and slender and angry. Her straight blond hair fell halfway down her back. Her jeans were tight. Her man's blue oxford shirt was untucked and hung loosely over her hips. Her icy blue eyes blazed. I guessed she was in her mid-twenties. She could have passed for a teenager.

Donald snapped off his radio. "Uh, sorry, Jill. Harold said this guy was okay."

"Yeah, well Harold is just a security guard like you, and his job is to maintain the security of this building, just like yours is. Neither of you is doing a very good job of it, and neither of you is what you'd call a shrewd judge of character." She turned her head and pierced me with those cold eyes. "And you. You're a lawyer, huh?"

"Yes. Brady Coyne. I—"

"You represent John Francis Costello, right? That sonofabitch sent you here with a bunch of papers, and you're supposed to sweet-talk me into signing them. Well, forget it."

"I never heard of any Costello," I said.

She cocked her head at me and frowned. "No, huh?"

"Nope."

"Honest?"

"Honest."

"No subpoena or anything?"

I shook my head.

She shrugged. "Well, shit. Sorry, then." She turned again to Donald. "That doesn't mean you're supposed to let anybody who says he's a lawyer into this building, and I don't care what Harold says. You know your job."

Donald succeeded in stifling the beginnings of a sarcastic smile. "Yes, ma'am."

"I'm Jill Costello," she said to me. "I'm the super here. What's up?"

I darted my eyes in Donald's direction. "Can we talk somewhere?"

"Sure. I guess. Come on."

She turned and I followed her into a corridor. She stopped where it opened into a stairwell. She fumbled a pack of cigarettes from her shirt pocket, got one lit, blew a plume of smoke at the ceiling, and said, "Look. I'm sorry about that back there. I'm behind in my studies, everybody's air conditioners are on the blink, and Johnny Costello is on my case. Okay?"

I smiled. "No problem."

"So you wanted to talk to me?"

I nodded. "I'm trying to contact Mary Ellen Ames. She lives in this building. I'm her mother's attorney. Susan Ames. She's got cancer. They give her maybe a month. She and her daughter have been estranged for eleven years, and Susan is very anxious to see Mary Ellen. There's the matter of the estate, which is substantial and complex. And mainly, I think Susan just wants to give her daughter a hug before she goes."

As I spoke I watched the angry tension drain away from

Jill Costello's face. Her mouth softened, and a glisten of tears doused the angry flames in her pale blue eyes.

"Ah, shit," she mumbled. "Ah, that sucks. Damn."

I touched her shoulder. "I'm sorry if . . ."

She wiped her wrist across her eyes. "No, see . . ." She snuffled into her shirtsleeve. "Ah, nuts." She looked up at me. "I'm just kinda strung out these days." She cleared her throat. "Actually, the truth is, my mom died a little over a year ago. She had a stroke. The doctors said she was gonna be okay, and I was in the middle of exams, preoccupied with Johnny, and so when—when she died, here I was in Boston, and her in some crummy hospital in Philadelphia, and I—I never even got to say good-bye to her."

Then the tears spilled out of her eyes. "Ah, dammit. Jeez," she muttered. She leaned her forehead against my chest. I patted her back awkwardly. Her arms snaked around my waist and she pressed herself against me. I could feel her shaking and shuddering. I hugged her against me and let her cry.

After a minute or two she snorted and stood back from me. "Thanks for the hug," she said huskily. "Boy, it's been a long time since I had one of them."

"My pleasure."

"I thought I was all over that."

"It speaks well for you that you're not."

"You touched a nerve. Pretty obviously. God, I wouldn't wish something like that on anybody. You live with the guilt forever, I guess. You know, I keep thinking if I'd only gotten there, maybe she wouldn't have died. Or at least she wouldn't have died alone. And your friend. Not seeing her daughter all these years, and knowing she's going to die . . ."

"Do you know her?"

"Miz Ames?" She looked up at the ceiling. "I guess I'd

recognize her. I've fixed a couple things in her place, but not when she was there. No, I couldn't say I knew her."

"Well, I really need to talk to her. I've been calling, and all I get is her machine. The post office has stopped leaving her mail because she hasn't been taking it from her box. Neither of your security men has seen her for over a week." I reached for her and touched her arm. "Can you help me?"

She looked up at me. Her blue eyes were not icy now. "You want to go up, check out her place, is that it?"

"Yes. Can we?"

She narrowed her eyes for a moment. Then she said, "Screw the rules. Let's go."

She took a final drag on her cigarette then ground it out under her sneaker on the marble floor. She took my hand and led me back toward the lobby. Suddenly she stopped. "God," she said. "I just had this awful thought."

"What?"

"What if—what if there's a body up there?"

I smiled at her. "Don't be silly," I said.

But I'd been having the same thought myself.

7

WE GOT into the elevator at the back of the lobby. It was one of the old-fashioned kind, with accordion barred doors that had to be opened and closed manually, and it moved up through the building slowly. It gave me time to imagine what we might find in Mary Ellen's rooms.

I have friends who are homicide detectives. They have described for me in gleefully colorful language the odor a human corpse gives off after a few days in a heated and poorly ventilated room. They have told me how a body bloats, how it discolors, how houseflies lay their eggs on it and how those eggs hatch into maggots. They have described bodies that were found hanging by the neck, how the eyes bulge, and bodies that left impossibly large puddles of dried black blood on a linoleum floor, and bodies that drowned in bathtubs, and bodies that lay in bed for weeks after they had ceased functioning.

I tried not to think about dead bodies. The harder I tried, naturally, the more vivid became the images that whirled in my brain.

Jill Costello stood beside me, operating the elevator. The top of her head didn't quite reach my shoulder. She was staring up at the blinking lights. I hoped, for her sake, that she didn't have friends who were homicide detectives.

The elevator opened into a large square hallway. Four doors opened onto it. Jill led me to the one marked 4-B. She paused outside it, then rapped on it with her knuckles. "Mary Ellen. It's Jill. Can I come in for a minute?"

She stood with her head cocked to the side for a minute. Then she looked up at me and shrugged. "Let's go in."

She took a ring of keys from her pocket, twisted one of them in the lock, and turned the knob. The door swung inward. It didn't come up against a chain lock. This I took as a small positive sign.

Jill pushed it all the way open. She gestured with the palm of her hand. "After you."

I stepped inside. I took a small, tentative breath through my nose.

It smelled musty, closed in, empty.

It didn't smell fetid.

I turned to Jill. "Come on in. I think it's okay."

"You were thinking . . . ?"

I nodded.

I switched on the light. The door opened directly into a large living room. A small area was sectioned off into a dining area. There was a rectangular drop-leaf maple table with eight matching chairs, matching buffet and china closet. Cherry, I guessed, with lots of fancy scrollwork. The larger half of the room contained a baby grand piano, two sofas, a big leather armchair, and a wall-sized shelved unit that held a television, VCR, stereo system, books, a few potted plants, and knick-knacks.

The knickknacks were pieces of pottery and crude statues and carvings. The pottery looked Indian. The sculptures and carved pieces were erotic.

The potted plants were dead.

Over the piano hung a huge oil portrait. I recognized the subject. It was Charles Ames, Mary Ellen's father, at least twice as big as life in her Beacon Hill living room. A craggy man of about sixty in the painting, with a magnificent head of curly steel-gray hair, shaggy gray eyebrows, long, lumpy nose, and the same sensuous mouth that I had seen in the photograph of Mary Ellen. I had seen photos of Charles at Susan's house in Concord. Susan had no oil portraits of her late husband.

A small floodlight attached to the ceiling, which had gone on when I'd thrown the room switch, illuminated the painting.

"So what are we looking for?" said Jill.

I shrugged. "I don't know."

We went into the kitchen. Appliances of every description lined the counters. Microwave, blender, toaster oven, food processor, cappuccino machine, coffee machine, coffee bean grinder. Other things the function of which was not apparent to me.

In the sink was a coffee mug and a bowl with a spoon in it. I bent to examine the bowl. A patch of green mold was growing on the bottom.

I opened the refrigerator. A few bottles of white wine lay on their sides. A brown head of lettuce in a plastic bag. Some Schweppes ginger ale. Half a dozen cans of Coors beer. A cardboard carton of milk.

I removed the milk and opened it.

"Whew!" said Jill.

The milk had soured long before.

"She hasn't been here for a while," I said.

"The bedrooms and bath are down this way," she said, gesturing with a jerk of her head.

I followed her. In the bathroom the usual array of feminine beauty aids was stacked on the back of the toilet and on a wicker shelf that hung over it. An opened box of Tampax sat on the floor beside the toilet.

Two towels lay crumpled on the floor. I picked one up and sniffed it. It smelled sour.

I slid open the medicine cabinet. Aside from one bottle of prescription drugs, the rest was over-the-counter stuff.

We went into the bedroom. The queen-sized bed was unmade. A pair of jeans, a couple of T-shirts, three pink silk panties, one bra, and about half a dozen white athletic socks were strewn about the floor. There were only a couple of empty hangers in the well-stocked wall-sized closet.

Jill fingered some of the garments that hung there. "Boy," she said. "This is all designer stuff."

"She has plenty of money," I said.

On the floor in the back of the closet sat four matching pieces of leather luggage and an Imelda Marcos collection of footwear.

"It doesn't look as if she packed a lot of stuff for a trip," I said.

Jill and I had been talking in low whispers, as if we feared being overheard. When the telephone beside the bed suddenly rang, she reached out reflexively and grabbed my wrist. "Shit," she mumbled. "I nearly wet my pants."

It rang three times. Then from another room we heard a muffled click and Mary Ellen's voice requesting, as it had of me when I tried calling, an "intriguing message."

This caller left no message.

I turned to Jill. "Where's that machine?"

"Must be in the other bedroom."

The other bedroom contained a sofa and a pair of bookcases and a desk with a Macintosh computer atop it. The room appeared to have served as Mary Ellen's study. The answering machine, along with a telephone, sat on the desk. The red light on the machine was blinking furiously. Jill and I both stared at it. I turned to her. "What do you think?"

"Oh, boy. It's an egregious invasion of privacy."

"You sound like a lawyer."

She shrugged. "I apologize."

"Let's listen," I said. "I won't tell if you won't."

"Fair enough."

I sat at the desk and depressed the button on the machine. It whirred, clicked, and clanked, and a man's voice said, "Hey, kiddo. You there? Thought we had a date. Give me a jingle."

Click, beep. A different male voice. "Mary Ellen? It's me. Just checking on tomorrow night. I've got the stuff. Talk to you later."

The same voice again, essentially the same message, no name or phone number given. Then a woman's voice, "Just wanted to shoot the shit."

There were several hangups. There was one computer-generated recording, a quick-talking high-energy voice that mainly kept repeating an 800 phone number. Each of the two male voices returned a couple of times, neither leaving a name, a time, a date, or what I would call an intriguing message.

My own voice startled me. Jill looked at me when it came on. I shrugged. At least I left my name and a message.

Then came a voice that jerked my head back, a heavily accented voice that I recognized instantly. "Mary Ellen," it said, "I must speak with you. It is imperative. Please call me at the office."

He didn't leave his name or a phone number. He didn't need to. It was Sherif Rahmanan.

Each of the two unnamed men called again. I called again. I used the word "urgent."

Sherif Rahmanan called again. He repeated the word "imperative."

The tape rewound. I held down the button so the recorded messages would not be lost.

"Lots of people looking for her," said Jill.

I nodded. "And not a damn one of them even left a name."

"Except you."

"I'm well bred."

"What do you think?"

I shrugged. "She's been gone for a while. Safe to infer that none of these callers knows where she is, or even that she planned to be away."

"As if she just decided to get away from everybody," said Jill.

"Like that."

"I wonder why."

"I don't know," I mused. "For all we know, there are plenty of people who do know where she is. They wouldn't bother trying to call her."

"Yeah, except some of these men who called, they seemed to know her well. I mean, they didn't even leave their names, as if they assumed she'd recognize their voices."

"They might be the very ones she wants to get away from," I said.

Jill went over and sat on the sofa. She lit another cigarette. I looked around for an ashtray and, finding none, slid a metal wastebasket toward her with my foot. "What if she already knew about her mother?" said Jill. "What if that's why she's gone away?"

"You mean to avoid the whole scene? To wait somewhere until she dies?"

She shrugged.

"How could she know?"

"Hey," she said. "You tell me. There must be doctors, friends, hospital people, whatever."

"Regardless," I said. "I've still got to try to see her."

Sherif Rahmanan, I thought. The bastard lied to me. His message came directly after mine. He had called her to warn her about me.

But she had been gone for a while already by then. If Rahmanan knew where she was, he wouldn't have tried calling her here.

I sat beside Jill and lit a Winston. "Now what?" she said.

I sighed. "I don't know." I smoked for a minute and watched the red light of the answering machine wink at me. Suddenly I snapped my fingers. I stood up.

"What?" she said. "What is it?"

"There was a prescription bottle in the bathroom. There must be a doctor's name on it."

"So?"

"So I don't know. So she's got a doctor. So she might be sick or something. Maybe she's in a hospital. Maybe he's treated her recently. Maybe she confides in him."

"Or her," said Jill.

"I stand corrected." I went into the bathroom. Jill followed me. I removed the bottle. It contained capsules of something called Pertofrane. I shook it. Half empty. Or half full, I suppose. I'm a half empty man, myself. I read its label. The prescribing doctor's name was McAllister. She was supposed to take two of the capsules by mouth every morning. The prescription had been filled on September 9. Less than a month earlier. She had three refills left.

"Let's find a phone book," I said.

The big NYNEX Yellow Pages was in the bottom drawer of the desk. I looked under Physicians. It listed three McAllisters. Arline, Peter, and Warren. Arline's office was in Cambridge, Peter's was in Chelsea, and Warren's in Brookline.

I took out my notebook and jotted all three names and numbers into it. Then I flipped the Yellow Pages forward to the section where the physicians were listed by their practice.

Arline was a gynecologist.

Peter turned out to be a plastic surgeon.

Warren was a psychiatrist.

I had no idea what the drug Pertofrane was for.

But I suspected that patients probably confided in their plastic surgeons and gynecologists. They certainly told secrets to their therapists.

I glanced at my watch. It was ten after nine. I'd call the three McAllister doctors in the morning. Maybe I'd give Sherif Rahmanan a call, too. I didn't like being lied to.

I stood up. "Let's go," I said to Jill.

"Don't you want to look through her papers or something? Maybe find a little black book, love notes, overdue bills, threatening letters, like that?"

"I'm already feeling like a rapist," I said. "I think I've violated her privacy enough for one evening. If I come back, will you let me in?"

She shrugged. "Why not?"

AS WE RODE DOWN in the elevator, Jill said, "This has been kinda fun."

"Fun?"

"I mean, playing detective."

I rolled my eyes. "Susan Ames is dying. Her daughter's missing."

She hugged herself. "Ah, shit. I'm sorry. You're right. It just—I kinda forgot about all the crap in my own life there for a while."

I patted her shoulder. "That's all right."

The elevator shuddered to a stop. "You want to stop in for a drink?" she said.

I shrugged. "Sure."

We walked across the lobby toward the stairwell. Donald watched us from his desk, smirking. We descended one flight of stairs and Jill unlocked the single door at the landing. Her apartment was small and cramped, just a single room divided by strategically placed furniture. It looked as if it had been built into the basement as an afterthought. A convertible sofa at the far end was pulled out and rumpled with a tangle of sheets, blankets, and pillows. A stand-up kitchen at the opposite end was separated from the rest of the room by a waist-high island. A large round table was piled with open books and yellow pads of paper. A single narrow window at head height over the sofa emitted yellow light from Beacon Street. Cheap prints of Andrew Wyeth paintings hung from the imitation knotty pine–paneled walls.

"Well," said Jill with a sweep of her hand, "such as it is."

I sat in one of the wooden chairs at the table. She pushed aside the books and papers. "I'm after my MBA," she said. "The damn technical courses are driving me nuts. I'm good at the people stuff. Leadership, human resources, shit like that. Computers, accounting, micro-economics? I don't know a spreadsheet from a bedsheet. Anyway, what do you like to drink? I've got beer."

"How about a beer?"

"Miller's or Miller's?"

"Got any Miller's?"

"Whatever you like," she said.

She took two cans of Miller's from her little refrigerator and sat across from me. We both lit cigarettes and sipped beer. She began to talk. She had grown up outside of Scranton. Her dad repaired automobiles. She got some loans and went to Penn State. Majored in sociology. Useless field. Met John Francis Costello. Married him and followed him to Malden, Massachusetts, where he took over the family restaurant. He wanted her to be the hostess there while they tried to make babies. She hostessed her ass off, hated it, finally told Johnny she wasn't doing it anymore. They were having no luck creating babies. She decided to get a master's degree in something with utility. John Francis Costello forbade it. He wanted his wife barefoot and pregnant, the way all the Costello women had been. She enrolled at Simmons anyway. He wouldn't forgive her for betraying him that way.

Finally she left him. Got this place to hide out in in exchange for watching over the building. She was good at fixing things. She'd learned a lot from her dad. Johnny kept harassing her. Long messages on her answering machine. Bribing Donald to let him into the building, then banging on her door for an hour, alternately yelling and cajoling, wanting her to open up, swollen with his bruised macho pride. And after she ordered Donald not to let him in, Johnny simply went around the side of the building to her private entrance and pounded and yelled out there. And she just sat inside at her table and cried and didn't open the door. So he tried a new strategy. If he couldn't bully her, he could divorce her. It was, she figured, his idea of revenge. Personally, she didn't much care whether she was divorced or not right now. She just had no desire to live with Johnny Costello. Somewhere along the way, love had transformed itself into hatred. Funny how things like that happened. She supposed she'd be needing a lawyer, but she hadn't gotten around to it.

As she talked it occurred to me that while she may have learned to hate him, she hadn't really stopped loving him.

She looked up at me. "What happens to people, anyway?"

I thought of Susan and Mary Ellen. I thought of me and Gloria. I shrugged. "I don't know. No wisdom here."

Our beer cans were empty. She got up, fetched more, came back, and sat down.

Her phone rang. It was sitting on the table in front of us under some papers on the end of a long cord that snaked into the kitchen. She let it ring twice, then pushed the papers off it. She lifted the receiver an inch off the cradle, held it there for a few seconds, then hung it up. She looked at me and shrugged. I lifted my eyebrows. She shrugged again.

She tilted up her beer can, took a long swallow, her throat working. Then she put it carefully down on the table. She rotated it slowly, staring at it as if she was studying the label. Then she looked up at me. She reached over and tapped my arm with her fingernails. "Hey," she said. "You're a lawyer."

I nodded. "I am."

"Do divorces?"

"You can't afford me, Jill. Have you thought of mediation?"

"Mediate with Johnny Costello? That's a laugh. I've destroyed his manly pride. He's just out to get me."

"What about a restraining order?"

"Hey. He's my husband."

"True." I took a swig from my beer can. "Tell you what," I said. "If that lawyer does come around with papers for you to sign, take them, don't sign them, and give me a call. I'll look them over for you."

"Yeah, well, you're right. I can't afford you. I can't afford anybody. Do they have public defenders for divorces?"

"I don't think so," I said. "I can look at papers, see what's involved. We can take it from there."

"I can maybe give you a hundred bucks as a retainer."

I smiled. "You don't need to. What do you want out of this?"

"The divorce? Not a damn thing. The divorce is his idea. His way of asserting himself. I don't care about a divorce one way or the other. I just want him to leave me alone. I couldn't possibly feel any less married to Johnny Costello if we get divorced than I do right now. He wants a divorce, he can have it. Just so I don't get screwed in the process."

"No custody issues?"

"I told you. We didn't make any babies."

"Golden retrievers, Persian cats, tropical fish?"

She smiled. "You're kidding, right?"

"No. Sometimes custody of pets is tougher than children."

She shook her head. "No pets."

"What about common property?"

"Nothing of mine. I haven't got any money. Just a clunky old Toyota. Had to get loans for school. He can have what's his."

"Everything is common property, you know. You're entitled to half."

"I don't want anything," she said. "I wouldn't take it."

I shrugged. "Well, I'll be happy to help you," I said.

"Really?"

"Sure. Really." I took out one of my business cards, wrote my home phone number on the back of it, and gave it to her. "Just give me a call."

She glanced at the card and dropped it onto the table. "Okay," she said. "I probably will."

I glanced at my watch. "Time for me to get going," I said. I drained the rest of my beer and stood up.

"Yeah," said Jill. "I still got homework to do."

I went to the door. She followed me. I opened it. She touched my arm, and I turned. "Hey," she said. "Thanks."

She put her hands on my shoulders, tiptoed up, and kissed my cheek.

"You're welcome," I said. I patted her shoulder and got the hell out of there.

I walked out of the building into the city night. I crossed Beacon Street and headed across the Common on one of the poorly lit diagonal paths that would start me back to my apartment on the waterfront. Jill Costello's daughterly kiss started me thinking about my impending date with Terri Fiori. It had been a week or so since I had seen Terri. Already her face had grown fuzzy in my memory. I tried to conjure it up, those great dark eyes, that jet black hair . . .

The hand that suddenly gripped my arm felt like a beartrap. The voice that hissed in my ear was rough and threatening.

"Hold it right there, buddy," that voice growled.

I stopped and held it right there.

Damn! I was about to become a statistic. I was about to get mugged on the Boston Common. If I was lucky I might not be murdered.

9

WITHOUT TURNING AROUND, and with his fingers digging painfully into the flesh above my elbow, I said, "What do you want?"

"C'mon. Over here, where I can see you."

He steered me toward a bench. I had never been mugged before. This was not how I would have imagined it.

"Siddown."

I sat. He sat beside me, still holding my arm.

"You can let go," I said. "I promise not to flee."

To my surprise, he let go.

I turned to look at him. He had closely cropped iron-colored hair, bushy gray eyebrows, a few days' worth of heavy black-and-white bristle on his cheeks. His eyes were small and dark and surrounded by puffy flesh. There was a large bump on his nose where it took a right-angle turn toward the left.

He looked more or less like Buddy Hackett in a bad mood.

"So who the fuck are you, anyways," he said.

"My name is Brady Coyne," I said. "Who the fuck are you?"

"Dave Finn," he said. "I'm a friend of Mary Ellen."

"You're not gonna mug me?"

Then he grinned. And he looked even more like Buddy

Hackett. "Nah," he said. "Sorry about that. Christ, you walk fast. I just wanted to talk to you."

"About Mary Ellen?"

"Yeah." He shrugged. "I knew she had another guy. Drove me nuts. She wouldn't admit it. She ever tell you about me?"

"I'm her—" I stopped. "No. She never did."

"You musta suspected, though, huh?"

I shrugged.

"I admit I was jealous as hell," he said, tugging at his nose. "But now I'm just worried. So if she's with you or something, okay, best man wins, all that shit. I just wanna know she's okay."

"Look," I said. "I'm her mother's lawyer, that's all. I don't know Mary Ellen. I've never even met her. I need to do some business with her."

"You're not that guy?"

"I told you, I've never met her."

He shook his head slowly back and forth. "Well, shit. I'm sorry."

"You don't know where she is either?"

"Nope. Been calling. Ever since she stood me up. Figured, fuck it, so she found some younger guy. What beautiful young gal like her'd wanna marry an ugly old bastard like me anyway? But, damn. She suckered me good, tell you that. Assumed it was you, comin' around to pick up some of her things. The guy at the desk said you was there earlier, might be comin' around again. I wanted to get a look at you." He cocked his head, looking at me. "Shoulda known when I seen you. Figured it hadda be somebody younger than you."

"Marry you? She's going to marry you?" I said.

"You think that's funny?"

I shrugged.

"Yeah, I know what you're thinkin'. Ugly old pug like me, rich lady like Mary Ellen, so beautiful and refined and all. Hey, I didn't believe it myself. But, yeah, we're plannin' on it." He took a deep breath. "I dunno. Guess maybe we're not. Guess she run off with the other guy. Not you, huh?"

"No. Not me. What do you know about this other man?"

"Nothing. Diddlysquat. I know there's some other guy. That's all."

"Guy with a ponytail and earring? Old hippie type?"

Dave Finn frowned. "Nah. I don't think so. I know who that is. That's some old buddy of hers. Fella name of Raiford. Sid Raiford. She usta work with him in some bookstore. No, this is some other guy. I don't think her and Raiford are like that."

"An Arab, maybe?" I said.

"Huh?"

"The other man. Is he an Arab?"

"Listen," he said. "I don't know *who* the fuck he is. I don't think it's Raiford, that's all. I thought it was you. He could be an Arab or a Greek or a fuckin' Russian for all I know. I mean, I oughta be able to figure it out, but I can't. Fuckin' detective, and I can't even get a line on some guy my gal's run off with."

"You're a detective?"

He snorted a quick ironic laugh through his L-shaped nose. "Not a very good one, I guess. Yeah, I'm a cop."

"Well," I said, "it would seem that between a cop and a lawyer, we ought to be able to find her."

"You really don't know where she is either, then?"

"No," I said.

"Gonna keep lookin'?"

I nodded. "Yes."

"If you find her, will you tell me?"

"If I find her," I said, "I will first ask her if she wants me to tell you. If she says no, then I will not tell you. What about you?"

"Me?"

"If you find her, will you tell me?"

"Same deal, I guess. What'd you say you wanted with her?"

"I'm her mother's lawyer. She's dying. It's about her estate."

"So Mary Ellen's gonna get even richer, huh?"

"Looks that way." I fished another business card from my jeans pocket, scratched my home phone number on the back, and gave it to Finn. "Here's my number. Home and office. I'd appreciate a call. From you or her."

He took the card, ran the ball of his thumb over the raised lettering, and shoved it into his pocket.

"You don't have any idea where she might've gone?" I said.

"I been lookin' for a week. Haven't got a clue."

"Do you know if she has a vacation place?"

"Yeah, matter of fact. She's mentioned it. She's got a cabin or something on some pond somewhere, I think. I never been there."

"No idea where it is?"

"Nope."

"Maybe she's there," I said.

"Hope so."

"Why?"

"Means she'll be back. But I doubt that's where she is."

"Why?"

"She woulda told me she was goin'."

Maybe not, I thought. But I remembered the inside of her closets. There didn't seem to be any empty hangers or missing pieces from the matching luggage. Her bed was unmade and there were dirty dishes in the sink. She left her prescription of Pertofrane in her medicine cabinet. Her place had not looked the way a woman would leave it if she was going away on an extended vacation.

I stood up. "Can I go now?" I said.

Finn grinned crookedly. "Hope you ain't mad."

I held my hand down to him. "It was good to meet you. A big relief that you didn't mug me."

We shook hands and I resumed my stroll down the path that crossed the Common. I glanced back over my shoulder. Dave Finn was still sitting there on the park bench, watching me.

JULIE HAD SET UP a morning full of conferences for me
on Tuesday, so I didn't get a chance to make any calls
until after lunch. That's when I took out my notebook
and punched up the first number on my list, Dr. Arline
McAllister, the gynecologist with the Cambridge office. The
woman who answered the phone sounded harried and informed me that the doctor was at the hospital and wasn't
expected back until late afternoon. I left my number and re-
quested she call me.

Next on my list was Dr. Peter McAllister, the plastic
surgeon whose office was in Chelsea. I tried the number I had
written down.

A woman answered. "Dr. McAllister."

"I'd like to speak to the doctor, please."

"I'm sorry, sir. The doctor—"

"I'm a lawyer," I said.

She hesitated. "Your name?"

"Coyne. Brady Coyne."

"Your client?"

"Let me speak to Dr. McAllister, please, miss."

"Just a moment."

She put me on hold. I lit a cigarette. It was less than half smoked when she returned. "The doctor can speak with you now, Mr. Coyne."

I heard a click, then, "Dr. McAllister. How can I help you?"

"I want to discuss Mary Ellen Ames," I said.

I heard a hesitation. Then, "Beg your pardon?"

"Mary Ellen Ames. Your patient."

"I have no patient by that name, sir."

"Has she been your patient? Have you done surgery on her?"

"Look," he said. "What is this?"

"You never heard of Mary Ellen Ames?"

"Never."

"Don't you want to look it up in your records?"

"I don't need to. I'd recognize the name of any patient I ever had."

"I find that hard to believe."

"Well, your credulity is of no interest to me, sir, and I don't appreciate being bullied by some ambulance chaser. So if you—"

"I'm sorry," I said quickly. "I'm not after a lawsuit, Doctor. Please. One question."

"I never heard of her. What else can I tell you?"

"Pertofrane. Do you prescribe Pertofrane?"

He laughed. "Hardly."

"Why not?"

"I'm a plastic surgeon, Mr. Coyne."

"So?"

"Pertofrane is an antidepressant."

"Oh."

"Listen. The reason I don't need to look up your client in my records? What was her name?"

"Mary Ellen Ames."

"Yes. The reason I don't need to look her up is that I just opened my office eight months ago. I haven't had that many patients. I'd remember her. Anyway, I don't prescribe Pertofrane."

"I'm sorry I bothered you."

"Me, too," he said. "I was hoping you needed some cosmetic work."

"I probably could use some," I said. "Guess I'll try to get by without it."

I hung up and glanced at my notebook. Warren, the third McAllister doctor, was a psychiatrist. Somebody had prescribed the antidepressant drug Pertofrane for Mary Ellen. Sounded like the shrink to me. If he prescribed drugs for her, it meant he treated her. Psychiatric patients met with their shrinks several times a week, I knew. If anyone was going to know where Mary Ellen had gone, it would be her shrink.

I tried the number for Warren McAllister and got his answering machine. My message simply stated my name and phone number and asked the doctor to return my call at his earliest convenience. I didn't know if gynecologists prescribed drugs like Pertofrane. If I struck out with Dr. Warren, and if Dr. Arline didn't return my call, I'd give her another try.

I thought of calling Sherif Rahmanan. He had lied to me, and it pissed me off. He knew Mary Ellen's phone number. Probably knew a lot more about her, too.

But if he knew where she was, he wouldn't have tried to reach her at home. I decided I had enough to do without making Professor Rahmanan sweat over his wife finding out that he had maintained a relationship with Mary Ellen all these years. I just wanted to know where she was. I just wanted to tell her that Susan was going to die.

I fooled around with paperwork for the rest of the afternoon, trying to get caught up. I'd spent a lot of time on Susan recently—billable time, theoretically, although Julie always accused me of being slipshod about keeping track of billable time.

Around four Julie buzzed me. "Line two," she said. "It's your wife."

"Gloria?"

"Of course."

"She's not my wife," I said gently. Gloria hasn't been my wife for a decade. Julie refuses to acknowledge that fact. She assumes that our divorce is merely a temporary hiatus in a lifelong partnership. I poked the flashing button on my phone and said, "Hi, hon."

"Brady," said Gloria without preamble, "do you know what William has done?"

"Drilled a hole in his ear?" I said. "Wild guess."

She hesitated for just an instant. "He told you?"

"I saw him last week."

"You visited him?"

"No, he was in town for an interview. He sponged lunch off me."

"Hm," she said. "He didn't tell me he was going to be in town."

"It was just a quick trip. He's trying for an internship at the Aquarium."

"Well, what did you do?"

"Do?"

"About his ear."

"Well, I asked him where it came from. He said he was drunk when it happened. I guess he figures that absolves him of responsibility."

"Yes," she muttered, "he would think that way. So would you." She paused. "Reason I called . . ."

"Hmm?"

"Wanna do lunch?"

"Do?"

"Meet for. Eat."

"Sure. When? Where?"

"How's Friday?"

"Fine. You coming in town?"

"Yes."

"Remember Marie's?"

"That little Italian place in Kenmore Square?"

"That's the one. Say twelve-thirty?"

"Fine," she said. "I'll be there."

"Um, hey, Gloria?"

"Yes, Brady?"

"What's up?"

"Oh, nothing much. It's been a while, that's all. I thought it would be nice to get together."

"It would be nice," I said.

After we exchanged good-byes, I swiveled around and stared out the window. Nothing much, she had said. My ex-wife was going to announce to me that she was getting remarried. To a lawyer. Ten years younger than her. A wuss. A dweeb. I wondered why she felt she had to tell me.

I returned to the papers on my desk, and at five Julie poked her head into my office. "I'm off," she said.

I waved to her without looking up. The very model of the hard-working attorney.

"Brady?" she said.

I sighed and lifted my head. "Yes?"

"What are you doing?"

I moved the back of my hand across the papers scattered over my desk. "My job. I'm a lawyer, see."

"No, I mean on the Susan Ames thing?"

"Still trying to catch up with Mary Ellen."

"And already you're way behind in your real work."

"Susan is my client. It's real work."

"Playing detective?"

"I'm not playing detective. I'm trying to do my job."

She shrugged. "It's your law practice."

"Precisely."

"Well," she said, "just have all that stuff on my desk in the morning."

I snapped her a salute. "Aye, aye, Captain."

After she left I slid the new Orvis catalog out from under a stack of manila folders. They had just brought out a great new line of fly rods. I really needed a couple of new rods. I swiveled around to face the window while I studied the catalog.

My phone rang around five-thirty. I picked it up. "Brady Coyne," I said.

"This is Doctor McAllister," said a deep male voice. "Returning your call."

"Thank you," I said. "I was hoping you might have some time . . ."

"Did you have a referral?"

"Pardon me?"

"Did someone refer you to me?"

"Oh." I laughed quickly. "No, it's not that. I don't need —well, maybe I could use it. Probably could. But I'm not looking for treatment, Doctor. I'm a lawyer."

I paused, and I could hear the hesitation in his voice before he said, "Yes?" Why is it that everybody assumes a lawyer is out to screw them?

"Doctor McAllister," I said, "is Mary Ellen Ames your patient?"

There was a long pause. "Sir, I'm sorry, but . . ." His voice trailed off.

"I don't want you to violate confidentiality," I said. "I know all about the privileged status of our patients and clients. But I'm Mary Ellen's mother's lawyer. I've been trying to find her. Susan Ames is dying, and—"

"She's my patient, yes."

"You prescribed Pertofrane for her?"

"What exactly do you want?" he said.

"I just need to talk with her."

Another pause. "I see."

"So do you know how I can get ahold of her?"

"You'd appear to be doing very well, Mr. Coyne. You know I treat Miz Ames, you know her medication."

"Well, I can't find her."

"Mr. Coyne," he said after a moment, "you asked me for some time. I can do that. But not now. If you'd like to get together . . . ?"

"Sure," I said. "That would be good."

"Let's see," he said. "Today's Tuesday. I've got my seminar tonight. How would nine be? Too late for you?"

"Tonight?"

"Yes."

"Nine is fine. Where?"

He gave me directions to his place in Brookline. His office was in his house. It sounded like a large house in a nice neighborhood.

11

D R. WARREN MCALLISTER'S big Victorian was exactly where he said it would be in Brookline, and I got there ten minutes early. A giant elm tree, apparently immune to the Dutch elm disease that has virtually extinguished that elegant old tree from New England, grew on the lawn. Its swooping limbs still clung stubbornly to a few clumps of leaves. Foundation plantings of rhododendrons had been allowed to sprawl unchecked across the front of the house, almost obscuring the porch that appeared to completely encircle it.

I parked on the street and sat in my car, smoking a cigarette and waiting for nine o'clock to arrive. I hate to be early. I also hate to be late. I like to get to my appointments just a few minutes ahead of time and then wait. I don't always make it, but it's how I like to do it.

Floodlights under the high eaves illuminated the driveway along the side of the house. The doctor had instructed me to go around to the back. At precisely nine I got out of my car, stomped on my cigarette butt, and followed the driveway around the house.

I climbed the wide steps onto the back porch and found two doors there, side by side, under a bright overhead light. One of the doors was heavy and solid-looking with no windows. In the center of it was a small brass plate on which "Dr. Warren McAllister" was etched in fancy lettering. The other door had a window in it with a curtain drawn across from the inside. Beside each door was a bell. Over the doctor's bell was a neatly hand-lettered sign that said "Ring and then come in."

I pressed the bell beside Dr. Warren's door, but I decided to wait rather than enter, and a minute or so later the door opened.

"Mr. Coyne?" he said.

He was a couple inches taller than my six feet, angular and a little stoop shouldered, with a bushy thatch of silvery hair that flopped over the tops of his ears. His eyes were deep-set and sharp blue. His face was seamed with what are called wrinkles on women, but on men are known as "character lines." I guessed he was in his late fifties.

He was wearing a Harris tweed jacket, with earth colors predominating, a blue oxford shirt that matched his eyes, a dark green tie, and tan trousers. He held a pair of steel-rimmed reading glasses in one hand.

He extended the other hand to me. I shook it and said, "Dr. McAllister. I appreciate your seeing me."

"No problem, Mr. Coyne. Glad you could make it. Well, why don't you come on up." He turned and I followed him up a flight of stairs that corkscrewed its way to the third floor. At the top was another door that opened into a small sitting room, the place where his patients waited until their fifty-minute hour session began, I assumed. It was furnished with an oxblood leather sofa and two matching easy chairs, a coffee table stacked with *New Yorker* and *Yankee* magazines, an aluminum coffee urn, and a large, densely populated tropical fish tank. Several cheerfully amateurish watercolors in cheap frames adorned the walls.

McAllister paused inside the waiting room for me to

catch up. Then he said, "We can talk in my office, if you don't mind."

"Fine," I said.

He pulled open a door and we entered a room nearly as big as my entire apartment. I noticed that there was another door, this one opening into the office. A double check on his patients' privacy, I deduced.

The floors were wide pine planks, with several braided rugs scattered about. Large windows on two walls looked out into the treetops. The other two walls were lined floor-to-ceiling with bookshelves. A wood stove stood in one corner. Two comfortable-looking armchairs sat facing each other in front of the wood stove. A big wooden desk, its top littered with papers and books, crouched under one of the windows. In another quadrant of the room was an upholstered chaise. A straight-backed chair sat by its head.

McAllister waved his hand. "Here's where I work," he said. "We can sit over here, if you want."

He led me to the two armchairs by the stove. I took one. He sat across from me. He fitted his glasses onto his face, leaving them low on his nose so that he looked at me over the top of them. "About Mary Ellen Ames," he said. "I'm sure it's redundant for me to reiterate the constraints that we'll have to place on this conversation. You must deal with matters of confidentiality now and then."

I nodded. "Happens a lot. I place a lot of value on discretion in my practice."

He nodded and smiled. "Yes, good. Both of us must be careful to protect our clients' privileged status with us. So if I appear less than forthcoming with you, Mr. Coyne, I want you to know that it's not because I don't care or am not as concerned as you are." He cleared his throat and arched his eyebrows at me.

"Sure," I said. "I understand. You are concerned about Mary Ellen Ames, then?"

He nodded. "Yes. She's my patient. I'm concerned about all my patients."

"Do you have a particular reason to be concerned in Mary Ellen's case?"

"Why don't you tell me what you want, Mr. Coyne."

So I did. I told him about Susan and my frustrated efforts to find Mary Ellen. He was a good listener. Those sharp eyes studied my face as I talked. He nodded frequently and murmured, "Certainly. Mm hm," when I paused in my narration, or, "Yes. Of course." When I mentioned going into her place and finding the prescription for Pertofrane with his name on it, he blinked but said nothing.

When I stopped, he said, "So you're asking me if I know where she is."

I shrugged. "Yes. That's what I was hoping you could tell me."

He slowly removed his glasses and gazed down at them as he held them in his lap. Then he looked up at me. "Perhaps you were wondering why I was so agreeable about meeting with you."

I nodded. "Well, yes, as a matter of fact. I didn't expect you to be so—cooperative."

"I wouldn't be normally. But Miz Ames has missed—let's see—we meet four times a week, so counting today's session, she has missed ten consecutive appointments. It is, quite frankly, a source of some concern to me, yes. She has not always been completely faithful about keeping her appointments, or informing me ahead of time if she's unable to meet with me. Many patients are irresponsible about this, and when they fail to show I am unlikely to be particularly concerned, although it's part of their therapy to keep the work going, even when it's painful for them, and their failure to keep appointments—often a rather transparent form of passive aggressiveness directed at the analyst, you see—inevitably becomes the topic of their subsequent sessions. But Miz Ames, as I said, has missed two full weeks plus yesterday and today, and as far as I know there is no reason for it. She's—"

"Has it been painful for Mary Ellen recently?" I interjected.

"Painful?"

"Your word, Doctor."

He frowned for an instant, then smiled. "Oh, yes. I see. Well, I shouldn't say it's been unusually painful for Miz Ames lately. Difficult, of course. It always is. We've worked very hard together for a very long time now. She has been making slow but steady progress. There have, naturally, been some, as you say, painful times. But, no, not currently." He cocked his head at me. "If you mean should I have anticipated her doing something, ah, desperate or destructive, no, I can't honestly say there's been anything particular."

"Desperate or destructive?"

"Pardon?"

"Your words again."

He shrugged. "She's a psychiatric patient, Mr. Coyne."

"Yeah, I see." I paused. "The drug, that Pertofrane—?"

"It's an antidepressant."

"So she's depressed, then."

He shook his head. The question was out of bounds, if I couldn't figure it out for myself.

"Has she spoken to you about a man named Dave Finn? Or Sherif Rahmanan? Or—" I squinted, trying to remember. "Or Sid Raiford?"

McAllister smiled. He reminded me of a Norman Rockwell *Saturday Evening Post* cover, the rural general practitioner about to remove a splinter from a tearful boy's finger. Kindly, gentle, wise, competent. "I can't discuss any of that with you, Mr. Coyne," he said. "Even if you are her mother's attorney."

"I need to know if she's said anything to you that would give us a hint as to where she's gone, that's all I'm after."

"I don't know where she is—"

"But—"

"But if I knew, I wouldn't tell you."

"But she could do something, um, desperate or destructive."

"I think I already indicated how I felt about that."

"You said, I think," I said, "that you didn't believe you should be held responsible for anticipating something like that, which is a little different. I'm not concerned with responsibility here."

"That's not exactly what I said." He smiled again. "I'll bet you're a pretty fair attorney, Mr. Coyne."

I waved my hand. "I'm sorry if it sounds like I'm cross-examining you. I'm just trying to find her. And I can't, and it worries me. Mainly on Susan's account. Nobody seems to know where she is. Mary Ellen's certainly got a right to her privacy, and you, I understand, are obliged to honor it. But if you have any idea how I can reach her . . ."

He nodded. "I apologize. This is a bit awkward for me. Normally I would refuse even to meet with you, for fear of inadvertently overstepping the proper bounds. Hence I find myself bending over backwards not to. All I can tell you is that Miz Ames's disappearance, or whatever we will call it, surprises me as it does you. And, yes, it does worry me. She has a great deal of work ahead of her before something like this would not disturb me. But as to the substance of our work together, I'm afraid that's simply out of bounds."

He arched his eyebrows at me. I shrugged.

"I'm sorry," he said.

"You have no idea where she might be, then?"

"If I did, it would be improper for me to share it with you." He hesitated. "I suppose I can tell you this, though. If she has gone somewhere, I have no idea where it might be or why she decided to go there. And I can say this, too. I do not believe Mary Ellen Ames is a danger to herself." He sighed. "And I would like to terminate this discussion at this point, if you don't mind."

"Not a danger to herself," I repeated. "You're talking about suicide?"

"Yes. Exactly. It's what we shrinks worry about. A patient's suicide is our ultimate failure, Mr. Coyne."

"But I can tell Susan not to worry about that."

"I would be absolutely shocked. Honestly."

"Can you think of a reason why she might want to run away?"

He shook his head. "I really do insist we close the subject."

I nodded. "Okay." I held out my hand to him. "I appreciate your time."

He smiled. "I'm sorry I couldn't be of more help." He stood up. "Look, would you care to join me for a drink?"

"Oh, I couldn't. I've taken enough of your time."

"I insist."

I shrugged. "Well, okay. Sure. Why not."

He held up his hand, palm facing me. "No shop talk, now."

"Agreed."

"Let me just find a couple things on my desk and we can go downstairs."

He went over to the desk under the windows and began

to rummage among the papers. I wandered over to the book-cases. He had an eclectic collection—old volumes of Freud and Jung, some Plato and Aristotle, Hemingway and Faulkner, Tolstoy and Chekhov—and on one shelf, by heavens, newer books by writers such as Brooks, Marinaro, Lefty Kreh, and Nick Lyons.

"Are you a fly fisherman, Doctor?" I said to him.

He turned and grinned at me. "I try. I do love it. Marvelous therapy. You?"

"To the point of obsessive compulsion."

"There, Mr. Coyne, is a subject which I can discuss without inhibition. The fly-fishing neurosis in all of its guises." He stared at the disarray on his desk and frowned. Then he shrugged. He looked up at me and grinned. "Come on. I bet you're a bourbon man."

He headed for the door. I followed him. "How'd you know that?" I said.

"What?"

"Bourbon."

"We shrinks are skilled at inferential reasoning, Mr. Coyne." He turned at the head of the stairs and smiled at me. "You're a smoker, too, aren't you?"

"That's amazing."

He tapped his head with his finger. "Medical school training, years of analysis."

"God, I hate to be that transparent."

"Nobody but a trained psychiatrist would ever figure out things like that about you, Mr. Coyne."

12

I FOLLOWED Dr. Warren McAllister down the stairs. At the landing he opened an inside door and we entered a large kitchen. Piano music—Chopin, I thought—filtered through hidden speakers. Ferns and pots of herbs and garlic braids and copper-bottomed cookware hung from big beams. There was a giant fireplace on the inside wall. In the corner stood a round table by a large window.

A woman was seated at the table. She had long dark hair sparsely streaked with gray and pulled back into a careless ponytail. She was wearing a pale blue T-shirt and faded and stained blue jeans. Her feet, under the table, were bare. A newspaper was spread open on the table in front of her. A coffee mug sat on one corner of the paper and an ashtray littered with butts sat on another corner.

She looked up and smiled when we entered. "Hi," she said. She had blue eyes almost exactly the same shade as McAllister's. Her face was long and thin, with prominent cheekbones and a wide mouth. She appeared to be about my age, which I guessed would make her about fifteen years younger than the doctor.

McAllister went over to her and kissed her cheek. "Robin, this is Mr. Coyne, a friend of mine and a fellow devotee of the angle. Mr. Coyne, I'm proud to present Robin McAllister, my wife and the best headshrinker in the family."

She held her hand out to me. I went over and took it. "Happy to meet you, Mr. Coyne," she said.

"Call me Brady," I said. "You're a psychiatrist, too?"

She made a face. "No, for heaven's sake. I'm a nurse." She tossed her head in Warren's direction. "He just gets spooked because I can see right through him so easily." She smiled.

"Well, now," said McAllister. "Since our business is done we can all get to first names. I'm Warren. So, Brady. Sour mash okay with you?"

"Perfect."

He reached up into a cupboard and took down a bottle of Jack Daniel's, which he showed me. I smiled and nodded. "Something, dear?" he said to his wife.

"A wee drop of the same would be nice, sure."

I sat across from Robin McAllister while Warren mixed our drinks. She shook a menthol cigarette out of a pack and struck a match to it. "You're obviously not a patient, Brady," she said to me.

"Is it that obvious?"

She smiled. "He doesn't bring patients down to drink with him. Otherwise, you just can't tell."

"You medical types are downright eerie, the way you draw these clever deductions. Your husband figured out that I smoked, for example."

"Winstons, I'll bet," she said.

"How the hell do you do it?"

"You've got a pack in your shirt pocket. It shows."

"Like I said. Amazing." I patted my shirt pocket, took out the pack, and lit a Winston. She laughed and pushed the ashtray so that it sat halfway between us.

She had a pleasing laugh, uninhibited and happy. I found myself liking her, liking the warmth of the McAllister kitchen, liking the casual intimacy so obvious between the two of them, liking the way Robin McAllister and I were sharing an ashtray.

He brought three short glasses to the table. Each of us picked up one of them. Daniel's, ice, no water. He lifted his. "To the insanity of trout fishing," he said.

"Amen," I said.

"Neurotic foolishness," added Robin.

We all toasted neurotic foolishness.

Warren McAllister and I exchanged tales of large trout, eccentric fishermen, and beautiful western rivers. Robin sipped her drink and paged through her newspaper, looking up occasionally to affirm something that Warren had politely addressed to her. She had accompanied him on a few of his trips, had done some fly fishing herself. Evidently the addiction hadn't afflicted her. I inferred that Warren wished it had.

Robin told me she was an emergency room nurse at the Newton-Wellesley Hospital. Her eyes sparkled when she discussed her work. She loved the variety of it, the unpredictability, the way the adrenaline sometimes pumped, the fact that nurses in the emergency room did real medical work, saved lives. That's how she and Warren had met. One of his patients had been admitted with gaping wounds on her wrists. Self-inflicted with an Exacto knife. Warren nodded. Robin had saved the girl's life.

We had a second round. We talked more fishing. Warren and I moved on to parts of the world we hadn't yet explored. By the third round the bottle was sitting on the table and he and I were making plans to take a month off in January for a trip to New Zealand. Robin had stopped reading. She sat back in her chair hugging her knees, her bare feet propped on the seat, watching the two of us and smiling.

After a while she stood up. She was taller than I had expected. Her jeans and T-shirt fit her snugly. She looked good in them. "I've got to be at the hospital at seven," she said. "Hate to be a party pooper, but I'm going to bed." She kissed her husband on the top of his head and smiled at me. "Good night, boys. Very nice to meet you, Brady."

I nodded. "Me, too."

After she left the room, Warren McAllister said, "Helluva lady, Robin."

"You're lucky," I said.

"The thing is, I know it. Sixteen years, all with the same woman, and it's still an adventure. Pretty rare. You're not married, Brady?"

"Divorced," I answered.

"Sure," he said. "I knew that."

"Any kids?"

He shook his head. "We never wanted any. Selfish, I guess. Our careers are important to us. And both of us see so much sadness in the world, all the ways that people go wrong, I guess we just haven't wanted to risk it." He shrugged. "We still talk about it. Robin just turned forty. A critical stage in a woman's life. The tick-tick of her biological clock. What about you?"

"Me? Oh, I've got two boys. Nice guys, both of them."

"You're fortunate." He sighed. "I don't know. We may yet try. Robin's getting restless. She's very dedicated to her work, but lately she's gotten into botany. By way of sublimation, I suspect. On her days off she's usually over at the Arnold Arboretum for classes or traipsing around the countryside looking for rare plants." He shrugged. "To each his own. I like fish, myself. Sunday is my day. I go fishing on Sundays."

I nodded and lifted my glass to him. "To fish."

He touched my glass with his. "To trout."

We drank, splashed a little more sour mash whiskey into our glasses, and drank some more. We tried to refine our New Zealand plans. We debated the relative merits of North Island and South Island. We took turns yawning. After a while, I pushed back from the table. "Better hit the road," I said.

"Not until I get some coffee into you. Otherwise you're likely to hit a telephone pole, instead."

"I'm okay."

"Like hell. You've had as much to drink as me, and I'm not okay."

"Coffee, then," I said.

He went to the counter and put on some coffee. Then he came back and sat down. "Listen," he said, "there's something I think I should tell you."

"What is it?"

He gazed up toward the ceiling. "That Dave Finn?"

I nodded.

He peered at me for a moment, then shook his head.

"What about Dave Finn?" I said.

He waved his hand. "Never mind. Sorry."

"Should we be concerned about Dave Finn?"

"Forget I mentioned it, Brady. Okay?"

"He's a cop. Says he and Mary Ellen are planning to get married. I know that already."

Warren got up and went to the coffeepot. He returned with two mugs. He slid one in front of me. "Black, right?"

"How the Christ did you know that?"

He smiled.

"What did you want to say about Dave Finn?"

"Please," he said. "Just drink your coffee."

13

TERRI FIORI answered the phone when I called the next morning. "It's Brady Coyne, General, sir."

She laughed. "Boy, that's the last time I refer to myself as a factotum, I'll tell you that. How are you?"

"I am excellent. How are the troops today?"

"She's right here. I'll put her on."

"Hey, General?"

"Yes?"

"We still on for Friday?"

"You bet. Hang on. I'll get Susan."

A moment later Susan said, "Hello?"

"It's Brady," I said. "How are we doing today?"

"We are doing fine, thank you," she said. "Have you talked to Mary Ellen yet?"

"Well, not exactly."

"Terri said you called the other day and that you'd found her."

"Well, I found where she's living."

"Meaning?"

"Meaning, she's not home. Hasn't been for a couple weeks. She's apparently on vacation or something."

There was a pause. "Brady, what's up? What the hell is going on?"

"Okay," I said. I had called to tell her everything, including what was becoming a bad feeling in my bones about Mary Ellen. Warren McAllister's allusion to suicide, even while denying that Mary Ellen was a candidate for it, had spooked me. But by the time Susan answered the phone I had decided to chicken out. Now I realized I couldn't do that. She had a right to know. "The truth is," I told her, "I've talked to several people—a man who's involved with her, people at the building where she lives, her psychiatrist—and—"

"Psychiatrist?"

"Yes. A Dr. McAllister."

I heard a sigh. "Oh, my."

"Anyway, none of them knows where she is. It probably just means that she's taken a trip, gone off with friends, but—well, she's missed two weeks of appointments with the doctor, and didn't cancel them or anything. I'm a little concerned, to tell the truth, Susan."

"What exactly are you thinking?"

"I don't know. Nothing, really. I'm sure she'll turn up."

"But?"

"Well, it might not be a bad idea to, um, file a missing persons."

"She's been missing for eleven years, Brady. I mean, the fact that she's not there doesn't mean she's missing, does it? She's somewhere. She's just not where you're looking. You file a missing persons thing when . . ." Her voice trailed off.

After a minute, I said, "Susan?"

"I'm here. I'm sorry."

"There are some more people I can talk to," I said.

"It's just that since you and I talked, I've been hoping—looking forward to—to seeing her. It's not just the will . . ."

"I understand," I said softly.

"I don't know how much time . . ."

"She'll turn up. I'm sure there's nothing to worry about. I just wanted to keep you posted."

"Yes. Thank you." She cleared her throat. "I'm sorry."

"I'll keep in touch, Susan."

I hung up, took a deep breath, let it out slowly. There wasn't much more I could really do. I took out my notebook and glanced at the notes I had taken. There was the bookstore, Head Start Books in Cambridge, where, according to Sherif Rahmanan, Mary Ellen used to work. Maybe she actually still worked there, or kept in touch with someone there. And there was a man named Sid Raiford, whom Dave Finn had mentioned and who, I assumed, was the same man described by the security guys at Mary Ellen's building. Possibly one of the nameless men who had left messages on her answering machine, meaning he didn't know where she was, either. There was Rahmanan himself, who had also tried to call her after telling me he had lost track of her. He obviously knew more than he told me at Hung Moon's. He knew where Mary Ellen lived, for one thing. But it didn't figure that he knew where she had gone.

Finn knew no more than I did. Dr. Warren McAllister wouldn't tell me any more than he already had, regardless of what he knew.

Most likely Mary Ellen Ames, with all her freedom and all her money, had just taken off for a while. Sick of analysis, feeling pressured by Finn, lured by warm sun and sand beaches. A spontaneous getaway with a new lover, perhaps— there were plenty of explanations that made more sense than the vague uneasiness in my stomach warranted.

I called Horowitz anyway.

Horowitz was a state police detective I had worked with before. I once helped him solve a murder case that indirectly involved one of my clients. He owed me one.

A secretary put me through to him at his office at Ten-ten Commonwealth Avenue. "Yeah, Horowitz," he said.

"It's Brady Coyne."

"Oh, yeah. How you doin'?"

"I'm fine. I need a favor."

"Huh," he said, half a laugh and half a grunt. "Figures."

"I'm looking for a young woman."

"Ain't we all, pal."

"Sure. Right. Listen. As near as I can figure, this particular one's been missing for two weeks."

"Missing?"

"Nobody knows where she is."

"Like her husband, her parents?"

"She's not married. Hasn't seen her mother in eleven years. Since her father died."

"She run away from school or what?"

"She's about thirty. Not in school."

"So she's not showing up for work, then, is that it? Roommate, lover can't find her?"

"Actually, I'm not sure she has a job. She lives alone."

Horowitz cleared his throat. "Excuse me, counselor. But who says she's missing?"

"Me, I guess."

"Because you don't know where she is."

"Well, yes."

"You think anybody looking for somebody can just come to the cops?"

"This is different."

"Sure," he said. "Any evidence that she might've been kidnapped or something?"

"No."

"She retarded? A mental patient?"

"Not exactly. She's being treated by a psychiatrist."

"Like about three out of every five Americans, you mean."

"I've got a bad feeling about it," I said lamely.

"On the basis of which you want to file a missing persons, is that it?"

"Listen, okay? Her name is Mary Ellen Ames. Her mother, my client, is dying of cancer. She's got maybe a month, maybe a little more. She wants to reconcile with her daughter before she dies. I told her I'd try to find her. I can't. I was wondering if you could help me out, for Christ's sake. That's all."

"Because I owe you one, right?"

"I wasn't even going to mention it."

He sighed. "So what do you want me to do?"

"What can you do?"

"Well," he said after a moment, "short of filing a formal missing persons, which doesn't really sound called for here, I suppose I could put the word out, circulate her photo, description, the usual. Massachusetts, contiguous states. How'd that be? Would that make us even, get you offa my back?"

"That would be great."

"Whyn't you come on down, we'll get the dope."

"I'll be there in an hour. And thanks."

"Just so you remember we're even, Coyne."

It was a short cab ride over to Ten-ten. Horowitz gave me a styrofoam cup of muddy coffee and settled behind his desk. I took the straight-backed wooden chair beside him. He rolled a form into his typewriter. "Okay," he said, his eyes fixed on the keys. "Name?"

"Ames, Mary Ellen."

He used the index and middle fingers of his right hand for the keys and his left thumb for the space bar. He typed fast. He kept his eyes on the keyboard and asked me questions without looking up at me.

"Address?"

I gave him Mary Ellen's Beacon Street number.

"Race?"

"White."

"Age?"

"Thirty."

"Hair?"

I removed her photo from my attaché case and looked at it. "Brown."

"Eyes?"

"Blue."

"Height?"

"I don't know. Average, I suppose."

He glanced up at me with his eyebrows arched.

"I've never seen her," I said.

He shrugged. "Suppose you don't know her weight, either."

"No."

"What about scars, tattoos, birthmarks, missing digits?"

"I don't know."

"I guess you don't know what she was wearing when she disappeared?"

"I don't know when she disappeared, period. You were probably going to ask me that. I'm not even sure she *has* disappeared. She's just—missing."

He nodded. "Yeah, you explained that." He looked back down at the form in his typewriter. "She have a car, do you know?"

"No. I don't know."

"Guess we can look that up," he muttered. "What about next of kin?"

"Her mother. Susan Ames. In Concord. But if you find her, I'm the one to inform, okay?"

"Sure," he mumbled, still whacking the keys. "Um, if you were to go looking for her, where'd you go?"

I shrugged, more for my benefit than his, since he wasn't looking at me. "To her place on Beacon Street. Where I already did go to look for her. She's not there. Otherwise, I have no idea."

He finished typing, sighed, and pushed himself back from his typewriter. "Hope you got a photo, at least."

I handed him Mary Ellen's high school graduation portrait. "This is about twelve years old," I said. "It's the most recent one her mother had."

"Can I keep it for a while?"

"I guess so. Susan would probably like it back eventually."

"I'll fax it out, see what happens." He yanked the form from his typewriter, clipped the photo to it, and put it into a wire basket on the corner of his desk. "You understand," he said, "this probably ain't gonna accomplish anything. Unless . . ." He peered at me.

I nodded. Unless they found a body, he meant.

He squinted at me. "That what you think, Coyne?"

I shook my head. "No reason whatsoever to think that, no."

"But maybe we ought to check the Jane Does down at the morgue, huh?"

"Oh, boy," I said.

"You wanna try to do this right?"

I shrugged. "It'd be good to eliminate them, I suppose."

He picked up his phone and depressed a button. Then he said, "Bring me the Jane Doe files, huh, sweetheart?"

I lit a cigarette. Horowitz unwrapped a stick of

Wrigley's, folded it up, pushed it into his mouth, and began chomping on it. "Been fishing?" he mumbled around the wad of gum.

Horowitz, I knew, did not fish, nor did he think it was an interesting pursuit. "Not enough," I answered.

He shrugged. "She should be in in a minute."

I smoked and he chewed in silence for a few minutes. Then his secretary came in. She plunked a sheaf of manila folders down on his desk, flashed me a quick smile, and left.

One by one, Horowitz slid the eight-by-ten glossy black-and-white photographs of dead women's faces in front of me. There were a dozen or fifteen of them. It appeared to be an accurate random sample of the Greater Boston population of women—just the right proportions of black, Hispanic, and white; young, middle-aged, and old; attractive, average, and downright ugly. Some of the faces were bruised, lacerated, or swollen almost beyond recognition. Others appeared to be sleeping.

None of them remotely resembled the graduation picture of Mary Ellen Ames.

I shook my head at each of them.

When I handed the last photo back to Horowitz, I said, "Nope."

"Good, I guess, huh?"

"I don't assume she's dead," I said.

"Well," he said, "if she's not, I probably won't be able to help you."

14

ON FRIDAYS during the best parts of the trout season I generally hang the "Gone Fishin'" sign on the office door at noon. Julie gets a head start on her weekend with Edward and Megan. I sneak out to the Swift River in Belchertown, or the Deerfield near Charlemont, to catch the afternoon mayfly hatch.

Sometimes I hang out the sign on Fridays even when I don't go fishing. Hell, it's my office, my law practice, my secretary. I'm supposed to be able to do what I want. I'm still working on not feeling guilty when I actually do what I want.

So at noon that Friday, the last one of September, I put up the sign, told Julie to switch on the answering machine, and sent her off. She did not argue. She wished me tight lines. I didn't tell her I was meeting Gloria for lunch. Julie would read an entire romance novel into that.

I got to Marie's a little early. Marie bear-hugged me, gave me her big gap-toothed grin, and led me to my table. A moment later a waitress put a carafe of the house red in front of me, compliments of Marie.

I'd sipped half an inch of my first glass when Gloria sat down across from me. She smiled quickly. "Hi," she said.

"Hi, hon." Her hair was shorter and straighter than it

had been the last time I'd seen her. The gray streaks in it had disappeared. "You got a new do, huh?"

Her hand darted up and touched her head. "You don't like it?"

I smiled. "I like it fine. It's different."

I poured some wine into her glass. She lifted it to her mouth and sipped quickly, in her characteristically nervous way. Maybe her nervous way was characteristic only when she was around me, I don't know.

I assumed I knew her agenda, but I didn't push it. We talked about the boys, ordered our lunches, exchanged business anecdotes. Gloria is a photographer who has, in recent years, landed some magazine assignments that have earned her a good reputation. No longer does she have to do weddings and bar mitzvahs and birthday parties. She told me she had been approached by a video company that needed someone to do the stills, and she was thinking of diversifying and taking on a full-time assistant. I thought, but didn't say, that she'd come a long way since our divorce. Farther than I had.

After our coffee arrived, she leaned toward me. "Brady," she said, "I've got some news."

I smiled. Here it came. "Good news, I hope," I said.

"I'm planning to put the house on the market."

"How come?" She was going to move in with Richard. I already knew how come.

She leaned back. Her eyes went to the ceiling. "Wellesley is too far from the action. I don't like working and living at the same place. If I take on an assistant, I'm going to need more work space. I'm looking at a studio in Harvard Square and a condo on Memorial Drive. Look. Joseph will be off to college in less than two years. I'll need less space to live and more space to work. This makes sense, don't you think?"

What about the dweeb lawyer, I was thinking.

I nodded. "Sounds good, I guess."

"Anyway," she said, "I thought before I talked to a realtor I'd give you a shot at it."

"At what?"

"The house. You lived there a long time. You did a lot of work on that house. You loved that house."

I hated that house, I thought. I hated painting and papering and lawn mowing and gutter cleaning and washer replacing and furniture moving. I hated the tension that crouched in every corner of every room of that house.

The house went to Gloria in the divorce settlement. It was the loss I regretted the least.

"Do I have to tell you now?" I temporized. I wondered when she was going to get around to telling me about Richard the lawyer.

She smiled and shook her head. "Of course not. I knew you'd need some time to think about it. I have a friend who'll give us an appraisal, and I'd deduct the broker's commission for you. We'll do a private sale. You can do the legal work. It would be a good deal for both of us."

"I'll have to think about it," I said. "This is kind of sudden."

"Fine. Two weeks, say?"

"You're in a hurry."

She shrugged. "I want to get moving on it. The market's soft."

"I'll let you know."

She smiled. "Good." She picked up her coffee cup and took a sip. End of subject.

And when we exchanged pecks on the cheek and parted outside Marie's, she still had not mentioned her marriage plans. I sure as hell wasn't going to raise the subject.

And I sure as hell wasn't going to move back to a

haunted house in the suburbs. Not that I was particularly enamored of my little apartment on the waterfront. But I liked the idea of renting. I liked my tenant-at-will lease. I liked the sense of transience it gave me, the irresponsibility, the absence of commitment. Some day I'd buy a ranch in Montana. In the meantime, I'd remain as unencumbered as possible.

I'd wait a week before I turned down Gloria's offer, so that she'd think I had given it serious consideration.

I had started back to my office when I remembered that the Gone Fishin' sign was hanging on the door. I stopped and glanced at my watch. Two o'clock. Too late to go home, change, and drive to a trout river. The sun would be setting around five-thirty. I thought of going back to the office anyway. I could get some paperwork done.

Bad idea.

So I descended into the underground at Kenmore and took the T to Park Square, where I changed to the Red Line outbound. I emerged in Central Square and began to walk along Mass Ave. toward Harvard Square. I had looked up Head Start Books in the Boston Yellow Pages. I had a general idea where I'd find it.

And it was there, more or less as I had imagined it—narrow in front, dirt-streaked windows, with a sign that read "Books, New and Used. Specializing in Occult and New Age."

I went in. It was dimly lit. The aisles between the tables and shelves of books were narrow. I browsed among the volumes, moving toward the back of the store, hoping to find some old trout-fishing tomes. Fly fishing for trout, I always thought, qualified as occult, though bookstores generally put their fishing books among those on golf and aerobics.

"Help you?" came a deep voice from behind me.

I turned quickly. I hadn't heard him approach me. "Jeez," I said. "You startled me."

"Sorry, man."

Sid Raiford. It had to be. His hair was the color of slush, pulled back in a ponytail at the base of his neck. Deep furrows bracketed his mouth and eyes. He was about sixty. A superannuated hippie, just as Donald, the doorman in Mary Ellen's building, had described him. He had gray teeth and gray eyes and a gold hoop in his left ear. A blue silk shirt was open to his bony sternum. A necklace of love beads showed across his chest. He was wearing bell-bottomed jeans with a red patch in the crotch and fringed moccasins on his feet.

"I was looking for trout fishing books," I said to him.

"Trout fishing." He grinned. "Far out."

"You don't have fishing books?"

He looked me up and down, taking in my lawyer's costume. His eyes narrowed. "Sorry, guy. Try the Coop."

I shrugged. "I was just on my way by, thought I'd take a look."

"The Coop's your best bet."

I nodded. I looked at him and frowned. "Say," I said. "I have a friend who I think used to work here. Maybe she still does."

"Who's that?"

"Mary Ellen Ames is her name."

His eyes shifted, returned to mine. "Ames?"

I nodded.

He shrugged. "Don't know any Ames chick."

"Well, guess I was mistaken."

"Guess so."

"The Coop, you say?"

He nodded.

"Maybe I'll try there, then."

He made a V with his fingers. "Peace, brother."

"Peace," I said.

I didn't go to the Coop. I went home. And all the time I was showering and changing and driving out to meet Terri in Acton, I tried to figure out why Raiford had lied to me. I came up with several scenarios.

I got to the restaurant before Terri. I waited outside the door, smoking a cigarette and looking up at the starry autumn sky and wondering if she would really show up.

When her Volkswagen putt-putted into the parking lot, I glanced at my watch. Seven-forty. She was only ten minutes late, and I had been, as is my unfortunate compulsion, precisely on time. I had only been waiting ten minutes. It seemed longer.

I went to where she parked and held the door for her. She was wearing a short dark skirt and a pale blouse and a bright red jacket. No jewelry, no makeup. She looked terrific.

I took one step back, clicked my heels, and snapped a salute. "Evening, General."

She nodded once. "At ease, mister."

She held her hand out to me. I took it. Then she grinned and tiptoed up and kissed my cheek. "Am I late?"

"Right on time."

We went in. The outside door opened into a large lobby. An inside door was marked "Ciao." The restaurant was small and dimly lit. A classical guitar played from hidden speakers. The windows, I noticed, were stained glass.

A silver-haired man greeted us and introduced us to the evening's specials. They all sounded delicious. Just their melodic Italian names sounded delicious.

After we were seated, we ordered a bottle of burgundy and snails in garlic and butter. While we ate our appetizers and sipped the wine, we talked about Susan. Terri seemed to know everything about her. It was clear that she was very fond of her, and I suspected that Susan thought of Terri as more than a factotum.

Terri had the chicken special and I had the veal, and we didn't talk much while we ate. We sampled from each other's fork and proclaimed it all excellent. When the coffee came, she said, without prologue, "I want you to know, I don't date, Brady."

I smiled at her. "What's this, then?"

She looked away. "I don't know. An experiment."

"Am I the guinea pig?"

"No. I am."

"Want to talk about it?"

She nodded. "I guess I'm just a little gun-shy."

"Something bad, huh?"

"I've got a ten-year-old daughter."

"Nothing wrong with that. I've got two boys myself."

She smiled. "I'm not married."

"Me neither. Divorced about ten years."

"I'm not divorced, either."

I shrugged.

She sipped her coffee and gazed into her cup. "The two best things I've ever done in my life," she said softly. She looked up at me. "Having Melissa, and not marrying Cliff."

I nodded.

"He's actually a nice guy," she said. "He wanted to put me into a white clapboard house in the suburbs where I could play bridge and join the PTA and clip recipes from the newspaper. I tried to imagine it. I couldn't make it work." Her gaze wandered around the restaurant. "We lived together for a year. Practice, we called it. But I was working, and it was okay. Then I got pregnant. Just dumb carelessness. Anyhow, Cliff was thrilled. I'd been resisting marriage. Now, he said, we had to. It made me really visualize it, and it just scared the hell out of me. I told him I'd be willing to continue living together for a while. He wouldn't buy it. Gave me the ultimatum. Marry him or we'd split. The choice was easy."

"But actually doing it must be hard," I said.

She shrugged. "Sure. It is hard. I like things that way."

"What about him?"

She laughed softly. "He was married within a year. He's got two little boys now. Melissa calls them her brothers. It's all very modern. Cliff married a nice lady who has a magnificent recipe collection. She and I are on decent terms. She's good to Melissa. Cliff and I are civil. He's a good father. Probably a good husband, for that matter."

"So you swore off men, huh?"

She nodded. "That was my firm decision, Brady. No men. No place in my life for a man. They either want to marry you and chain you to a house, or they just want to— you know. Either way, they steal your soul. I've got a daughter who needs me. I've got Susan, right now, and she needs me. I'm busy. My life is full." She shrugged.

"What about this, then?"

"This? Our date?"

I nodded.

She smiled. "Would you believe, you're so handsome I couldn't resist?"

"I wouldn't believe that. No."

"That's good." She reached across the table and put her hand onto mine. "You *are* kinda handsome, though. But, no, that wasn't it. When you asked me the first time, I said no. Reflex. Anyhow, it was my weekend with Melissa. Cliff and I swap every other weekend. I look forward to my time with her. With all the hours I'm putting in with Susan, I hardly see

Melissa during the week. But I got to thinking. Want to know the truth?"

"Yes."

"I was dreading this weekend. Without her. Being alone. Maybe after all these years I'm getting a little sick of being alone every other weekend, I don't know. I used to love being alone. I called it solitude. Lately it seems more like loneliness. Anyway, the more I thought about seeing you, the more I liked the thought. It seemed like a risk. But maybe a risk worth taking. You don't strike me as the kind of guy who wants to capture a woman's soul." She smiled quickly. "If I'm wrong, you better tell me now."

"I'm still trying to get a line on my own soul," I said. "That's pretty much a full-time job."

"Well," she said, "so far I don't regret it."

"I'm glad," I said. I squeezed her hand. She didn't pull it away.

I paid the bill and we walked out into the night. The sky was clear and the air cool. Terri hooked her arm through mine as I walked her to her car. I squeezed her arm against my side.

She fumbled in her pocketbook, found her keys, and unlocked her car. Then she turned to me and put her arms around my neck. "Thank you," she said softly.

"I enjoyed it," I said.

Her kiss was hesitant at first, as if she had never done it before. Then her mouth yielded and her lips parted and it became a real kiss. Her arms tightened around my neck. In her throat she murmured a little two-tone noise that sounded like "Oh-oh," and for an instant her body pressed against mine.

She pulled away from me abruptly. "I'm sorry," she mumbled.

"Why?"

She shook her head. "I told you. I'm gun-shy."

"Don't worry about me," I said. "I'm harmless."

She didn't smile. "You better be."

"We'll play by your rules."

"You'll have to be patient with me."

"I can do that."

"I swore off men a long time ago."

"I know."

"I don't know if I can handle it."

"I don't know if I can, either," I said.

She tilted her head back and peered at me. After a moment she nodded. "Okay," she said. I realized she was talking to herself. "Okay, then."

"How about next weekend?"

She frowned. "I told you. I've got Melissa."

"Good. Bring her."

She shook her head. "I don't think so."

I shrugged. "Your rules."

"Melissa's never seen me with a man."

I thought of Billy's reaction to seeing Gloria with her lawyer dweeb. "Sure. I understand."

"You'd want to go to dinner with me and my daughter?"

"Sure. I like kids."

"Let me think about it."

"Okay."

She got into her Volkswagen and started it up. She needed a new muffler. She cranked down the window. "Hey, Brady?"

"Yes, General?"

She put her face to the open window. "Kiss me?"

"Sure."

I did. It was a good long one.

"I don't know what I'm getting myself into here," she said.

"Me neither," I said.

15

SATURDAY NIGHT. No lonelier than any other night. I was alone, but not lonely. I had my fly-tying table and my books and a briefcase full of paperwork and my little black-and-white television for company.

I wondered what Terri was doing. It was her weekend without Melissa. I thought of calling her. My instincts told me that it wouldn't be a good idea.

I was working on a bowl of Ben and Jerry's New York Super Fudge Chunk, the best ice cream ever made, and watching a PBS documentary on the strange and wonderful fauna of Australia, when the phone rang. I glanced at my watch as I got up to answer it. It was a little after ten.

"Hello?" I said.

"Brady? Mr. Coyne?" A woman's voice, hesitant and shaky.

"Yes?"

"It's Jill. Jill Costello."

I had to think for a minute. "Oh. Hi."

"I couldn't think of anybody else to call."

"It's nice to hear from you."

"He's—I don't think I can take much more," she said. "I don't know what to do."

"Your husband?"

"Yes. Johnny."

"What's happening?"

"It's been all night. Since suppertime. He started with the phone calls. First I just let it ring. So my machine came on, and he talked into it until the tape ran out. Just saying crazy things. Then he kept calling back and I'd just disconnect each time. Finally I left it off the hook. So then he came banging on my door. I just—"

"You didn't tell the guy at the desk not to let him in?"

"Oh, sure. But I've got a private entrance. He knows where it is. He was out there for about an hour, banging and yelling. I feel—I feel like a prisoner. I wish the hell he'd just divorce me and get it over with."

"He's gone now?"

"I think so. I haven't heard him for a while. That's why I called. I couldn't have called before. I was crying too much. You know, if I had a gun I think I would've just blasted away through my door at him. I really wanted to kill him. I'm afraid he wants to kill me. I can't . . ."

I heard her gasp and sob. "Hey," I said.

She snuffled into the telephone. "I'm sorry. I'm probably overreacting. I hate being a hysterical female. I just didn't know what to do."

"You called a friend. That was fine."

"I feel dumb. I don't have anybody else to talk to."

"It's not dumb to be frightened. It sounds like a reasonable way to feel under the circumstances."

"I want to get out of here. But I don't dare."

"Keep your door locked. There's nothing he can do."

"That's what I mean. I'm a prisoner. Damn him!"

"It sounds like you could get a restraining order, Jill."

"Yeah, well I thought of that. This started as soon as he found out where I was living. I talked to a lady at one of those women's support groups about it. She said she doubted a judge would grant a restraining order. He's never actually hurt me, and he is my husband. That's what they go by. You've got to get hurt first, I guess. And the way it works, if you've slept with a guy it seems like he's got the right to harass you all he wants. Like that means he owns you and anything he does is okay. A woman judge might understand. Most of them are men. This woman I talked to, this counselor, she did some role playing with me. Her the judge, me being me. Shit, she made me cry. I mean, I know how rape victims feel. Like it's their fault. She made me feel like I was wrong here, like he was the victim and it was me who was antagonizing him. Like I should go back to him and tell him I was sorry, it was all my fault, and just be happy I got a man."

"I'm sorry" was all I could think of to say.

"Yeah," she said quietly. "Well, thanks for listening." There was a pause. "I didn't think you'd be there."

"I'm here."

"I'm probably keeping you from company."

"No. I was just having some ice cream and watching TV."

She laughed quickly. "Wild night, huh?"

"Yeah. Wild."

Another pause. "Hey, Brady?"

"Yes?"

"No, sorry. Forget it."

"What?"

"I was just wondering. Do you play chess?"

"Chess? Yes, I play sometimes. I'm not very good."

"Me neither." Pause. "Hey, you don't feel like coming over, having a game, do you?"

"Negative question, huh?"

"Dumb question, I guess."

"It's pretty late, Jill."

"Yeah, you're right. Bad idea."

"No," I said, "it's not a bad idea. If it's not too late for you, I'd enjoy a game of chess."

"Really?"

"Sure."

"Hey, great. You can park right beside the building. There's a service entrance around back and a driveway goes around to it. My door's on the side. You'll see my little Toyota there. You can just park right behind it. Knock on my door. Just—just don't bang and start yelling, okay?"

I laughed. "Sure."

"Well, good. See you real soon?"

"I'm on my way."

As soon as I hung up I regretted it. Jill Costello's problems with her husband were not anything I wanted to become enmeshed in. But on the other hand, she was a maiden in distress, and she had called me. I was her noble knight.

Get real, Coyne, I told myself. I'd been thinking about Terri all evening, wondering if I'd see her again. She had said it well. Sometimes solitude becomes loneliness.

Nobility. Right.

Some knight.

I slipped on my sneakers and sweatshirt and went down to my car. It took me about fifteen minutes to get to Beacon Street. One game of chess, one beer, I promised myself. Then I'd get out of there.

The driveway was barely the width of two compact cars or one full-sized delivery truck. Jill's little Toyota was parked right against the building. I pulled in behind her. A bare bulb glowed over a plain steel door. I rapped on it and called, "Jill. It's Brady."

A minute later the heavy door creaked open. She was

wearing a baggy orange sweatshirt and a pair of black running shorts. Smooth bare legs, bare feet. Her hair hung loose down her back, held there by barrettes behind each ear. Her face was scrubbed and clean. Her lipstick looked as if it had been freshly applied. So did her smile. She looked like one of the high-school volleyball players my son Joey dated.

"Oh, hey, this is great," she said. "Come on in."

She reached out, grabbed my hand, and pulled me in. Quickly she closed the door and threw the dead bolt. We were standing in an unfinished hallway that disappeared into darkness on the left and right. Straight ahead of us a door stood ajar. She tugged me through it and into her apartment.

The chessboard was all set up on her table. Her books and papers were neatly stacked on the side. Down the other end of the room her bed was folded back into a sofa. I deduced that she had cleaned up for me.

I sat at the table. She got a couple of bottles of Miller's from the refrigerator and sat across the chessboard from me. She took a white pawn in one hand and a black one in the other, held them behind her back for a moment, then extended her closed fists across the table to me. I tapped one. She opened it. I got black.

"I wasn't sure if this was proper," she said.

"What?"

"Me calling you. I mean, you said you'd look at my papers for me, that's all."

I waved my hand.

"I've been married for a while," she went on, her eyes studying the chess pieces. "I don't know how to . . ." She looked up at me.

I smiled. "Your move."

It took about six moves for me to realize that I was overmatched. She used an opening I'd never seen before, forced a pawn swap that prevented me from castling, and soon got both of my knights for just one of her bishops.

"I concede," I said.

She grinned. "So soon?"

"I may not be good, but I do know when a game is over."

"Want to try again?"

"One more."

I took white, tried the conservative King's Gambit opening that was most familiar to me, and played a cautious, defensive game. It took an hour for her to maneuver a passed pawn into a position where I couldn't stop it. I tipped over my king.

"That was a good game," she said. "You've never studied chess, have you?"

I shook my head. "It shows, huh?"

She nodded. "You do unconventional things. You make me stop and think. But you make mistakes."

"I have some friends who play," I said. "They've showed me some things. Mostly I play with my sons. We play fast and wild."

"You'd be good if you studied it. You've got a feel for it."

I shrugged. "I guess I don't care if I'm good at chess. I'm not patient enough to think more than a few moves ahead. I tend to react rather than plan. I like to improvise. Old sports habits, I guess. I'm sorry I'm not better competition."

"You take white again. I'll get us another beer and we'll try one more game."

"One more," I said. "That'll be enough humiliation for one night."

I managed a draw this time. I suspected she took it easy on me, but I didn't mention it.

She sat back in her chair and drew her feet up so that she

was hugging her bare legs with her chin on her knees. "It's really nice to have you here," she said.

"This was fun."

"It makes me feel almost—I don't know—normal."

"I'm glad you feel better."

"So how's it going with Mary Ellen?"

I shrugged. "I still haven't caught up with her. Her mother's pretty upset."

She nodded solemnly, her blue eyes big and tragic as she looked at me. "And I think I've got it tough," she said softly. "That poor woman."

"I just hope she shows up before . . ."

She nodded. We sat in silence for a minute or two.

"Hey," she said. "We can go sit where it's more comfortable." She jerked her head in the direction of her sofa. "Watch a little TV? I could put on some music. Or we could just talk."

"I think I should get going, Jill. It's pretty late."

"One more beer?"

"No, I don't think so."

"Sure. Right." She smiled and dropped her eyes.

"It's not that . . ."

"No, you're right." She unfolded herself from her chair and stood up. "Coffee or something before you go?"

"No, thanks. I'm fine."

She took my hand and led me into the hallway. We stood inside the steel door. I turned to her and she put her arms around me. She hugged my waist and put her face against my chest. I had forgotten how short she was. She mumbled something into my sweatshirt. I patted her back awkwardly. "I didn't understand what you said," I said.

She tilted her head back to look up at me. It had the

disconcerting effect of pressing her pelvis against me. "I just said that you're a nice man."

"Thank you."

"No, I mean it. You could've stayed. You could've stayed the night, probably. I think I would've let you. Maybe I wanted you to. But I really didn't. Do you understand?"

"Yes."

She bowed her head and mumbled, "You find me attractive, though, huh?"

"Very. But you're married."

"Yes, I am. It makes everything confusing and complicated for me."

She hugged me again. Then I left. I waited outside until I heard the dead bolt clank into place on the steel door. Then I went to my car.

I was just inserting the key into the door lock when he hit me. It was a heavy blow on my right temple, and it sent me sprawling against the side of my car. Then he hit me again, a hard fist against my cheek. I staggered dizzily and went to the ground. He kicked me in the ribs. I brought my arms around my head and tucked my knees into my chest.

"Just stay away from her," he growled. He kicked my shoulder. Pain arrowed into my stomach. "I mean it, pal. You leave Jill alone or I'll kill both of you."

16

HE WENT OVER to the steel door and pounded on it. "Jill! Hey, baby, come on," he yelled. "We gotta talk. Come on, honey. Open up, willya."

He sounded pitiful.

I managed to get to my feet. I leaned against my car and conducted a quick survey of my body. Small lump beside my ear. Tender place on my cheekbone. Sharp pain in my ribs. Duller pain in my shoulder. No blood. No broken bones. No concussion.

He'd been wearing sneakers when he kicked me. And I sensed that he'd held something back. Johnny Costello was not an accomplished or wholeheartedly enthusiastic mugger.

But he'd made his point.

He was still banging on the door, but not yelling anymore. After a minute he stopped. He came over to where I was standing. He was breathing heavily. "You okay?" he said.

"Oh, sure. Pisser."

"Look, I'm sorry, okay?"

I shrugged. "Forget it."

"Just stay away from her. She's my wife."

"She was frightened."

"That's none of your business. You keep out of it."

"I'm her lawyer," I said. "So it's my business."

"Lawyer, huh? Well, fuck you. Both of you."

I turned and unlocked my car door. I opened it and started to get in. He grabbed my arm. "Hey," he said. "Hey, Mr. Lawyer. I'm talking to you."

I yanked myself out of his grip. "I heard you," I said.

"I mean it, buddy. I don't give a shit who you are. Next time . . ."

I slammed the door, started up my car, and backed out of the driveway, leaving Johnny Costello standing there staring into my high beams with his arms hanging down at his sides. He looked young and helpless and miserable.

And as I drove home through the deserted back streets of Boston, I found myself feeling almost sorry for him. More than anything, I guessed, he was bewildered by Jill's behavior. He had no context for it. In his experience, a wife didn't do the things she had done—defy her husband, enroll in college for a degree more advanced than his, walk out and find a new place to live, get a job, refuse to talk to him. A wife stayed home, kept house, brought up children, did as she was told. Like Johnny Costello's mother probably had. Jill had forced him to see himself as a failure, according to a hoary but still widely held standard: He couldn't control his own wife. Lacking philosophy or theology on it, he reacted the only way he knew. He banged on doors, he yelled plaintive threats and angry endearments, he halfheartedly beat up people like me who happened to get in the way.

I thought about Jill. I wondered if there wasn't a gentler, more understanding way for her to handle her problems with her husband. I wondered if she wasn't purposely antagonizing him. I wondered if that hadn't been precisely the reason she'd invited me over. She probably figured Johnny would still be lurking around her door. She knew he'd see me. She knew it would drive him nuts. Maybe she even knew he'd try to beat the shit out of me.

I caught myself. I was thinking like one of those male judges who refused to grant restraining orders to frightened young women, whose instinctive sympathies went to men whose masculine pride got wounded. I knew better. Jill's fear of Johnny Costello was well founded.

The hell with it. I'd had enough chess for one night. I hadn't enjoyed being punched and kicked. But I didn't like the idea of being Jill Costello's pawn, either.

But I remembered the tears that I'd seen in her eyes. Her fear, her desperation seemed genuine.

Women had fooled me before. Many times.

When I got back to my apartment I stripped and took a long steamy shower. The aches in my body were superficial. I'd probably feel worse in the morning.

And I did. I ached all day Sunday, but by Monday I felt fine, and except for a few bumps and bruises I was none the worse for my encounter with Johnny Costello.

The bruise on my cheekbone showed, a faint purplish patch. Julie didn't even comment on it, which meant she didn't notice it.

Around ten in the morning she tapped on my door.

"Enter," I called.

The door opened and she stood inside it. "There's someone here to see you," she said. She was frowning, and I detected a tense stiffness in the way she hunched her shoulders.

"What's up?" I said. "What's the matter?"

She shook her head slowly. "I don't know. It's Lieutenant Horowitz."

"Oh, Christ," I muttered.

I got up from behind my desk and went to the door. Julie

went back to her desk. Horowitz was standing there. "Come on in," I said to him.

He came in. I closed the door behind us. Without preamble, he said, "We found a body."

"Mary Ellen Ames?"

"Looks that way. But we can't be sure."

I let out a long breath. "Jesus," I said, thinking of Susan.

"We haven't made a positive ID," said Horowitz.

"You want someone to . . . ?"

He shook his head. "Floater. We need dental charts."

I waved him to the sofa in my conference area. He sat down. I took the leather chair across from him. "Tell me," I said.

He fumbled a stick of gum out of his pocket, unwrapped it, folded it up, and fingered it into his mouth. I lit a cigarette.

"I faxed out the description and picture," he said around his wad of gum. "Massachusetts, the other New England states, New York. Got a call this morning from a DA in Concord, New Hampshire. Said they might have a hit. A Jane Doe they'd had on ice for a week or so. The general descriptors seem to fit. White female around thirty. She—"

"There must be dozens of bodies that fit that description," I said quickly.

Horowitz looked at me with his head cocked to the side. "You want to hear this or not?"

"I'm not sure," I said. "Yes. Sorry. Go ahead."

"Some kids waterskiing found her down the shallow end of a place called Teal Pond. That's near Keene. Southern part of the state. Apparently a kind of exclusive setup with a couple dozen cottages scattered around it. Drowned. She was nude. They found a capsized canoe in a different part of the pond."

"That doesn't answer my question," I said. "What makes you think this is Mary Ellen?"

Horowitz shrugged. "One of the cottages on Teal Pond belongs to her."

"Yeah," I said. "I see."

"See, the New Hampshire cops, they wouldn't have made the connection. I guess everyone closes up their places on Labor Day. Turn off the water, board up the windows, crank up the docks, bring in the boats. Nobody reported anybody of her description missing, nobody saw it happen. She'd been in the water a couple weeks before they found her. Nude, like I said. No ID."

"So," I said, "if they've had her body for a week, and if they guess she'd been in the water two weeks before they found her . . ."

He nodded. "Yeah. It figures she died about three weeks ago."

"Which," I said, "is about how long since anybody's seen Mary Ellen."

"Anyway," said Horowitz, "they want to make a positive ID. That's the first thing. I assume you can help us."

I sighed. "I'll have to check with Susan. Her mother. Find out who her dentist is. Or was. Are ten-year-old dental records helpful?"

He nodded. "Sure."

I stubbed out my cigarette. "She drowned, huh?"

"They haven't autopsied her yet. They were waiting to identify her. But the preliminary, evidently, points to that. They don't suspect anything else, if that's what you're getting at. There was a capsized canoe and a dead body floating in the weeds."

"You said she was nude?"

He nodded.

"Kind of strange, don't you think? I mean, who goes out canoeing without any clothes on?"

"I dunno. Not me." He shrugged. "Might've been one of those warm nights we had in September. Maybe she was skinny-dipping by moonlight, decided to take a turn around the lake. After Labor Day there's nobody around to see you. Who knows?"

"Yeah," I said. "Who knows."

"Well, anyway," said Horowitz, "I'm just cooperating with my counterparts up there in Concord. If you can scrape up the name of Mary Ellen Ames's dentist, give me a call, and we'll take it from there."

"Sure," I said. Already I dreaded the phone call I'd have to make. "And you'll let me know?"

He nodded, then stood up.

I walked him to the door. "Hey, Horowitz," I said as he pulled it open.

He turned. "Yeah?"

"Listen. Thanks."

"For what?"

"You could've done this by telephone. I appreciate it."

He waved away the sentiment. "Ah, I needed to get out of the office, that's all."

After Horowitz left, I went back and sat behind my desk. I lit another Winston and stared at the telephone for the length of time it took me to smoke the cigarette. Then I called Susan.

Terri answered.

"Terri? It's Brady."

"Oh, hi." She hesitated. "You didn't call me General."

"Sorry, sir."

She laughed quickly. "That's all right."

"I had fun the other night," I said.

"Me, too."

"Can you talk?"

"Not really."

"Have you thought any more about next Saturday?"

"Yes."

"And?"

"I don't know."

"Well, okay." I cleared my throat. "How's Susan today?"

"Just fine," she said. I thought I detected a false cheeriness in her tone.

"She's standing right there, is that it?"

"That's right."

"Not really that good, then, huh?"

"No, not really."

"I see." I hesitated. "I need to talk to her. It won't be pleasant for her. What do you think?"

"I guess so. Why?"

"The police think they've found Mary Ellen's body."

There was a pause. "Yes, I see."

"They need dental records. I've got to ask Susan how to find them. It's going to upset her."

"Of course." She paused. "Okay. Just a moment, please."

I heard muffled voices. Then Susan's voice. "Brady. What's up?" She sounded tired.

"I talked to the police the other day," I said. "They agreed to help us look for Mary Ellen, so—"

"Do you really think that's necessary?"

"I thought it would be good to get some help. Anyway, I let them borrow her picture and described her as best I could. They'd like to have her dental records on file, so I—"

"What?"

"Dental records. Just for their files."

"Brady Coyne," she said sharply. "You tell me the truth."

"I am. If they're going to—"

"Please," she said quietly.

"Yeah, okay. They found a body. It might be her or not. Dental records will tell them."

"Why do they think it's Mary Ellen?"

I told her what Horowitz had told me. She didn't interrupt. When I was done, she said, "Dr. Silver. He was her orthodontist. His office is in Concord. I assume he's still there. Her regular dentist was Dr. Frazier. Same building in Concord."

I wrote them down. "Thank you, Susan. I'm sorry."

"Don't try to keep things from me, Brady."

"I know. I apologize."

"I want to know."

"Yes."

After I disconnected from Susan, I called Horowitz's office and gave his secretary the names of Doctors Silver and Frazier.

17

TWO DAYS LATER, on Wednesday, I found Horowitz waiting outside my office door when I got there around eight-thirty in the morning. I lifted my eyebrows to him and he nodded.

"It's her," he said.

"You sure?"

"Positive."

"Oh, boy," I sighed. "Come on in."

I unlocked the door and he followed me in. I put on the coffee. We went into my office. I lit a cigarette. He sat on the sofa. I remained standing.

"So tell me," I said.

He shrugged. "Not that much to tell. The boys in New Hampshire got the dental records and made the match. They wanted to know how to notify next of kin. I told them I'd take care of it. Figured I better talk to you first."

"Thanks."

"They have to investigate it."

"I thought you said she drowned."

He nodded. "She did. The autopsy verified it. Pretty straightforward, looks like. No unusual bruises or anything. Looks like she fell out of her canoe and drowned. But you know how it is. Unattended or accidental death, it's a medical examiner's case. I guess the guy up there is pretty good. Stickler for doing things right. He wants to have us talk to some people."

"He think she might've been murdered?"

Horowitz flapped his hands. "I don't really know what he thinks. What I understand, there's no particular reason to think that. Suicide, maybe. Murder? Could be, I guess. Most likely an accident, and he just wants to eliminate the others. Murder, suicide, those're the null hypotheses. Try to prove one of 'em. If you can't, you're left with an accident."

"So who's he want to talk to?"

"I don't know. They've got no witnesses except the kids who found the body. Hoped you could give us a hand. I remember you saying she had a shrink."

"Yes. Dr. Warren McAllister. He's in Brookline. And there are people in the building where she lives. I haven't talked to any of her neighbors there, but there are some security men and the superintendent of the building who could maybe help. Oh, and there's a man, guy named Dave Finn, a cop who I ran into, said he was going to marry her. He was looking for her, too."

"Marry her, huh?"

I nodded. "That's what he told me."

Horowitz had pulled a notebook out of his jacket pocket and was scribbling into it. He looked up at me. "And this Finn guy, he's a cop?"

"A detective, yes. So he told me."

"What about the mother?"

"Boy, I hope nobody feels they have to talk to her. She hasn't seen Mary Ellen in about eleven years."

"No?"

I frowned. "Well, that's what she told me. Look, she's dying of cancer. I mean . . ."

Horowitz waved his hand. "Don't worry. This is a pretty routine thing. I don't really know if they're going to talk to anybody. I'm just cooperating. They wanted names, I figured you could give me some names."

"Well, a couple others for you. Guy named Sherif Rahmanan, a professor at the Fletcher School. And another, name of Sid Raiford, works at a bookstore called Head Start Books, near Central Square."

Horowitz wrote for a minute, then looked up and smiled. "Okay. Great. I did you a favor, and what do I get? I get you doing me one. You're probably gonna say I owe you again now."

"You do," I said. "One more. Keep Susan Ames out of it, if you can. She's next of kin. I'll talk to her, break the news to her. She hasn't seen her daughter in eleven years. She knows nothing. The last thing she needs is a cop—even a pleasant fellow like you—quizzing her."

"I can't promise," he said. "It's up to the ME in New Hampshire."

"So try."

"I'll try. You can tell her this, anyway."

I walked Horowitz out. Julie had arrived while we were in my office. She was sitting at her desk watching us. After he left, she said, "I don't like the looks of this."

I went over to the coffee machine and filled two mugs. I took them to Julie's desk and put one in front of her. "They've identified Mary Ellen Ames's body," I told her.

"Oh, boy."

"They figure she accidentally drowned."

"Just a young woman."

I nodded. "About your age."

"And her mother . . ."

"Yeah," I said, sipping my coffee. "I've got to tell Susan."

Julie reached over and put her hand on my wrist. "Oh, Brady."

For once, no flippant remark occurred to me.

I went back into my office. I sat behind my desk and lit a cigarette. I smoked and sipped my coffee and stared at my telephone. I tried it out in my head.

"Susan, I have some terrible news."

"Susan, are you sitting down?"

"It's about Mary Ellen, Susan."

"Your only daughter's dead, Susan."

How the hell had those officers in their crisp uniforms managed to march up to front doors with news from Vietnam? They must have been professionals, especially trained for the singular task of informing parents and wives that their sons and husbands had been killed. It was their job, their livelihood. I wondered if they learned how to do it without feeling.

In the World War, I thought I remembered they used telegrams. Quick, efficient, impersonal, and painless, at least for those with the responsibility for conveying tragic news. I doubted if the recipients of those telegrams handled it any worse than those who a generation later had to answer a doorbell and see a Marine uniform standing on the doorstep.

There was no good way to do it.

I crushed my cigarette and pecked out Susan's phone number. Terri answered.

"Thank God it's you," I said.

"Brady?"

"Right. Is Susan with you now?"

"No, she's still upstairs."

"Good. I've got to come see her."

There was a long pause. "Bad news, right?"

"The worst, Terri."

"Mary Ellen, huh?"

"Yes. She drowned."

"Susan's been waiting for this. I think she expected it."

"Well, if she's prepared, that's good. But I've got to see her. I want to talk to her in person."

"Of course. Today?"

"This morning, if you think it's all right."

"She's been sleeping a lot lately. Sometimes spending most of the day in bed. I'll make sure she's up and around before you get here."

"I'll be there before noon."

"Should I tell why her you're coming?"

"She'll know why."

"Yes," she said. "She'll know. I'll tell her."

"That will be hard for you."

She laughed ironically. "It's what we factotums are for."

I paused, then said, "Hey, General, sir?"

"The answer is yes."

"Saturday?"

"Yes. If you still want to."

"I do."

"How about the Rusty Scupper around six?"

"Sure. I know where it is."

"It'll be an early night. Melissa conks out by nine."

"That's fine. It'll be fun."

"I guess we can both use a little fun, huh?"

"I guess so. Anyway, tell Susan I'll be there around noon."

I hung up and lit another cigarette. I stared out my window while I smoked it. Sooty clouds hung low over the city. It looked like rain, one of our New England line storms that would suck a cold front in behind it. The rain and the wind would strip the foliage from the trees, and when the storm had passed it would leave winter in its wake.

A good day for telling a mother that her daughter was dead.

By the time I pulled into Susan's driveway, small raindrops were beginning to sprinkle my windshield. Terri answered the door. A yellow ribbon was tied up in her short black hair, and her blouse matched the ribbon. Her gray tailored slacks fit her trimly. She was quite beautiful.

I had the urge to hug her. Her body language told me not to.

I guess I was staring at her, because she said, "Is something wrong, Brady?"

"No. Sorry. You look nice, that's all."

"Well, shucks, thanks." She smiled quickly and stepped back from the door. "Come on in. Susan's in the library. I'm sure she knows why you're here."

I went in. "Any change in her health?"

"She has good days and bad days. In the last week or so, more bad ones. No pain, at least not that she complains of. She's lethargic, no appetite." She shrugged. "I'm no nurse. She's dying. That's all I know."

"It can't be easy for you."

"It's not. Sometimes she's bitchy as hell. That's on her good days. But I like her. I feel that I'm helping her. She seems to appreciate my company. It's all I can do."

Susan was sitting on the sofa in the big library, where the walls were lined floor to ceiling with bookshelves crammed with old volumes. She had dressed up for the occasion. She was wearing a blue dress, stockings, and heels. Her gray hair was wound into an intricate braided crown atop her head. Her face was pale and pasty. There was a touch of gloss on her lips and liner around her eyes. She looked elegant and composed as she sat there with a magazine open on her lap.

I went over to her. "Hello, Susan."

She smiled up at me. "Brady, you're a dear to come out here to convey tragic news to me. I expect you've been rehearsing speeches to yourself. You can relax. I know why you're here."

I nodded. "I'm very sorry."

She patted the sofa beside her. "Do sit with me and hold my hand."

I sat and took her bony hand.

"What can you tell me?"

"It looks like a canoeing accident. A place called Teal Pond near Keene, New Hampshire, where Mary Ellen apparently owned a cottage. It happened about three weeks ago, according to . . ." I let my voice trail off.

"The coroner? Come on, Counselor. You can speak candidly with me."

"Yes. The medical examiner. They hadn't identified her body until I spoke to the police about her. The dental records were what they needed."

Susan squeezed my hand. "Well, this is just bullshit," she said.

"Susan, dental records are very—"

"Oh, I'm not saying they've misidentified her. But there is simply no way Mary Ellen would drown. She was a magnificent swimmer from the time she could walk. She was a regular fish in the water."

"There could have been a storm," I said. "She might've gotten a cramp."

"Nonsense. If they're trying to make an accident out of it, they're simply wrong."

"Susan—"

"Now don't you try to patronize me, Brady Coyne. I am very saddened by this news. I had my heart set on seeing my daughter one time before I died. But it has been a long time, and she is just a memory for me. That's as plain as I can say it. I'm not doing a denial thing. I'm simply saying that she did not drown in an accident. Or do they say she hit her head or something?"

"No. Apparently they've discounted anything like that. There were no bruises or contusions or anything. She just—drowned."

She cocked her head at me. "Suicide?"

"Oh, Susan . . ."

"I want to know, Brady."

"I don't know about suicide."

"You told me she was seeing a psychiatrist."

I nodded. "He doesn't think she was suicidal. I imagine the police will talk with him. He might help."

"The other possibility," said Susan, her voice firm, "is murder."

I shrugged. "All I can tell you is what I've been told. There's no evidence of either suicide or murder. But they are looking into it."

Her hand loosened in mine. She let herself slump back against the sofa. She closed her eyes. "Well," she said quietly, "now it doesn't matter."

I patted her hand and said nothing.

"Willard Ellington," she murmured, "will be thrilled."

"Who?"

"I mentioned him to you." She opened her eyes and turned her head to me. "The man from the Concord Historic Places Commission. You passed him in the driveway when you were here before. My daughter has predeceased me. The commission will have the Ames estate any day now. Willard will dance a jig when he hears."

I found myself disliking Willard Ellington, whom I had never met, intensely.

18

WARREN MCALLISTER called me at the office Friday morning. "I just heard," he said. "My God."

"I should've told you," I said. "I'm sorry. I guess Susan—Mary Ellen's mother—has been on my mind."

"I can't believe it." He sounded genuinely shaken.

"How did you hear?" I said.

"That's why I'm calling you. I had a call last evening from a state policeman. He wants to interrogate me."

"Interrogate?"

"Interview was the word he used, I think. Evidently the circumstances of her death . . ."

"She drowned," I said. "There were no witnesses. It's an unattended death. Therefore a medical examiner's case. It's routine."

"Anyway," he said, "this policeman is coming over this evening." He hesitated. "I want to have an attorney with me."

"Why?"

"I've never been interrogated—interviewed—by the police. In my profession, confidentiality is everything. I don't know what the law says about privilege after the client has died, but I know how I feel about it."

"The law is vague, as it usually is. The Massachusetts Supreme Judicial Court has held that for lawyers, at least, privilege continues after the death of the client. Remember the Stuart case? For doctors, it's safe to assume the same rules would apply. Obviously whatever a client tells you in confidence about other people is privileged. Or at least it's obvious to me. Otherwise, I would assume one would want to be of help. It could be tricky."

"Exactly," said McAllister.

I waited.

"So," he said, "I wondered if you'd help me."

"Don't you have a lawyer?"

"I've got friends who are lawyers. One of them has helped me and Robin with financial things. Taxes, investments, real estate. He did our will for us. I've got the impression that you're more familiar with situations like this one."

"I'm sure any lawyer could do the job," I said.

"Well, this guy is more of a family friend than a family attorney. Anyway, I think you told me that, um, discretion, I think was the word you used, is more or less your forte."

"It's true. It is." I paused. I could think of no reason not to help him out. "Sure, okay. I'd be happy to be there for you, Warren."

"Boy, that's terrific. This policeman said he'd be here at eight tonight. Is that okay?"

"I'll be there."

I pulled my car in front of his Victorian in Brookline on the dot of eight. Warren answered the doorbell out back and led me upstairs to his office. He was wearing a blue flannel shirt, tan corduroy pants, and boat shoes. He looked more like a clerk at the corner hardware store than a psychiatrist. He sat me down in one of the chairs by the wood stove, but he continued standing. He offered me coffee, which I refused. He moved around the room touching things and glancing out the window.

Finally I said, "Warren, relax. This is a routine thing."

"They'll want to know if Mary Ellen could've committed suicide, won't they?"

I nodded. "I imagine so. That's a question you should try to answer."

"Well, I guess that doesn't bother me, although somehow the very idea of it seems like an accusation. But listen. I know about her lovers, her parents, her friends and enemies. I don't feel comfortable with any of that."

"Tell the police that, then. If you're uncertain, consult me."

He nodded. "Okay. It sounds easy."

He sat down across from me. "Mainly," he said, "I'm very upset by this thing. One gets to know one's patients very well. Professional distance and everything, sure, but still, you care very much about them. Mary Ellen was . . ."

He stopped. I said, "Was what?"

"So—so vital. So alive and enthusiastic. Oh, she was quite neurotic. But her depression was well controlled by the medication. I just can't believe she's dead."

"I understand," I said.

"But you never knew her."

"True. It's different, I know."

Warren jumped to his feet at the buzz of the doorbell. He left and returned a minute later.

Horowitz was behind him. He looked at me and grinned. "Well, well," he said.

"Hi." I lifted my hand in greeting.

Horowitz turned to Warren. "You don't need a lawyer, you know, Doctor. We're just trying to get some information. You're not being accused of anything. If you needed counsel, it's my job to remind you of that."

Warren nodded. "I know that. I feel more comfortable."

Horowitz shrugged. "Your privilege. Why don't we get started. It shouldn't take long."

The three of us sat by the cold wood stove. Horowitz took out a notebook. "Okay," he said, looking at Warren. "Mary Ellen Ames was your patient, correct?"

"That's right."

"For how long?"

"She came to me nearly four years ago."

"Why?"

"Pardon me?"

"Why did she come to you? What was her complaint?"

Warren glanced at me. I nodded. He turned back to Horowitz. "She was depressed. She had problems with relationships. She'd never held an important job or done anything that she felt was worthwhile. She'd had a basically unhappy childhood. She was trying to mourn her father's death, something that had happened several years earlier." He shrugged. "These are typical of the reasons why people seek psychiatric help, really."

"You said she was depressed," said Horowitz.

Warren nodded.

"Was she suicidal?"

He hesitated and glanced at me before answering. "I was concerned at first, yes. But as we proceeded with our work I no longer was concerned. Her depression was mild and well controlled."

"Controlled how?"

"I prescribed Pertofrane for her. It's a very good drug, widely used now. And she was doing well with our work together."

"Doctor," said Horowitz, "Miz Ames's death appears to be accidental. We would like to be able to rule out suicide.

Can you say that at the time of her death she was healthy and well balanced?"

Warren shrugged. "She was as healthy and well balanced as most people. I'm quite confident that she did not kill herself."

"No crises in her life? No recent breakups with lovers, financial worries?"

"There was nothing," he said carefully, "that would lead me to believe Mary Ellen Ames was suicidal."

"Okay." Horowitz paused. "Now, then. The other possibility, Doctor, is that she was murdered."

Warren said nothing.

"There's no evidence of it," said Horowitz after a moment. "But it would help us to know of anybody who might've had reason to kill her. Spurned lovers, for example."

Warren turned to me.

I said, "You don't have to talk about anybody else."

Warren looked at Horowitz and shrugged.

"You're refusing to answer my question?" said the policeman.

"Yes, I guess so."

"You saying that if you knew someone who might have a motive to kill her, you wouldn't tell me?"

"Lieutenant," said Warren, "I don't want to be uncooperative. If Mary Ellen Ames was murdered, I would be outraged and I would very much want her killer to be apprehended. But you've got to understand. My patients tell me all their secrets, things they tell absolutely nobody else. Many of these things they don't even know for themselves until we've commenced our work. We must wrestle these things up to the surface of their consciousness from where they have been buried and repressed. Painful, difficult, very personal, and sensitive things. Once these things are brought out, we must then examine them, analyze them, test them against objective reality. Psychiatric patients—indeed, virtually all people—have distorted concepts of reality. Their versions of reality may not be what is in fact real. A patient may think somebody is out to get her, wants to kill her, hates her, whatever. Paranoia is almost universal among psychiatric patients. So if—and I'm just saying if—if Mary Ellen had told me that someone she knew wanted to kill her, I would not accept that as truth. I would accept it as *her* truth, yes, but not as objective truth. Everything I know about her and everything I know about all the people in her life came to me distorted through that peculiar filter we call her consciousness. Her ego, her idea of herself and her world and her place in it. It was my job to help her reduce that distortion. That takes a very long time." He shrugged.

"Meaning," said Horowitz, "you're not going to answer my question."

"Yes, sir. It would be irresponsible of me and a violation of Mary Ellen's privacy."

"She's dead," said Horowitz.

Warren shrugged.

"What about a guy named Dave Finn?" said Horowitz.

Warren shook his head.

Horowitz sighed. He turned to me and gave me a wry smile. "Thanks a lot, pal."

I nodded. "We're all doing our jobs here."

"Yeah." He closed his notebook, shoved it into the inside pocket of his jacket, and stood up. He held his hand out to Warren. "Well, thanks, Doctor. You helped on the suicide thing, anyway. And really, there doesn't seem to be any reason to suspect murder here, so unless something pops up, I guess they'll be calling it an accident." To me he said, "How's the mother doing?"

I shrugged. "She's all right, considering. But listen. The mother told me that Mary Ellen was an excellent swimmer, for whatever that's worth."

He nodded. "Okay. That's something. I'll tell them. I'm just a helper here, trying to keep the jurisdictional relationships healthy. When the ME gives his verdict, Coyne, I'll let you know. I assume the mother will want to know, huh?"

"Yes," I said. "So will I."

"Thanks again, Doctor. See you, Counselor." Horowitz headed for the door. Warren got up and followed him out. I stayed where I was.

Warren was back a minute later. He sat down heavily across from me. "There are some things I didn't tell him," he said.

"I imagine there was plenty you didn't tell him."

"Well, I want to tell you. I can trust you to keep it to yourself?"

"Do I infer that you've hired me?"

"Of course. I didn't expect you to come over here on a Friday night out of friendship."

"It's always best to keep friendship and business separate," I said. "I'll have Julie send you a bill. So, yes, you are my client. What you tell me is privileged."

He stared at me for a moment, then let his eyes slide away. As he began to talk, his eyes remained focused on something beyond my left shoulder. "Mary Ellen Ames was an extraordinary young woman," he said. "It's a shame you didn't know her. It would help you understand my problem with all this better. She was brilliant, witty, creative, mercurial. She suffered tremendously from her father's death, and it affected all of her subsequent relationships. There was a deep anger in her, and at the same time a powerful love, both directed toward this man whom she was denied the opportunity to make peace with. She blamed her mother, believed she was caught in an Oedipal-type contest with her, knew it was completely irrational, but couldn't help herself. She avoided her mother because she knew that her anger toward her was unwarranted, and that made her feel profoundly guilty. She sought—obsessively—that unconditional father's love that she felt had been cruelly stolen from her by his death."

"Penis envy, huh?"

Warren smiled quickly. "Sure. If you want."

"That's why she ran off with the professor," I said. "Still trying to seduce her father."

Warren looked up at me. "Yes. But it didn't work for her. That man wasn't her father. Nor was he any kind of reasonable substitute. But she wasn't attracted to men her own age. Mary Ellen had many lovers, and many men who simply used her. All were older men. Men in her father's image."

"Like Dave Finn."

He nodded. "Finn was just the current one. A crude, uncomplicated man, if I have inferred accurately from all that Mary Ellen said to me. Another doomed relationship for her." He ran his fingers through his thatch of white hair. "You understand why I couldn't tell these things to the police."

"You think Finn could have murdered her?"

He shrugged. "I have no idea. I don't know the man. I only know Mary Ellen's perceptions of him. She saw him as quick-tempered, possessive, lonely, professionally unsuccessful. A murderer?" He shrugged again.

"What do you mean, unsuccessful?"

"According to Mary Ellen, he was suspended from the Boston police force. I'm not sure what the charges were, or if his case has been resolved. But when Mary Ellen heard about it, it burst Dave Finn's balloon as far as Mary Ellen was concerned. No father figure would fail so dramatically at his work. Any Charles Ames substitute would be successful and respected, as she believed Charles himself was. She expressed fear of Finn, however. Whether her fear was appropriate or not, I couldn't tell you. She wanted to break from him, but she felt she could not predict his reaction. So when you told me she had disappeared, I simply assumed that disappearing for a while was the way she had chosen to separate herself from Finn. It would have been consistent with the Mary Ellen I knew. She was an avoider, not a confronter."

"Christ," I said. "I think the cops should know this."

Warren nodded. "I agree. But I can't tell them. And now, neither can you."

I lit a cigarette. "I met Finn. He didn't strike me as a murderer. I mean, when I met him, Mary Ellen was already dead. He just struck me as a man in love who was looking for his girl. He seemed too ingenuous to play-act that whole scene while knowing she was already dead."

"He was a cop," said Warren. "Anyway, there's more."

"I still don't know why you're telling me this."

"I've got to tell somebody," he said simply.

I nodded.

"Mary Ellen also had another lover. A woman." He peered at me with his eyebrows arched.

"That doesn't shock me nowadays," I said.

"I suppose not. This was a new thing for her, though. Recent. Within the past few months. She was very excited by it, but very confused, too. We hadn't done much work on this issue when she stopped showing up for appointments, so I don't know how—or if—it fits in." Warren ran the palms of his hands over his face as if he was very weary. "I mean, I suppose she simply drowned accidentally, and none of this has any relevance whatsoever. But it's her life, and it's hard for me not to continue to ponder it and analyze it and try to figure out how to help her with it."

I nodded. "Who was her woman lover?"

He shrugged. "She didn't tell me. She told me very little about her. When she talked about it, she talked about herself. How it felt to her, how she responded to this other person, what it was like to her, being, um, involved with a woman in this new way. Emotionally. Sexually."

Warren stood up, walked over to his desk, looked at some papers on it, came back and stood in front of me. "There's more," he said.

I looked up at him. "More?"

"Me," he said.

"You?"

"I was her lover, too."

19

I STARED at Warren McAllister. "You were Mary Ellen's lover?"

He shrugged.

I blew out a short laugh. "Jesus Christ."

"Look," he said. "You don't understand."

I nodded. "I think I do."

"No you don't. You're making judgments."

"A psychiatrist screwing his patient? I shouldn't judge that?"

"It wasn't like that."

"Look," I said. "You told me, okay? You got it off your chest. You want me to comfort you?"

"No," he said, "but I'd appreciate it if you'd try to understand it."

"Why? Why me?"

He smiled. "Who else?"

"Okay." I sighed. "What am I supposed to understand? That fucking Mary Ellen Ames was part of her treatment? Sex therapy?"

"No, of course not. It's ethically indefensible. There is no justification for it. I'm ashamed. I'm guilt ridden. What we did wasn't calculated or planned. It's much simpler."

"Lust," I said.

He nodded. "That's about it."

"This is odious."

"Thank you for your objectivity, Brady."

"We have this girl," I said. "She comes to you for therapy. She could've been your daughter. She becomes dependent on you. She opens her soul to you. Classical transference. She is vulnerable. You are weak. So you seduce her. And you toss it off as simple lust."

"No," he said. "I don't toss it off. And lust isn't simple. But never mind any of that. It happened, it was wrong. But it wasn't bad for Mary Ellen. And, in fact, now it has nothing to do with anything. She is dead."

"Which must be a vast relief to you."

He stared at me for a long moment. "I have been completely candid with you, Brady. So listen, and I will be candid some more. I am shattered by Mary Ellen's death. Not because I was unforgivably indiscreet and unprofessional with her, but because she is a human being whom I knew better than anyone else on earth knew her, and about whom I cared as I care for all my patients. I am not relieved. I am bereaved."

"Look," I said. "I'm no one to judge anybody else. But I'm having these thoughts."

"Such as?"

"Such as, if you screwed her then spurned her, she might want to kill herself."

"No," he said. "I don't know what eventually would've happened. But I never spurned her. My inability to spurn her is what led us into that—that situation in the first place. I feel guilty for many reasons. But I can tell you right now, Mary Ellen Ames did not kill herself, for me or for anybody else."

"Or," I said, "you panicked. She threatened to go public. Or tell Robin. Or sue you. So . . ."

"So *what?*"

"Obvious," I said. "So you killed her."

"Jesus Christ, Brady. What kind of man do you think I am?"

"I don't know you that well, Warren," I said quietly.

"Yeah, well I'm no murderer, I can tell you that. She never threatened anything. I didn't kill her. My God."

"You didn't get me over here for your interview with Horowitz to protect your right against self-incrimination, then?"

"Of course not."

"You didn't kill her."

"No. Listen. If I did, I know I could tell you. It would be privileged, right?"

I nodded.

"I didn't kill her."

"Okay."

"And I'm positive she didn't kill herself, either."

"Positive?"

"Yes."

I sighed. "Does this happen a lot?"

"What?"

"Shrinks screwing their patients?"

He shrugged. "It happens. Some justify it. It takes some convoluted reasoning, but they rationalize it for themselves. Some end up marrying their patients. Some get sued. They almost always settle quietly, out of court. Mostly, I guess they just—I don't know—break up. Like lovers do. Some psychiatric patients suffer more than other people might from it. Some probably suffer less. The psychiatrists suffer, too. Everybody's human. I suppose it happens more than people think. It's not something the profession is eager to make public."

"Does your wife know?"

"Robin? God, no. Nobody knows. Only you."

"I just hope your conscience is clear, Warren."

"Of course it's not. But I feel no responsibility for Mary Ellen's death, if that's what you're getting at."

"And now if the cops come back and start asking questions about your relationship with her, you've got me, fully informed, to help protect your rights. That's why you're telling me this, right?"

"Partly, I guess. Mainly, I felt I had to get it off my chest."

I nodded. "Anything else while we're on the subject?"

"No. That's all of it."

"Well," I said after a minute, "she was quite the young lady. If I've got it right, she was simultaneously sleeping with a policeman named Dave Finn, who was convinced she was going to marry him, seducing her shrink, or vice versa, and exploring the joys of Lesbos with a mysterious woman."

"It sounds worse when you say it than it actually was for her."

"But not exactly a conventional love life."

"No," he said. "But not exactly an unhealthy one, either."

"Well, I don't sit at the head of a couch for ten hours a day, so I probably have a poor handle on what's healthy."

He smiled. "And I do sit there. So my idea of healthy is probably distorted, too." Warren looked at me. "Can we still be friends, Brady?"

"Hell, I don't know. Sure, I guess so." I shrugged. "Like I said, I'm in no position to judge anybody. Especially when it comes to matters of lust. I suppose in one way or another, we all take advantage of situations."

"Don't say that," he said. "What I did was wrong, and it should be judged. So go ahead and judge me."

"Okay. Consider yourself judged."

He held out his hand to me. I took it.

"Thanks," he said.

"This couldn't have been easy for you."

"No," he said. "But not telling somebody hasn't been easy, either." He rubbed his jaw with his knuckles. "Listen. What about a drink? I think we could both use one."

"Will Robin be there?"

"Probably."

"Jeez, I don't know."

"Please?"

I shrugged. "I guess so. Why not."

I followed Warren McAllister down the two flights of stairs and through the door into the kitchen. I was greeted by the melodramatic strains of Wagner over the speakers and the unbearably nostalgic aroma of apple pie in the oven. Robin was at the sink loading the dishwasher and humming to the music. Her long dark hair was pulled into two pigtails which hung in front of each shoulder. She was wearing yellow rubber gloves that came nearly to her elbows.

She looked up when we entered. "Hi, fellas."

Warren went to her and kissed the back of her neck. "Hi, babe."

"You guys have impeccable timing. The pie'll be out of the oven in about two minutes. What say a scoop of vanilla ice cream on top, huh?"

"Perfect," I said.

She frowned at Warren. "How'd it go?"

He shrugged. "Okay. I don't think I was of much help."

"Was he mean to you?"

"The policeman? No. It looks like a drowning accident. I guess they have to rule out suicide."

"It was nice of you to help out, Brady," she said to me.

I shrugged. "No problem."

A little bell dinged.

"There," said Robin. "The pie's done. We'll let it cool for a few minutes. Why don't you boys sit at the table."

"I'm getting drinks," said Warren. "Want one, hon?"

"Sure."

I sat at the table. Warren rummaged in the cabinets while Robin finished at the sink. Then they sat down, too, and we sipped Jack Daniel's while the pie cooled. Robin talked about her day in the emergency room. There was only one automobile accident, no fatalities. Two cardiac arrests, one saved. A high school soccer player with a compound leg fracture, a toddler who had swallowed a marble, a couple of nursing home admittances, one drug overdose, several lacerations requiring stitches. A quiet day, she said. The night shift, she said, was usually worse. More bad accidents, more gunshot and knife wounds, more strokes and heart attacks. She liked night shift work better. More exciting, more demand on her expertise. But since her marriage she preferred working normal hours. Otherwise she'd never see Warren.

She had reached over and put her hand on top of his as she talked. I found myself feeling envious. Warren McAllister, who had been screwing one of his patients, had a beautiful and obviously adoring wife who had great enthusiasm for her work and baked aromatic apple pies. He didn't deserve her.

Once the phone rang. Neither of them got up to answer it. I heard Warren's recorded voice answer it in another room.

I stopped at one drink. I allowed Robin to talk me into a second helping of pie, however. Afterward we had coffee.

It was nearly midnight when I left, balancing a wedge of

pie on a paper plate. Warren and Robin McAllister stood in the doorway to watch me leave. They had their arms around each other's waist. Robin's head was tilted against her husband's shoulder.

I SLEPT LATE the next morning. I generally sleep late on Saturdays and Sundays, unless I've got a fishing plan, in which case I have no problem arising before the sun. I spent what was left of the morning sorting old newspapers and magazines and catalogs and bottles and cans into recyclable groups. It took longer than it should have, since I couldn't resist flipping through the magazines and catalogs, and I kept finding things I hadn't read and pictures I hadn't seen.

But while the top part of my mind was attending to these activities, the bottom part chewed on the questions raised by Mary Ellen Ames's death. She had drowned. No evidence that it had been anything else. Yet Susan said she was a strong swimmer, unlikely to drown by accident in a small pond. She could've killed herself, but Warren McAllister vowed she was not suicidal, and I thought I believed him.

Somebody could have killed her. There seemed to be plenty of candidates with possible motives. But the New Hampshire medical examiner's conclusions seemed to rule out murder.

On one level, it didn't matter. Like most people, Mary Ellen undoubtedly had allies and enemies, some people whose lives would be diminished by her death and others who would not mourn—and might secretly celebrate—her death. They would continue, diminished or enhanced by the fact that Mary Ellen Ames was no longer part of their lives. For better or worse, though, her death was irreversible.

But on another level, I found not knowing intolerable. I had tried too hard to find her to let it go now. I had agonized with Susan. I had wanted to be the one to bring her and her daughter together for one final hug before Susan died. Now it wouldn't happen. I needed to know why.

But what could I do? The medical examiner would submit his finding and Mary Ellen would be buried. And soon enough, so would Susan.

I could do some checking around. Playing detective, as Julie called it. A weakness of mine.

Around five I showered and shaved and headed for Acton. I found myself nervous about meeting Terri's daughter. I hadn't had much experience with ten-year-old girls. I wanted her to like me.

I found Terri waiting in the lobby of the Rusty Scupper. "Hi, General," I said.

"Oh, hello, Brady." She gave me her hand and tried to smile. It was a poor effort.

"Where's Melissa?"

"Wandering. She'll be back."

I touched her arm. "You okay?"

"I'm fine."

"Regret this?"

"No. I'm just not sure how Melissa's going to react."

I shrugged. "I'll try to behave."

She smiled. "Don't try too hard. Kids can tell."

She appeared a minute later, a miniature of her mother. The same clear olive complexion, the same black hair, the same dark chocolate eyes, the same head-turning beauty.

"There's a bar upstairs," she said to Terri. "They've got four televisions."

Terri touched her shoulder and turned her around to face me. "This is Mr. Coyne," she said.

"Brady," I said. I held my hand out to her.

She took it solemnly. "Nice to meet you, Brady," said the girl. "Do you like rodeos?"

"I've never been to one."

"All the TVs upstairs are showing rodeos. These cowboys try to ride Brahma bulls. They almost always get thrown off, and they never get hurt. It's pretty neat."

"Sounds like fun," I said.

The hostess led us to a table. "Nonsmoking," Terri whispered to me. "Hope you don't mind. Melissa hates smoking."

"I'll survive."

Melissa ordered spaghetti from the kids' menu. Terri asked for scallops, and I settled for shrimp scampi.

Melissa told me about her soccer team and her fifth-grade teacher and a boy named Benjamin, whom she hated because he kept telling everyone he had kissed her, which he certainly hadn't done. I learned that her favorite food was Brussels sprouts and that she hated shrimp and that she was going to be an archaeologist when she grew up and that she was going to get married when she was thirty and have three children.

Terri sat quietly and smiled.

"Are you married?" said Melissa.

"I'm divorced."

"Why?"

"My wife and I weren't good for each other."

"Didn't you love each other?"

"We did," I said. "We still do, sort of. Marriage just wasn't right for us."

"I understand," she said solemnly, as if she was consoling me. "It's the same with Mommy and Daddy, except they were smart. They didn't get married at all, so they didn't have to get divorced. But I still think that being married can be good, don't you?"

"Yes, I do."

When our meals arrived, Melissa gave me a dissertation on the various methods of eating spaghetti. "You can twirl, like me," she said. "Italians can twirl. Nobody else can do it right. People who aren't Italians, when they twirl, they have to use a spoon. Or else they just twirl the whole bowlful until they've got a humongous big glob on their fork, and they try to jam the whole thing in their mouth. Some people suck. That Benjamin sucks, I've seen him in the lunchroom. He gets a string in his mouth and starts sucking, and when he gets to the end it kind of pops in, and he gets sauce all over his chin. It's disgusting. Little kids have their parents cut it up and they eat it with a spoon."

Melissa, I noted, twirled expertly and got no sauce on her chin. She was polite and charming and at ease. I found myself regretting that I'd had no daughters.

Terri and I had coffee afterward while Melissa had a dish of ice cream. I wanted to ask about Susan, but it didn't seem appropriate in front of Melissa.

I walked them to Terri's Volkswagen. Melissa held her hand out to me. "Thank you very much, Brady," she said. "I had a nice time."

"So did I. Maybe we can do it again."

"Mommy should make her gnocchi for you. It's awesome."

"I'd like that."

Melissa climbed into the passenger seat. I went around

and held the other door for Terri. "Thank you," she said softly. "All my fears were unfounded."

"Kids are tougher than we give them credit for," I said. "She's a doll."

She gave my cheek a quick kiss. "We can do it again, if you want."

"I want."

"Next Saturday?"

"Sure."

"I'll make you my gnocchi."

"Great. I'll bring the wine."

I watched Terri's Volkswagen chug away. Then I trudged over to where I'd parked. I was vaguely envious of Terri. She was going home to read a story to her daughter and tuck her in for the night. I found myself missing my boys, missing them when they were young and innocent and unskilled at twirling spaghetti, and when they demanded a story before bedtime.

When I got back to my apartment, the message light on my answering machine was blinking. I played the message. It was Jill Costello. "Hi," she said. "It's Jill. Give me a call, okay?"

I called her.

"Jill, it's Brady Coyne."

"Oh, hey. Thanks for calling. How are you?"

"I've recovered."

"Recovered from what?"

"Sort of a long story. What's up?"

"Oh, nothing, really. I just wondered if you'd like to come over, have a rematch."

"I'm not much competition for you, I'm afraid."

"To tell you the truth, I was kinda lonely."

I realized that I was, too. Somehow, being with Terri and

Melissa had made my apartment feel empty. "I could come over for an hour or so," I said.

"Great."

I changed into jeans and a sweatshirt, pulled on a windbreaker, and walked to Jill's place on Beacon Street. It was a cool October evening, crisp and dry after the rain earlier in the week. Frost would surely settle upon every pumpkin in New England this night.

I banged on the steel door outside Jill's apartment. "It's Brady," I called to her.

She had on the same outfit as the first time I had seen her —snug-fitting jeans, sneakers, and an untucked man's blue oxford shirt. Her handyman costume, I figured. Her hair was braided down her back. She looked very vulnerable and very sexy. And very young. I guessed she was as close to Melissa's age as she was to Terri's.

She grabbed my hand and tugged me inside. Once we were in her apartment with all the doors bolted shut, she snaked her arms around me and pressed herself against me. I patted her back paternally for a moment, then pulled away from her. She looked up at me with her eyebrows arched. Then she shrugged. "Beer?" she asked.

"Sure."

I sat at the table. She fetched two bottles of Miller's from her refrigerator and sat across from me. She propped her feet up on the seat and wrapped her arms around her knees. "Well," she said, "let's have it."

"Have what?"

"Your long story. You said you had a long story for me. I love stories."

"I guess it's not that long. When I left here the other night, your husband attacked me. Didn't you know?"

Her hand flew up to her mouth. "God, no. Did he hurt you?"

"Nah. I'm tough. He's not that good at it. He caught me by surprise, that's all."

"Aw, Jeez. I'm sorry, Brady."

"Not your fault. I'm surprised you didn't hear anything."

"Well," she said slowly, "I did hear him banging on the door out there sometime after you left. I didn't respond, of course. I didn't realize . . ."

"It's okay." I took a swig of beer from the bottle. "I almost felt sorry for him. I mean, he hit me and knocked me down and kicked me, but somehow it seemed more pitiful than vicious."

She pulled her long blond braid around to the front and began to twist it in her hand. "Pitiful: good word. I guess the whole situation's pitiful."

"Well, anyway, that's what happened." I looked at her. "You haven't heard, have you?"

"Heard what?"

"About Mary Ellen."

"Miz Ames? No. What about her?"

"She's dead."

Jill's eyes widened. "What?"

"They found her drowned in a pond in New Hampshire."

"Drowned," she whispered. "Oh, shit."

I watched her face crumble. Tears abruptly welled up in her eyes before she squeezed them shut and covered them with both hands. She put her forehead onto her knees and began to sob quietly.

I let her cry for a minute or two. Then I said, "Jill."

My voice sounded harsh to my ears, and Jill jerked her head up and frowned at me. "What?"

"No policeman has been around this week to question you?"

"Question me? No. Nobody. I didn't know."

"What would you have told them if they did?"

"What do you mean?"

"Would you have told them the truth?"

She shook her head slowly back and forth. "What truth? What are you talking about?"

"About you and Mary Ellen."

"Brady—"

"You were lovers, weren't you?"

"Of course not. We hardly—"

I reached across the table and put my hand on her knee. She stared at me. "Jill, it's all right. I just want to know."

She shook her head back and forth, then let out a long breath. "How did you hear this?"

"I know she had a woman lover. I figured out it was you."

"But how?"

"You're a terrible liar, for one thing."

"You never asked me anything about this."

"No. But you implied that you barely knew her, and when you had your wits about you, like just a minute ago, you referred to her as 'Miz Ames.' But a couple times you slipped and called her 'Mary Ellen.' And twice, now, when I've mentioned something about her to you, you've cried in ways that strike me as an overreaction for someone who barely knows her."

She hugged her knees hard. "God," she said. "If Johnny ever knew this . . . I think it would be worse than if I had a man for a lover. Brady, this is so embarrassing. And now. Now you say she's dead."

I nodded.

"What can I say?" she said.

"Well, you surely don't have to tell me about it. I'm not accusing you of anything, or judging you. The only reason I bring it up is because the circumstances of her death are not clear. I thought you might've been questioned."

"Well, I wasn't. What would they want to question me about, anyway?"

"They're wondering about suicide."

"Mary Ellen? Hardly."

"She wasn't depressed or unhappy?"

"Lately? Hell, no. She was in love."

"With whom?"

Jill chuckled. "Not me, if that's what you mean. With us it was—different. You wouldn't understand."

"No, I guess I wouldn't."

"With us it was—it was comfort, it was—shit, the words don't work very well here. It was intimacy, escape. It was a new thing for both of us. I mean, we like men. We really do. Neither of us had ever—at least, I hadn't. Mary Ellen said she hadn't, either. I went up one evening to look at her oven. The self-cleaning setting wasn't working. She's like the only person my age in the whole building. It was so good for me to see somebody of my own generation, and I guess I just babbled away to her. I couldn't fix the damn oven. She made tea, and I stayed and we talked. Shared life stories, sort of. Hers was much more complicated than mine, though I don't think she was telling me very much of it. And I told her about my dumb, frustrating marriage. I guess I cried. I'd only left Johnny a couple weeks earlier. She came over and hugged me. And . . ."

"It's okay," I said. "Jill, who was she in love with?"

"I don't know. She was funny about that. As if she thought I'd be jealous. Look. We mostly just lay down and hugged each other. It wasn't dirty or anything. I mean, it didn't *seem* dirty. It was—comforting. We held each other. And we talked and we slept. I know this doesn't make sense to you. She was—she sort of played my mother, and I was her child. She'd hold me and hum to me and tell me everything was okay, and I'd relax and snuggle up in her arms. And that's how it was. I mean, I knew she wasn't really telling me her secrets. I told her everything, but she kept things back. The way it would be with mother and daughter, do you see?"

I nodded. "Did she tell you about Dave Finn?"

"Dave?" She nodded slowly. "She talked a little about a man named Dave, yes. She called him Huckleberry sometimes. She liked him. Thought he was funny." She stopped and nodded. "Oh, I get it. Finn. I never knew his last name. Huckleberry Finn."

"Well, what did she say about him?"

Jill shrugged. "He was a man in her life. I don't know." She narrowed her eyes. "Why are you asking me these questions? You said she drowned. What difference does any of this make? She's—she's dead."

"I want to try to understand it. For Susan. Her mother. I think she'd feel a little better if she was convinced that Mary Ellen did not take her own life."

Jill nodded slowly. "Sure. Of course she would." She shrugged. "Maybe I didn't know her that well. I always knew she was holding things back. It was me who got consolation from her, mainly. But she certainly didn't seem suicidal or anything."

"Did she talk about other men besides Finn?"

"Well, yes and no. There was another man, I think. She

never said his name or who he was. But the way she talked, there was somebody else. Somebody she was more interested in than Huckleberry. I'm not sure if they ever got to the point of, you know . . ."

"Johnny didn't know about the two of you, huh?"

"How would he know?"

I shrugged. "I don't know."

"I'm sure he doesn't know." She smiled at me. "Want another beer?"

"No, thanks."

"Do we have to talk about this anymore?"

I shook my head. "I guess not."

"Good. This is awfully upsetting." She put her chin on her knees and peered at me. "Maybe we could go sit on the couch and you could hold me for a little while, huh?"

"No," I said gently. "I don't think so, Jill."

"You think I'm some kind of freak, don't you?"

"No. Not at all. You're a beautiful young woman. I just don't think it would be a good idea."

She tipped her head so that her cheek rested atop her knees. She closed her eyes and sighed. "I really miss being held," she said quietly.

"I know," I said. "Sometimes I do, too."

21

HOROWITZ CALLED ME Monday afternoon. "Just wanted you to know," he said. "The medical examiner up there in the Granite State isn't prepared to release the Ames body yet. I figured your client should know. Figured you'd be the one who should tell her."

"Thoughtful of you," I said. "What's the holdup?"

"He's still trying to figure it out. He's still going for a drowning accident, I guess. But I passed along the word that she was supposed to be a good swimmer. That's a small pond, Teal Pond. Water's still pretty warm in September. Seems like if she tipped over in her canoe, she'd either grab ahold of it and float to shore or just swim. She could've banged her head or something, except he couldn't find any evidence of it. Anyhow, he wants to run some more toxicology tests."

"Drugs, huh?"

"I suppose so. It's one way of accounting for what happened. Listen, you informed the mother, right?"

"Yes."

"She okay?"

"About what you'd expect."

"Well, the pathologist wasn't too happy about me turning over that chore to you. Not the normal way it's done. Informing next of kin is one of the official duties. I told him you were the lawyer, sort of an arm of the court, and you could handle it. Explained how the mother was sick, hadn't seen her daughter in a long time."

"Well, I did it."

"So now you can tell her she can't have the body for a while longer."

"Sure. It would be a pleasure."

"Well, good," he said, missing my sarcasm entirely. "It wouldn't be a pleasure for me."

"Are you still investigating?" I said.

"Me?"

"You *did* talk with Dr. McAllister. I gave you other names."

"Well, he discounted suicide pretty emphatically, as I'm sure you recall. That's what we were wondering about."

"You don't plan to talk to anybody else?"

I heard him expel a breath into the telephone. "Coyne, they don't pay me these big bucks to work on New Hampshire medical examiner cases, okay? Especially when they aren't real cases. This is what they call your basic *quid pro quo* deal. If I help Doctor Dead up there, one day he'll help me. So I helped. Talked to the authority on the dead woman's frame of mind. Suicide? No way. Good enough for me. Good enough for the doctor, too, by the way. You might not believe it, because you don't hang around with the right people, but we actually have murders and rapes and arson fires and bank scams and multi-million-dollar drug deals right here in the good old Bay State. The good doctor up there in New Hampshire wonders about this body they found in a pond that looks like it drowned, and in fact did drown, and because he's a very meticulous guy with not much work to do, since they don't have all the murders and rapes and multi-million-dollar drug deals we have, he says, 'Hey, let's check out suicide.'

Well, I'll tell you, if her body showed up here in the Commonwealth, say in Jamaica Pond there, by now Mary Ellen Ames'd be signed, sealed, delivered, and cremated, on the theory that what looks like an accident probably by God *is* an accident, and on to the next fifty cases."

"Christ," I said. "I'm sorry I asked."

"Just so you don't accuse me of not knowing my job."

"Far be it from me."

I called Susan right after hanging up with Horowitz. She answered the phone herself with a brisk, businesslike, "Yes?"

"It's Brady."

"Hello, Counselor."

"Hi. Feeling okay?"

"Fine."

"Yeah? Good?"

"For heaven's sake," she muttered. I heard her take an exasperated breath and let it out slowly. "What's up, anyway? Or did you just call to inquire after my health?"

"I care about your health, Susan," I said. "I also wanted you to know. They're not ready to release Mary Ellen's body yet. They want to run some more tests."

"Brady, what the *hell* is going on?" she said. "They know who she is, they know she drowned. What more do they want?"

"They've got to decide what happened. It's the medical examiner's job. He's got to rule out—other explanations."

"Suicide, you mean."

"Well, that, yes. But also, if she was intoxicated or under the influence of a drug, that would help explain why a good swimmer like Mary Ellen might drown."

"There's something else, isn't there?"

"What do you mean?"

"Murder. They think somebody murdered her."

"I don't believe they think that. There doesn't seem to be any evidence of it."

"But maybe they'll find something."

"Yes," I said. "Maybe they will."

"And you'll continue to keep me informed."

"I will."

"Well, you should know that Willard Ellington is eager to tidy things up."

"The Historic Places guy?"

"Yes. Him. Now that—since Mary Ellen has, um, predeceased me, of course, the place goes directly to the commission upon my imminent demise. He wants to be sure the transfer is smooth and quick. He's afraid of the whole thing landing in probate."

"There will be no delay, Susan."

"Well, good. You can reassure him."

"Me?"

"I suspect he will want to discuss it with you."

"And I should be polite to him."

"How gracious you are is entirely up to you."

"Actually," I said, "it's entirely up to him."

And, as it turned out, it was difficult to be gracious to Willard Ellington, who did, in fact, appear in my office on Tuesday afternoon.

Julie ushered him into my office and ventured a sly quizzical grin behind his back. This particular sly quizzical grin of hers meant she either didn't like him, or had found him amusing, or had concluded he was a crackpot. I'd just have to find out which for myself. He took the wood-frame chair beside my desk without my invitation. In fact, by a subtle tilt of his head he managed to invite me to sit in my own chair, thereby taking command of the meeting. Neither of us offered to shake hands.

"I am here," he said abruptly, "to discuss the matter of Susan Ames's estate. I am a busy man, and I have driven here from Concord, taking me away from my business, so I trust we can be direct and to the point."

"There is nothing I'd like better," I said, "inasmuch as I am in the middle of my own business hours myself."

Ellington, I judged, was in his mid-sixties. He reminded me of a vulture in both appearance and demeanor. He had a sharp, hawklike nose and a jutting pointed chin and a completely bald head that was a bit undersized for his angular, hollow-shouldered frame. The skin was stretched so tightly over his skull that all the planes and angles of his bones stood out sharply. He had pale bushy eyebrows. They might have been blond or white, I couldn't tell. His eyes were the color of slate.

"Very well, then," he said, after impaling me with those eyes for a moment. "Quite simply, I want to verify that there will be no delay in the transfer of the deed to the Ames place once Mrs. Ames passes."

"Her will was drawn up by a competent attorney, if that's what you're getting at."

My remark called for a witty—or at least, sarcastic—rejoinder. After all, that competent attorney had been me, which he, of course, knew. But instead, Willard Ellington said, "Yes. Precisely." Obviously, a man for whom humor was too time-consuming.

"Well, Susan Ames seems satisfied with it"—I shrugged—"and she's paying for it. So I guess it'll have to do. The Concord Historic Places Commission will get the place once your death dance works its magic."

He narrowed his eyes. "That was uncalled for."

I shrugged.

"Susan Ames is elderly," he said. "Death is inevitable.

The Ames mansion, however, is timeless. It belongs to history. It's a rare thing nowadays for a monument of such historic significance—and in such excellent repair—to become available. I do not want this transaction bungled or delayed in any way."

"Well, sir, it's a damn good thing you reminded me. Otherwise I probably would have bungled the hell out of it." I gave him my most courteous smile. "And how else may I be of service, Mr. Ellington?"

"I would like my own attorneys to examine the will."

"You can't wait for Susan to die first?"

"Is there a problem?"

"Your attorneys helped us frame the language in the will. If Susan wants to release her copy of it to them, I can't stop her. Frankly, I don't know what your rush is."

"My rush, as you put it, is none of your affair, Mr. Coyne."

"But Mary Ellen Ames's untimely death certainly has worked to your advantage."

He thrust his beaky nose at me. "And what are you implying?"

I shrugged and smiled. "Nothing. I will discuss the matter with Susan. Have your attorney call me."

"Very well." He stood up. "And I thank you."

"Oh, it's been a pleasure."

I walked him out of my office and we shook hands just like gentlemen at the door. After he left, I muttered, "Asshole."

Julie looked up. "Huh?"

"I've found one person who is rejoicing that Mary Ellen Ames has died," I said. "I suspect there are others."

22

I WAS SITTING at Julie's desk at around two the next afternoon. Julie was in my office negotiating the extension of our lease with our landlord. He wanted to jack up the rent. Julie had complaints about the management of the building.

Julie was skilled at that sort of thing, which worked out well since I had little patience with it. Besides, it fell under her job description. She also handled our insurance, ordered supplies, and generally left me completely free to do the lawyer stuff. Actually, she did a lot of lawyer stuff, too. I had tried once to elevate her status from secretary to office manager. To my bafflement, it just pissed her off. She wanted to be called a secretary. She believed that a sexist male business world had created the negative connotations on the title "secretary." Secretaries, she said, were vital cogs in the corporate wheel. Without secretaries, said Julie, offices could not function. So why belittle them by giving some of them phony titles?

Pay secretaries what they're worth, said Julie. That's all.

Secretary, office manager, either way Julie was the boss. She ran the show.

So while she hammered it out with the landlord, I sat at her desk answering the phone, as she had instructed me to.

And when it rang, it was I who picked it up.

"Brady Coyne, attorney at law," I said, the way Julie insisted I do it.

"Is that you, Brady?" It was Terri.

"Oh, hi, General. How goes the battle?"

"Not very well, I'm afraid."

"Susan?"

"She's started having a lot of pain. And she's very despondent. The doctor wants to put her on morphine, but she's refusing. I think it's really hitting her now."

"That she's going to die?"

"Well, yes. That. But also that her daughter is dead. I think up till now she's kept herself going by sheer will power. Mary Ellen's death seems to have sucked that out of her. The last few days have been bad. According to the doctor, it's not going to get any better. There's a tumor, and it's just going to keep growing and eating her up. She says it's kind of like being pregnant. This thing inside of her grows bigger and bigger and then one day—it's over. Like giving birth. Except she calls it giving death." Terri laughed quickly. "That's her. Trying to make a joke out of it. The doctor would like to hospitalize her. She won't hear of it. She feels that if she goes to the hospital, she'll never come home."

"Oh, boy," I said. "This is just all around lousy. What can I do?"

"You're one of the few people she'd like to see, Brady."

"When would be a good time?"

"Anytime, really. Late afternoon, early evening would probably be best. But whatever is convenient for you."

"I think I could be out there later today, if that would be all right."

"That would be wonderful."

"Look for me between five and six, then." I hesitated. "Hey, Terri?"

"Yes?"

"We still on for Saturday?"

"Why wouldn't we be?"

"I don't know. Good. Look, I'll see you this afternoon."

"That will be nice."

It was actually a little after six before I pulled into Susan's driveway. Terri answered the door. She smiled and held her hand out to me. "Hi, there."

"Hello, General."

She rolled her eyes. "You *can* call me Terri, you know. We factotums don't like to stand on ceremony."

"Okay. How is she?"

"Eager to see you, I think. She's in the library having tea. Want some?"

"Sure."

Susan was propped up on the big leather sofa. A bulky comforter was wrapped around her so that only her head was poking out, and she was watching the news on a small table-top television. Her hair had been brushed and her face made up. But nothing could erase the pain lines etched around her mouth and eyes.

"Brady," she said. A hand snaked out from under the comforter.

I went to her and took it. I bent and kissed her cheek. "Hi, Susan."

"Turn off that damn machine and sit with me."

I shut off the television and sat beside her. Her hand reached for mine again. I squeezed it gently and kept holding it. "Not too good, huh?" I said.

"I can't decide which pain is worse," she said softly. "The one in my gut or the one in my soul. But you didn't come here to listen to an old lady's complaints."

"You can complain all you want. I don't mind."

Terri came into the room with a teapot and a mug. She poured mine full and refilled Susan's, which sat on the table beside the sofa. "Anything else I can get you?" she said.

Susan shook her head. "No, thank you, dear."

Terri left the room.

"Lovely young lady. Very capable. Beautiful, isn't she?"

I nodded.

Susan looked at me sharply, then smiled. I wondered if Terri had let it slip that she and I had been seeing each other. "I want to do something for her. She has a young daughter, you know."

I shrugged. I didn't know what Susan knew. I figured it was up to Terri to tell her if she wanted to.

"I'm very fond of her. She doesn't have a lot of money. I'd like to establish a trust fund for little Melissa Fiori."

"That can be done," I said. "I'll have Julie put together the paperwork."

"We better do it quickly, Brady."

I nodded. Before she died, she meant.

"I'd just as soon give everything to her," said Susan. "She's—she's been like a daughter to me."

"Your predatory friend wouldn't like that."

"Willard? You met him, then."

"Yes. He was in yesterday. He's starting to circle around."

She smiled. "He is a buzzard, isn't he? Still, the commission must get the place, regardless of Willard Ellington. But there is a little money there for Melissa, I trust."

"There is actually quite a bit," I said.

She closed her eyes. "Good. This feels like a good thing. I think of Terri and her little Melissa, and I think of—of Mary Ellen."

I sipped my tea.

"I was thirty-two when Charles and I married," she said. "He had just turned forty. Both of us, I think, were surprised by it. We had more or less resigned ourselves to single life. I don't know if it was what they call love. It felt more like convenience. Both of us were independent sorts, fixed in our ways, not accustomed to partnership. I think Charles felt the breath of advancing years on the back of his neck. He had no heirs. His brother did not survive a Japanese prison camp. Both of his parents were dead. We never really talked about it. But the deal, I think, was that I would give him an heir. It took nearly ten years to accomplish. We were both deep into middle age by then. I don't think either of us had a great capacity for love. At least not the kind of love a parent is expected to have for his child. Not the kind of love Terri has for her Melissa. Maybe if you don't have much money, you make up for it with love. And, by the same logic, if you have plenty of money you shortchange the child in the love department. I don't know. I have limited experience. I do know that we didn't do right by her."

"I'm sure you did the best you could," I murmured.

"Oh, I'm sure we didn't," she said. "We—" She stopped suddenly. I turned to look at her. Her eyes were squeezed shut and her forehead glistened with perspiration.

"Susan?"

"Take my hand, Brady."

I found her hand. She gripped mine hard. "Oh, shit," she whispered through clenched teeth. She panted rapidly through her mouth, the way women are taught in natural childbirth classes to control labor pains. When giving birth. Or giving death.

After a minute or two, her grip on my hand relaxed and she let out a long, deep breath. She opened her eyes and looked at me.

"Okay?" I said.

"It comes so quickly. I don't know when to expect it. I'm sorry."

"What about medication, Susan? You shouldn't have to tolerate that."

"I do not want to die in some fuzzy drug world. I don't have much time. I want at least to be aware of what there is left of it for me."

I nodded. "I understand."

She breathed deeply again. "I'm all right now." She closed her eyes for a moment. "Anyway, Mary Ellen was a wild, brilliant child. Very bright, very uncontrolled, very manipulative. Neither Charles nor I understood that warmth and love was all she needed. He coped with her willfulness by buying things for her. I did not approve. I believed in discipline. Punishment. So Charles spoiled her and I alienated her. She learned how to play us off against each other by the time she could talk. I have been over it and over it in my mind ever since you told me she—was dead. And I realize now what happened. I tried to blame him. It *was* his fault. But mine equally. We both killed her. Charles and I. Because, God help us, we didn't love her. And she knew it."

"You're being too hard on yourself, Susan. Blaming yourself isn't right. There is no evidence that Mary Ellen committed suicide."

"I'm not necessarily talking about suicide, Brady. I just mean the whole course of her life, which took her to the place where she had to die young. Charles and I, we had power over that."

"Replaying it doesn't do anybody any good."

"It does me good," she said. "I want to figure it out. Listen. We put her in private schools. She got terrible grades. All her teachers said she was brilliant, gifted. But her energies went into manipulation, not schoolwork. One of her male teachers got fired when she was thirteen. Do you know why?"

I nodded. "I guess I can figure it out."

"The school persuaded Charles not to press charges. If I'd had my way, that man would have gone to prison. But you know Charles."

"No," I said quietly, "I never knew Charles. You hired me after he died, remember?"

She touched my arm. "Of course. I'm sorry. Anyway, I was wrong. That poor teacher didn't victimize Mary Ellen Ames. It wasn't his fault. He was *her* victim. She was a mature woman—physically—at thirteen, and more skilled at deceit than most adults. She had an abortion at fifteen, Brady, and another a year later. She somehow graduated and got into college. Her father's name and her father's money—and his connections—did it for her. She had terrible grades and astronomical scores on her standardized tests. Anyhow, then Charles died, and she left with that Arab person, and . . . well, dammit, anyway."

"Mary Ellen had a big portrait of Charles in her condominium. It occupied a place of honor on her wall."

"She was a complex person, even as a child," said Susan. She looked up at me. Her smile was wan. "Probably no portraits of her mother, huh?"

I put my arm around her shoulder and held her against me. I didn't answer her question. I couldn't think of anything to say.

After a moment, she said, "I'm sorry, dear Brady. You came here to cheer me up. I haven't been very cooperative, I'm afraid."

"That's okay, Susan."

"It's just that when you're at the end of your life you

have nowhere to look except back. And what I see doesn't please me."

"We don't always get to pick our lives for ourselves," I said. "We bumble through them, doing the best we can at the time. Second-guessing ourselves is pretty fruitless."

She snuggled against me. Her voice became dreamy. "She loved him, you know. She worshipped him. And all he ever did for her, all he ever gave her, was money. It's not what she wanted. I—I tried to make her a good person. She hated me for it. It wasn't fair. But somebody had to try. At least I tried. He wouldn't."

Her voice trailed off. I continued to hold her. After a few minutes, I realized she was sleeping. I eased myself off the sofa and lifted her thin legs up onto it. She shifted, moaned. I tucked the comforter around her, propped a pillow under her head, and left the room.

Terri invited me to stay for a drink. I declined. I wanted to put some distance between myself and the old Ames mansion in Concord.

23

WHEN I GOT BACK to my apartment that evening, the little red light on my answering machine was winking. Blink, blink, pause, blink blink, pause. Two messages. I took off my jacket and tossed it onto the sofa. My necktie followed it. My shoes tumbled under the kitchen table.

Then I went into my bedroom and stripped down to my underwear. I tried to decide who I wanted to be trying to reach me. Either of my sons. Even if they wanted money, or wanted to complain about their mother. I always liked to hear from them. Or Terri. But I'd just seen Terri.

I pulled on my jeans and sweatshirt and padded back to the living room in my stocking feet. I pressed the button on the machine.

"Brady, it's Gloria" came the first voice, as though I needed her to identify it. "It's Tuesday, a little before seven. Give me a call. I'm here all evening."

There was a beep, then another voice, this one belonging to a man. "Ah, Mr. Coyne, this is Dave Finn here. Remember? Your mugger?" He laughed. "Mary Ellen's friend. I wanna talk to you, huh? You, um, shit, I guess I gotta try you again. I ain't got a phone. Anyways, like I said, I'll try you again. I guess that's the message."

The machine clunked and rewound its tape. I went to the cabinet and took down my bottle of Rebel Yell. I poured an inch into a tumbler, plopped three ice cubes into it, and sat at the table with it. I took a long sip, lit a Winston, stared out the window at the dark ocean, and then pecked out the Wellesley number.

Gloria answered with her throaty "Hello?"

"Hi, hon."

"Oh, Brady. Thanks for getting back to me."

"Is everything okay?"

"Sure. Why wouldn't it be?"

"I don't know. The boys, whatever."

"The boys are fine, as far as I know. Of course, I never hear from William."

"Me, neither."

"Well," she said after a pause, "the reason I called was just to check on your thinking about the house. You said you'd get back to me. It's been over a week."

It sounded to me like an accusation. Gloria had a way of making the most innocuous statements sound like accusations. And no matter how outlandish her accusations were, or how clearly I realized that they were not intended to be accusations, they always made me feel defensive. "A week?" I said. "You sure?"

"Positive. We had lunch a week ago Friday. I think I told you I could wait a couple weeks. But I just figured maybe you'd made up your mind, and I'd really like to know."

"Well," I said, "I honestly haven't given it much thought. I've been pretty much preoccupied with a very complicated matter for a client."

"If you don't want the house, you can just say so."

I *didn't* want the damn house. I didn't have to give it any thought whatsoever. But for some reason I was reluctant to say it. "Give me a few more days. It's a difficult decision."

"Fine. Call me by Friday, then, okay?"

"Sure. Will do. Listen, is Joey around?"

"Joseph is hardly ever around. Since he got his license . . ."

"Well, give him my love."

"I will, Brady. Talk to you by Friday, then, huh?"

"You bet."

"Don't forget."

"I won't."

I might, I thought as I hung up the phone. I might forget.

The phone rang a few minutes later. When I answered it, a woman's voice said, "Brady?"

I couldn't place the voice. I was vaguely disappointed to realize it wasn't Terri. "Yes. Who's this?"

"Robin McAllister. I tried you a few minutes ago. Your line was busy. Can I talk to you?"

"Sure. Go ahead."

"Not on the phone."

"What's up, Robin?"

"It's Warren. I'm—concerned."

Oh, shit, I thought. She's found out about Mary Ellen. "We can meet somewhere, if you want," I said.

"You name it."

"It doesn't matter to me."

She hesitated. "How about that revolving lounge on top of the Hyatt on Memorial Drive? What's it called?"

"The Spinnaker," I said. "Cute, huh?"

"Yes," she said. "Cute. That's more or less equidistant for us, I think."

"That's fine. When?"

"An hour?"

"Okay."

I had to change my clothes again. I avoided a necktie by pulling a sweater over a shirt. I shrugged into a sport jacket and drove over to the Hyatt.

The Spinnaker Lounge on the top floor of the Hyatt Regency rotates at the rate of about one revolution every fifteen minutes. Some people find it disconcerting. Some people claim to get motion sickness up there. But it offers a good and ever-shifting view of the Charles River and, beyond it, the city. I can pick out my office building from up there.

Robin McAllister was already there, rotating. She was wearing a red dress with a low neckline. She had makeup around her eyes. I had never seen her dressed up before. She looked spectacular.

I sat across from her. "Hi," I said.

She smiled. "Thanks a lot for coming," she said. "I had to talk to somebody . . ." She waved her hand in the air. "Somebody discreet."

"A lawyer."

"That's not what I meant. Somebody—a friend. Who knows what's going on."

She knows about Warren and Mary Ellen, I thought again. I didn't want to be in the middle of this one.

"Where's Warren tonight?" I said.

"It's Tuesday. He's got his seminar at the hospital on Tuesdays."

"Right. I remember."

A waitress came to the table. Robin asked for a glass of white wine. I ordered a bourbon old-fashioned.

When the waitress left, Robin reached across the table and touched my hand. "He's taking this hard."

"This?"

"The death of his patient there. That young woman."

"Mary Ellen Ames."

She nodded.

I revised my guess. She didn't know. But she suspected.

"Brady," she said, "what's going on? Do they think she killed herself? Warren won't talk about it. He just broods. It's unlike him. He acts—guilty, or something. Was it suicide?"

"I don't know. They haven't figured it out. It could be. They haven't discounted murder."

Her eyes widened. "Murder," she whispered.

I nodded.

"Do they have a suspect?"

"Not really. Which means, at this point, that everybody's a suspect. They're trying to sort it out."

"I thought she drowned."

"She did. I guess it was probably an accident. They just haven't said so officially yet."

Our drinks arrived. After the waitress left, Robin said, "No wonder Warren's upset. I don't know what to say to him. I'd like to help. Make him feel better. He's taking it so hard. I wish he'd talk to me. But he's so damned circumspect and proper when it comes to his patients."

"I guess all you can do is love him."

She smiled. "That's easy. But I worry about him. He hasn't even gone fishing lately. He used to go every Sunday. It was good for him. He'd always come back rejuvenated." She touched my hand. "You could take him fishing, Brady."

I nodded. "Sure. I could do that."

"Would you?"

"I'd be happy to. Maybe not this weekend, but soon."

"Don't let on that we talked about it, okay?"

"Of course not."

"He wouldn't want me to be doing this. He's a very private man. Very proud."

"I understand."

We sipped our drinks quietly for a minute or two. Then Robin said, "Brady?"

"Yes?"

"If there's anything you can tell me that will help me to understand, to help him—will you?"

"There's not much, Robin. Like I said, they're just trying to rule out suicide or murder, that's all."

"But if something should come up?"

I shrugged. "Within the boundaries of my profession, sure, I'll tell you."

"Thank you. You've made me feel better."

We finished our drinks and took the elevator down to the parking garage. Robin gave me a quick hug and drove away.

I got home around eleven. Dave Finn called a little before midnight. When I answered the phone, he said, "Man, I hope you can tell me that what I think I'm hearing ain't true."

"You heard about Mary Ellen, then?"

I heard him expel his breath. "Oh, shit. It's true, then, huh?"

"She's dead. Yes. How did you hear it?"

"I'm a cop, remember?"

"I understood you were suspended."

"I didn't tell you that, did I?"

"No."

"Well, yeah. I got shafted is what happened. Suspended without pay. I mean, I didn't do nothin' everybody else doesn't do. Anyways, that's not important. I want to know about Mary Ellen."

"You haven't been interrogated about it?"

"Why should I be?"

"I gave your name to a state policeman."

"Oh, boy. Thanks. Just what I need. Who, Horowitz?"

"Yes."

"No, nobody questioned me. I just caught a rumor that Horowitz was investigating something. Not even her name. It just—sounded like her. I figured, I'm so worried about her I'm just imagining it. God. It *is* her, then."

"Yes. I'm sorry."

"What happened?"

"She drowned in a pond in New Hampshire."

"No way she drowned. She was a fuckin' porpoise in the water."

"I'm just telling you what I was told."

"Only way that girl drowns is if someone holds her head under water. Even then, I doubt it. She's a strong kid." He paused. When he spoke next, his voice had a brittle edge to it. "They trying to make it out she killed herself?"

"I don't think so. They haven't figured out how it happened. I guess that's still a possibility."

"Like hell it is. She was in great shape. She was going to her shrink there like every day, talking about the future, happy and laughing all the time, just a happy kid. I'm telling you, Mr. Coyne, she didn't drown by no accident, and she didn't commit suicide, either."

"There's only one other possibility, Dave."

"Don't I know it." He whooshed out a breath into the receiver. "I wasn't a detective for twenty-two years for nothin', you know. Somebody killed her is what happened."

"Well, okay. The sixty-four-dollar question, then."

"Who? Hell, I oughta be able to figure that out. Gotta think about it."

"Well, when you do, let me know, okay?"

"Maybe."

"Or maybe what else?"

"Lissen. I was gonna marry that girl. What'd you do, somebody killed the girl you were gonna marry and you figured out who it was?"

"I'd turn him over to the authorities."

His laugh was ironic and short. "Well, pal, I usta be one of them authorities of yours, and I know how all of 'em operate, and I'll tell you this. If I was looking for justice here, the authorities ain't where I'd be looking."

"Well, I'm not one of those authorities, myself," I said. "So maybe you could share your insights with me before you go searching for justice."

"Maybe I will. I've got your number."

"I don't have yours, though," I said.

"I ain't got one is why. I'm living in a trailer, for God's sake. You go six or eight weeks without a paycheck, you've gotta scramble a little. Friend's letting me stay here for a while. I'm out here in the boonies. Little trailer in the woods. I'm at this friend's house right now. Just down the road from my cozy happy home. And I gotta get off, because they're getting ready for bed. So look. Anything comes up, maybe I'll give you a jingle."

"Okay. Do that."

I hung up the phone slowly. Another vote against an accident and against suicide. By process of elimination, a vote for murder.

Dave Finn didn't sound like a man who had murdered his girlfriend. But I still didn't like the way he sounded. He certainly sounded capable of murdering somebody.

24

"**T**HOUGHT YOU MIGHT LIKE to hear about those toxicology screens," said Horowitz when he called me the next morning.

"Absolutely," I said. "What'd they find?"

"Small amount of alcohol. Equivalent of one shot of booze, can of beer, glass of wine. She wasn't drunk. Traces of cocaine and marijuana, too, but the ME says that was old stuff, not relevant to her death. But something pretty interesting."

Horowitz paused, so I said, "Well, I trust you're going to tell me."

"You mentioned that drug Pertofrane, right?"

"Yes. She had a prescription. It's an antidepressant."

"Well, the ME ran a screen for Pertofrane, and guess what?"

"Come on, Horowitz."

"Well, he found it. Not just in her blood, but in her stomach, too. You understand what that means?"

"Obviously. She took her medication the morning she died." I hesitated. "Well, sure. I know exactly what it means. It means, assuming the drug was doing its job, that she wasn't depressed. And if she wasn't depressed, she'd be unlikely to kill herself. Hell, if you're intending to kill yourself, you probably aren't real conscientious about taking your medicine anyway."

"The ME agrees with you."

"Also," I said, "it means she was home the same day she died. The prescription bottle was still in her medicine cabinet on Beacon Street. So she must have gotten up, taken her pills, then driven up to Teal Pond. Where, eventually, she drowned."

"Yup," he said. "They found her little Porsche tucked under the pine trees beside her cottage."

"And of course they're doing all sorts of forensics on the car and the cottage, right?"

"Hell," said Horowitz, "I don't know about that."

"But," I said. "Somebody must have killed her. That's the only explanation left."

"The New Hampshire guy is going for an accident, Coyne. Everything points to it."

"Except for the fact that she was a strong swimmer."

"So she panicked. Got a cramp. Who knows?"

"Christ," I muttered.

"Well," said the cop after a moment, "I just thought you'd like to know."

"Did those toxicology screens show anything else?"

"You know how they work," said Horowitz. "They've gotta be looking for it if they're gonna find it. They always check out alcohol, coke, grass, some of the other nasty stuff. That's routine. I told them to look for Pertofrane. If they hadn't of looked, they wouldn't of found it."

"So what are you going to do?"

"Do? Me? In this case, I'm doing what the ME asks me to do. It's his case. It's all I can do. And he's not asking me to do anything. He said thanks for all my help, he can handle it from here. That's what I'm doing."

"That's it?" I said.

"Coyne, it's not like I've got nothing else to worry about."

"I wasn't accusing you of anything."

"Yeah, well I got a boss here, you know. And he's already pissed about all the time I've taken away from a whole bunch of good high-profile Massachusetts cases to help out our friend up there in New Hampshire. So . . ."

"You agree with me, don't you?" I said. "You think somebody murdered her, don't you?"

"I don't know. Yeah, maybe I do. But it's their case."

"This doesn't seem right."

"Tell it to the judge, Coyne."

I had nobody to tell it to. But I thought about it for the rest of the morning, and I was still thinking about it after lunch when Julie buzzed me. "Call on line one," she said. "An attorney named Elizabeth McCarron."

I pressed the button and said into the phone, "Brady Coyne."

"Mr. Coyne," she said, "I have just spoken to Susan Ames's associate, a Miz Fiori, and she asked me to confer with you." She had a deep voice that managed to sound both sultry and masculine. "I wonder if I could buy you a drink at, say, around six this afternoon."

"I'm available," I said, "and I hardly ever turn down a free drink. What's up?"

"It has to do with Mary Ellen Ames's will, and I'd rather discuss it in person with you, if that's all right."

"Okay. That's fine. Where do you want to meet?"

"Well, you're in Copley Square, so how about J. C. Hillary's? That should be convenient for you."

"It is. There are booths in the bar. Where are you coming from?"

"My office is on State Street."

"I'll try to get there early and grab a booth," I said. "How will I recognize you?"

"I'll be the tired-looking redhead." She laughed. "I've got on a lime green suit, which matches my eyes and sets off my hair, which is the color of a pumpkin. I'm about five-ten. Really, I'm hard to miss. What about you?"

"Oh, I'm a handsome devil. Fortyish. I'll be wearing a lawyer suit."

"Gray pinstripe, huh?"

"You got it. With a vest. And a blue tie with a school of little rainbow trout swimming on it. So Mary Ellen had a will, huh?"

"Yes. We'll talk about it. See you at six."

I got to J. C. Hillary's at quarter of six and slipped into the only available booth by the bar. I sat facing the entry so I'd see Elizabeth McCarron when she came in. A waiter appeared with a menu. I told him I didn't expect to be eating, but I could use a shot of Jack Daniel's on the rocks.

I had just taken my first sip and lighted my first cigarette when she appeared. As promised, she was hard to miss. None of the businessmen at the bar missed her. They all swiveled around and stared. The little narrow lime green skirt stopped several inches above her knees, leaving what looked like several yards of slim, shapely leg showing below. Her magnificent mane of red hair flowed over her shoulders. It was burnished brown, not really orange—more the color of autumn oak leaves than pumpkins. She had a wide mouth, snub nose, and lots of freckles. In her high heels she looked as if she'd be able to stare Kevin McHale straight in the eye.

She paused in the doorway, frowning myopically. I

waved. She smiled and came over. She held out her hand to me. "Liz McCarron," she said.

I took her hand. "Brady Coyne. Come on. Sit down. You look beat."

She slid in across from me. "Boy, you got that right. I was in court all afternoon. Old Judge Crocker had a hair up his ass."

"Crocker usually does," I said. I held up my glass of Blackjack. "I already started. What'll you have?"

"Scotch." She looked around.

The waiter was already staring at her, so when she caught his eye he came instantly to our booth. "Ma'am?"

"Cutty on the rocks."

He left. She put her elbows on the table and her chin in her hands. "So. You're a smoker, huh?"

I glanced down at the cigarette that was smoldering in the ashtray. "Yes. Afraid so."

"Ugh."

"I'll put it out if it bothers you."

She waved her hand. "Naw. Give me one."

I held my pack out to her. She plucked one out. I held my Zippo for her. She steadied my hands with hers and lit up. She blew out a long plume of smoke. "Ahh, this is evil," she murmured. "Damn, I miss these things."

The waiter slid her drink in front of her. She picked it up and sipped. Her tongue slithered out and touched her upper lip. "This, too," she said. "Evil. Delicious." She looked at me. "I've heard a lot about you, Brady Coyne."

"Oh-oh."

"Nothing bad." She waved her hand. "Seems like every lawyer in town knows you except me. You've got an, ah, interesting reputation."

"Interesting?"

"You've managed to corral the wealthiest folks in Greater Boston for clients. Most everyone I know envies you."

"That just makes them work harder to beat me," I said. "Being envied is not such a good thing."

She smiled. "Well, you and I aren't likely to be adversaries here, so we needn't worry about envy." She sipped her drink, puffed at her cigarette, and cleared her throat. "Mainly, I just was hoping we could smooth out some things."

"Good. I like things smooth."

"Here it is. I did a will for Mary Ellen Ames about three years ago. As you know, she has died. The main beneficiary is her mother, Susan Ames, who is your client. I spoke with her secretary this afternoon, a Miz Fiori?"

I nodded. "Yes. Her general factotum. Terri Fiori."

"Okay. She referred me to you. She indicated that Mrs. Ames is unwell."

"She's dying."

"Right. Which complicates things."

"It sure as hell does, since Mary Ellen was the primary beneficiary of Susan's estate, too."

"Yes. But if you and I work together, we should be able to simplify it. Agreed?"

"Agreed," I said. "But not over drinks."

"No. Of course not. I just wanted to meet you and make sure we were on the same wavelength."

The waiter came to the booth. "Another round, folks?" he said, looking only at Liz McCarron.

"Not me," she said. "One more'll put me on my ass."

I waved my hand. "I'm fine."

The waiter hesitated, then left with a show of reluctance.

"You said Susan was the main beneficiary," I said. "There are others?"

She nodded.

"Can you tell me who they are?"

"I don't know why not. You'll see Mary Ellen's will soon enough. There are two others. A Sidney Raiford and a Sherif Rahmanan. Mary Ellen had many assets. These two gentlemen stand to inherit one hundred thousand pre-tax dollars apiece from this."

"No shit," I muttered.

"No shit, Counselor." She was grinning. "You know them?"

"Raiford and Rahmanan? A little. I wonder if they know about this will."

"I have no idea. They'll find out soon enough."

"Did you know Mary Ellen well?" I said.

She shook her head. "I didn't really know her at all. She came to us for a will, as I said, about three years ago. Somebody referred her, I guess. Can't remember who, if she ever mentioned it. It was a just a will, no big deal. They gave it to me. She had a lot of money, but it was a very simple will. As I said, everything went to her mother except for the cash to the two other guys. I haven't seen her since then."

"Well, we ought to get together soon," I said. "Best if we clear away the underbrush while Susan's still alive."

"Yes. Good. I'll call you and we can set something up."

"Want some supper while we're here?" I said.

She shook her head. "It sounds delightful, but I've got a desk I haven't seen the top of in a month waiting for me."

"You're going back to the office at this hour?"

"I go back to the office at this hour every day," she said. "Except on those days when I haven't had an excuse to leave it in the first place. Then I just stay there. Saturdays and

Sundays, usually, too. Sometimes by the time Sunday evening arrives I actually get to see a little patch of desktop. Of course, by Monday morning it's covered up again."

"Why," I said, "does anybody want to be a lawyer?"

"They think their practice will be like yours," she said. "You're probably going home now. You don't have a desk piled with half-written briefs and volumes of precedents and correspondence, overflowing manila folders, unopened mail, right?"

I smiled. "Nope. I've got a very efficient secretary. Mostly, my desk is piled with L. L. Bean catalogs."

"See?" she said. "That's why every lawyer in town envies you. I'd love to have dinner with you. Hell, I'd love to have another Scotch, and a couple more of your cigarettes. But I can't."

"Well," I said, "another time, maybe."

She smiled. "I'd like that."

She reached into her pocketbook and took out a couple of bills. She put them on the table.

"I'll get it," I said.

"My invitation," she said, "my treat." She smiled. "It *was* a treat."

I shrugged. "Okay. Thanks. Next time'll be mine."

After she left I decided to have another Jack Daniel's. I tried to imagine how Susan would feel when she realized that Mary Ellen had bequeathed most of her estate to her.

25

WHEN I CALLED Charlie McDevitt the next morning and asked him to meet me at Marie's for lunch, he must have detected something in my voice, because he didn't give me a lot of shit about who owed whom a favor, or how much busier than me he was, or how much more important his work was than mine. He didn't tell me a rambling joke or cautionary tale or shaggy dog story.

He just said, "Sure. Of course."

And he was waiting at our table nibbling a breadstick when I got there.

I slid into the seat across from him. "Boy, thanks," I said. "It was short notice."

He shrugged. "Does this have something to do with that phone number I got for you?"

I nodded. "Yes. The way it started, I was just looking for the daughter of one of my clients. They'd been estranged for about eleven years, and the mother's got terminal cancer so she wanted to reconcile with her daughter. Now it looks like the daughter's been murdered."

Charlie arched his brows. "Whew," he breathed.

"It's complicated," I told him. "Let's order. I'll tell you about it."

Charlie ordered the calamari, the way he always does at

Marie's. I had the stuffed ziti. We declined Marie's standard complimentary carafe of wine. We both had an afternoon's work facing us.

And while we ate, I tried to summarize what I was coming to think of as the Mary Ellen Ames Case for him. Talking about it to Charlie, trying to be logical and sequential in my recitation, identifying the connections that I recognized and pinpointing the gaps as they appeared, all helped me to see things a little more clearly.

And Charlie, good listener and good friend that he was, didn't interrupt. He nodded here, frowned there, and pursed his lips at the other places.

We were sipping coffee when I told him about my tête-à-tête with Liz McCarron. Then he started grinning. I guess I embellished her physical appearance more than was necessary for the smooth continuity of my tale.

"Anyway," I concluded, waving my hands, "it looks to me like someone murdered her."

Charlie nodded. "You do tend to overthink problems, Coyne."

"You don't agree with me?"

"I follow your logic, all right. But you keep forgetting the first rule of all science and philosophy."

I frowned.

"Occam's razor," said Charlie with a shrug.

"Huh?" Charlie had a way of making me feel ignorant sometimes.

"The first rule. It states that the simplest explanation for any unknown phenomenon is preferable to a more complex one, and that you should attempt your explanation on the basis of what is known rather than assuming there are unknowns that need to be discovered."

"Indulge my ignorance," I said. "But, if you will please, apply Mr. Occam's wisdom to the present conundrum."

Charlie grinned. "Okay, Counselor. Answer me this. What quacks like an accident, waddles like an accident, flies like an accident, and lays eggs like an accident?"

I nodded. "Sure. Except—"

Charlie held up his hand. "Hey, Brady?"

"Yeah?"

"What does this *not* quack like?"

"It does not," I admitted, "quack like a murder. No physical clues. No witnesses. No single outstanding suspect."

"Nevertheless . . ."

"If it's murder," I said, "it's a cleverly plotted and executed one."

"Which," said Charlie, "is the least simple explanation of all. As you know."

"Nevertheless," I said, "I think one of these folks murdered Mary Ellen Ames."

"You are a stubborn son of a bitch," he said Then he nodded. "However, sometimes Occam's razor doesn't apply."

"Right," I said. "It's just a matter of figuring out which one of these people stands to gain the most from her death."

"Or," said Charlie slowly, "the other way 'round."

"Huh?"

"You know. Who stands to lose the most from her living."

I stared at him for a minute, then nodded. "Sure. You're right."

We talked about it some more while we finished our coffee. Then I paid for our lunches and we walked out. We turtled into our trench coats against the slicing wind that swirled around Kenmore Square. A miniature tornado of brown leaves twisted down the sidewalk. An odd sight, inasmuch as no trees grew in Kenmore Square.

Charlie waved down a taxi. "What're you going to do?" he said to me.

"I don't know," I said. "Shake a few bushes, see what flies out quacking."

"Watch out something doesn't fall on your head, Counselor."

"Thanks for the advice."

The last time I had eaten at Marie's was with Gloria a couple of weeks earlier. That day I had taken the T to Central Square in Cambridge to visit Sidney Raiford in his bookstore. I did the same thing this time.

Head Start Books still had its sooty windows and its hand-lettered signs. Inside, it was gloomy and empty of customers, just as it had been the first time I was there.

I worked my way through the narrow aisles between the bookshelves, pretending to peruse the merchandise. As I approached the back of the store I saw Raiford. His long gray ponytail was tied back with a pink ribbon. He was seated at a messy desk talking on the telephone. He glanced up when he saw me, held up one finger, and went back to his conversation. I picked up a book on Eastern religions and paged idly through it.

A minute later Raiford came up to me. "We still got nothing on fishing, man. Did you try the Coop?"

"You remember me?"

He grinned. "Shit, guy, you're like one of my best customers."

I held my hand to him. "I'm Brady Coyne."

He grabbed my thumb in what I took to be an alternative handshake. "Sid Raiford. Sole proprietor. Listen, man. I can order something if you know what you want. You don't see it, I can get it. New, used, whatever. Dig?"

"I dig," I said. "What I'm really after, though, is some information."

He rolled his eyes. "Ah, fuck. So you're a cop, huh?"

"No." I fumbled a business card from my jacket and handed it to him. "I'm a lawyer."

He glanced at it and shrugged. "Six a one, half a dozen a the other. Look, mister. I've been clean a long time, okay? I don't even hang around with those dudes anymore. Who is it this time, anyway?"

"Mary Ellen Ames."

Up close, Sid Raiford looked even older than from a distance. He was over sixty. His face was crosshatched and weathered like the sheer side of a rock cliff. He had a high sloping forehead. The hair that was pulled straight back over his head was thin, so that his skull shone through. And when he attempted to smile, his teeth showed gray and stubbed.

"Who?" he said.

"Come on, Mr. Raiford," I said. "I'm not a cop. But I know many cops. I just want to talk with you about Mary Ellen."

He shrugged stubbornly. "Sorry, man."

"She's dead, you know."

His head jerked back. "Say what?"

"Mary Ellen died a couple weeks ago."

"What happened?"

"I was hoping you could tell me."

He cocked his head and stared at me for a moment. Then he said, "I can't tell you what I don't know. But you want to talk, I'm cool. Come on out back."

He went to the front door and flipped around the sign that hung there, so that potential patrons would know that he was out to lunch, expected back soon. Then he led me through the store to a back room. It was piled with books of all descriptions, cardboard boxes, old magazines, empty Coca-Cola cans, and a large coffee urn. There were two threadbare upholstered chairs. He gestured for me to take one.

"Coffee?" he said.

I nodded. "Sure. Black."

"Black's all we got, man."

He handed me a styrofoam cup of coffee. Then he took the other chair. "You're jiving me about Mary Ellen, right?"

I shook my head. "No. She's dead. She drowned."

"Damn," he muttered. "She was a nice little chick."

"How well did you know her?"

He smiled at me. "I wasn't boffing her, if that's what you mean. Shit, man, I coulda been her grandfather, practically. I gave her a job a long time ago. She was one messed-up little bird, I can tell you that. Too much money, too little of anything else. She wanted to do something, you know? I let her handle the cash register. In those days, we actually got a customer now and then. She lasted a couple months. Then she stopped showing up." He looked at me and flapped his hands. "Sayonara," he added.

"You haven't seen her since then?"

He shook his head.

"How long ago would you say that was?"

"I dunno. Six, eight years."

I stood up. "Thank you, Mr. Raiford."

He looked up at me. "That's it? That's all you wanted to know?"

I nodded. "I just wanted to know whether you intended to tell me the truth. Since you don't, I'm not going to waste my time. I expect you'll be having other customers coming around pretty soon. I'll recommend your place to some of my friends."

"Wait a minute."

"No, that's okay. Have a nice day, Mr. Raiford."

"Hey, shit, man. Sit down, huh?"

"Why?"

"I don't need any cops coming around, okay? Lawyers either. Come on. Sit down. I'll talk to you."

I sat down. "Okay. Talk to me, then."

"I will," he said. "But first tell me how you know about me and Mary Ellen."

"The security people in her building have seen you coming and going. Some of her friends know of you. Besides," I added, "you're one of the beneficiaries in her will."

"Say what?"

"You're inheriting some money from her."

"You're bagging me."

"I'm not bagging you, Mr. Raiford. You didn't know about it?"

"Would you believe me?"

"I don't know."

He shrugged. "I didn't know. Honest, man. Jesus, no wonder . . ."

"No wonder what?"

"Well, you must think I killed her or something, huh?"

"I think somebody might have. What do you think?"

He shook his head slowly. "Listen, okay? She was this wasted little bird, maybe twenty-one or -two. She was trying to get away from some guy who was giving her a hard time. I didn't know her from Adam and Eve, but she kept coming in here, hanging around, not buying anything, just sitting cross-legged on the floor in the corner reading my books. Shit, didn't matter to me. Those days, lots of kids from the

Square'd wander in here. It was a safe place for them while they waited to finish their trips, come down, sober up, whatever. I got to know her, talked with her. She was different from the others. Older, for one thing. Lot of those kids were like thirteen or fourteen. Mary Ellen was on her own, not trying to hide out from rich parents in Dover or someplace. And she had plenty of bread, dressed nice, always wore makeup. So I gave her a job; we got to be friends. We'd blow a little weed now and then. After she stopped coming to work I didn't see her for, I don't know, a few years, anyway. Then she came by. Looking really together. She—"

"When was this?"

He rubbed his chin. "Three, four years ago? Yeah, about four years ago. She tells me she's got her shit together, in therapy, got herself a nice place to live, car, all that. I'm happy for her. We go out to dinner. Over at the Charles Hotel, no less. Hey, she was paying, right? She tells me she's found a guy, only he don't know it yet, whatever that was supposed to mean. Funny broad, Mary Ellen. Anyways, she comes around to telling me that what she'd really like is to get ahold of some good stuff."

"Dope, huh?"

He shrugged. "Just grass, a little nose sugar, that's all. She wasn't into anything weird. I tell her, this is no problem. Look, honest. I gave up dealing. I mean, I'm losing my ass on this store, but I can't afford to fuck around anymore. People look at me, they see this poor old hippie who did it all. Shit, I tripped with old Tim Leary over at Harvard. I was in Chicago in '68, Woodstock, you name it. I was a Deadhead for about a year. Cops all know me. So I gotta stay straight. But for friends, I can help out. Mary Ellen wants to get ahold of some good stuff . . ." He spread his hands and smiled.

"And you did."

"Sure. And I helped her smoke it and sniff it, too. I didn't make a profit or anything. She'd give me some bread, I'd get her a baggie or two. We'd crash at her pad for a few days. What's wrong with that?"

"I guess that's a matter of opinion," I said. "But what's a matter of fact here is that she is dead. And you stand to inherit a hundred grand."

"A loyal chick, Mary Ellen," he said.

"Mr. Raiford," I said, "somebody killed her."

"I feel terrible about it," he said. "I really do. But it wasn't me, friend."

"Who, then?"

"You asking me?"

I nodded.

"How the hell would I know?"

"She must have talked about people."

"I suppose she did."

"Who'd have reason to kill her?"

"Mr. Coyne," said Raiford slowly, "obviously you didn't know her."

I shook my head. "You're right."

"Because if you did, you'd know. Nobody would want to kill her. She was easy to love. Guys fell for her. Women liked her. I think you're on the wrong track."

I remembered the conversation Charlie and I had an hour earlier. "It seems to me," I said, "that there were people who stood to gain from her death. And," I added, "vice versa."

He looked at me and shrugged. "So what do you want?"

"Who'd she talk about?"

"Her father. Her mother."

"You mentioned she was in love."

"Yeah, well, she didn't say with who. Or if she did, I

don't remember. Understand, we were mostly stoned when we had these conversations."

"Does the name Dave Finn ring a bell?"

He squinted at me. "Yeah, maybe."

"Sherif Rahmanan?"

"The Arab? Yeah, she talked about him. In the past tense."

"What about them?"

"They loved her. Like I said, she was a lovable chick. But she didn't love them."

"Well, who did she love?"

"Just one guy."

"Who?"

"Her father."

"What about her mother?"

He smiled. "Oh, Mary Ellen hated her mother."

26

IT BECAME CLEAR to me that Mary Ellen Ames had not confided much in Sid Raiford. He knew nothing of her entanglement with Jill Costello or her affair with Warren McAllister, for example. When they were together, they were just a pair of potheads, both of them old-timers at it despite the thirty-odd years separating them. They'd sit cross-legged on her living room floor sipping red wine and toking and snorting and listening to Mary Ellen's collection of Beatles and Moody Blues compact discs and reminiscing about the good old days. I got the impression that Raiford did most of the reminiscing. Mary Ellen was still sucking pacifiers during Sid's good old days.

The fact that Mary Ellen glorified her dead father and had alienated herself from Susan was not news.

Raiford seemed sincerely touched that Mary Ellen would have remembered him in her will, even though he recognized it as a symbolic gesture. After all, she must have assumed that she'd outlive him.

He said he could surely use the money. He'd rather sell the bookstore, but nobody wanted to buy it. One hundred thousand dollars would keep him going for a long time.

Sid Raiford did not strike me as a man who'd kill for an inheritance. On the other hand, if a lawyer learns anything, it's that predicting people's behavior on the basis of a personal judgment of their character is folly. Nice people commit crimes. Sometimes violent crimes. Sometimes murder. No one is immune from greed or jealousy, lust or anger.

After a while, he meandered into a nostalgic narrative of his adventures in Selma, Alabama, of candlelit vigils outside LBJ's White House, of pig-taunting demonstrations in Harvard Square, of acid and speed and heroin. Sid Raiford took kids under his wing, sat out bad trips with them, pulled them out of the paths of club-swinging rednecked policemen, encouraged them to go back home to their parents in Oregon or Michigan. He had been, I understood, a superannuated hippie even then.

So after the undrinkable coffee had cooled in my styrofoam cup, I gently interrupted Raiford and asked him if I could use his phone for a local call. "Help yourself, man," he said.

My call to the Tufts switchboard was shuttled to the Fletcher School, and thence to Sherif Rahmanan's office, where a secretary, asking no questions, put me through to him.

"Rahmanan," he answered, pronouncing it with a guttural "R."

"It's Brady Coyne, Professor."

"Pardon me?"

"You helped me locate Mary Ellen Ames, remember?"

He hesitated. "Oh, yes. Of course."

"I need to meet with you," I said.

"I thought we had an agreement, sir."

"I remember no agreement, Professor. But if we did have one, things have since changed."

"And how is that?"

"Mary Ellen is dead."

The silence at the other end of the line lasted so long that finally I said, "Professor? Are you there?"

"I am here," he said.

"Did you hear me?"

"I did. I assume you are attempting to shock me."

"No. I'm just telling you the truth. And we must talk."

"Why?"

"Because you lied to me the first time."

A pause. Then, "Yes. I see."

"Do you know the Charles Hotel?"

"I know it," he said.

"The bar. Top of the stairs on the right. In an hour."

"Mr. Coyne, I am in the middle of office hours."

"Cancel them."

"Yes. All right."

It was a twenty-minute stroll from Head Start Books in Central Square down Mass Ave. to Harvard Square with the biting autumn wind in my face the whole way. I wandered around the Square for half an hour, ducking into several bookstores to check out their fly-fishing stock. I exercised admirable restraint and resisted making any purchases. I climbed onto a barstool at the Charles ten minutes before Sherif Rahmanan. I was halfway through a Bloody Mary when he arrived.

We shook hands. "Thank you for being prompt," I said.

"This is a grave matter."

"Pun?"

He frowned.

The bartender, a young blonde in a short skirt, came over. "Drink, sir?" she said to Rahmanan.

He waved his hand. "Soda water." He turned to me. "What has happened, Mr. Coyne?"

I told him the parts of the truth I wanted to tell him.

While I was talking his drink arrived. He ignored it. I concluded by saying, "So, Professor, whether you like it or not, you are involved."

"I am *not* involved, sir. Anything between Mary Ellen and me ended a long time ago."

"That's not true."

"I beg your pardon?"

"I said it wasn't true. It's a lie." He opened his mouth to speak, but I held up my hand. "Understand me, Professor. I did not ask to meet with you in order to threaten you. But as far as I'm concerned, it's not at all certain that Mary Ellen's death was an accident. I am quite prepared to turn over the information I have to the state police."

This was a mild distortion. In fact, I had already mentioned Sherif Rahmanan's name to Horowitz, who had so far chosen not to pursue it.

"You *are* threatening me, sir."

"No. I am simply clarifying my position for you."

He nodded. "What," he said softly, "do you want from me?" He was stirring his glass of soda water with the swizzle stick that protruded from it, studying the way the ice cubes swirled in it.

I spread my hands. "Just the truth."

"I did not kill the girl." He looked up at me. "I loved her."

"The one does not preclude the other," I said.

He nodded. "Yes. Quite so. All right, then. The truth." He paused, took a deep breath, sipped from his glass. "I couldn't let her go. It was she who broke off with me. That was ten years ago. My feelings for her never changed. I kept track of her. Yes, I knew where she was living. Yes, I tried to contact her. Oh, many times. I spent many evenings, evenings when my wife thought I was at my office working on a mono-

graph or grading exams, standing in front of her building on
Beacon Street, gazing up at her lighted window, wondering
who was with her, what she was doing, whom she loved. I
telephoned her. She screened her calls, Mr. Coyne. She allowed her machine to answer for her. She talked with only
those whom she chose to talk with. Alas, I was not one of
them. I left her messages. Plaintive, querulous messages. I
told her I knew she was there, listening. I begged her to speak
with me. But she didn't. Not once. Not ever." Rahmanan
shook his head slowly back and forth. "She was more mature
than I, of course." He sipped from his drink, then shrugged.
"This is pitiable, sir. I know it. I am deeply embarrassed. Do
you understand why I was not forthcoming with you?"

I shrugged. "I don't like being lied to."

"There was no good reason for me to tell you the truth,
Mr. Coyne."

"There is now."

"Of course. And I have." .

"You haven't spoken with her or been with her?"

"Not for ten years."

"But you wanted to."

He smiled. "Desperately."

"This must have been very frustrating for you."

He shrugged. "Love creates complex emotions."

"She must have made you angry at times."

"Anger is one of those complex emotions, yes."

"And jealousy, too. She had other men."

He nodded. "I suppose so."

"Greed as well."

His head jerked back. "Greed?"

"Money, Professor."

"I'm afraid you lost me, Mr. Coyne."

"You knew of her will, of course."

"Whose will? Mary Ellen's? She had a will?"

"Yes."

He frowned. "What about it?"

"She bequeathed a substantial sum of money to you, Professor."

He smiled. "Now I know you're trying to manipulate me, sir. Mary Ellen and I have been out of touch for ten years. She would have no reason to bequeath anything to me."

"She did. One hundred thousand dollars."

He shook his head. He frowned. He cocked his head and peered intently at me. "This is the truth?"

I nodded.

He blew out a long, worried breath. "This is terrible. Something must be done."

"Excuse me?"

"Don't you see, sir? I cannot accept any bequest from Mary Ellen Ames."

"You can't use money?"

"Of course I can use money. But that's not it. How in the name of heaven could I explain it to my wife?"

"I don't know," I said. "You could try lying to her."

He smiled. "You are a cruel man, Mr. Coyne."

"I'm a lawyer," I said. "What did you expect?" I laid a five and a one on the bar and swiveled off my stool. "An attorney named Elizabeth McCarron will contact you about Mary Ellen's will, Professor," I said. "She may be less cruel than I."

I left Sherif Rahmanan sitting there poking with his forefinger at the half-melted ice cubes in his glass of soda water. I took the T back to my office and got there a few minutes before five. Julie was just pulling the dust cover over her computer when I walked in. She looked up, widened her eyes, and said, "Oh, my. What a lovely surprise. It's Mr. Brady Coyne."

"Come off it, babe," I said. "What I don't need right now is a bunch of shit from my secretary."

"Oh, but just to catch a glimpse of you. I didn't dare hope."

"Julie . . ." I tried to inject a hint of warning into my voice.

Julie was skilled at ignoring my hints. "I left a stack of phone messages on your desk. You might want to glance through them since you've chosen to honor us with a brief visit."

I went over to her and kissed her cheek. "Thank you, sweetheart. Have a nice evening. I'll see you tomorrow."

She made an exaggerated O of her mouth. "You will? Wow!"

"That is my present plan. A long day of paperwork. I will be entirely at your disposal."

"How unprecedented."

"Go home," I said.

She grabbed her coat and swirled out of the office. She paused in the doorway to blow me a kiss. I feigned a swoon. Then I went into my office. I sat behind my desk, lit a cigarette, and glanced through the dozen or fifteen telephone messages Julie had left for me. All but two were from clients or lawyers with no business I judged urgent. The other two were from Dave Finn, one at 3:10 and one at 4:30. Both of his messages were identical: Will try again. In neither case had Finn left a phone number where I could reach him. I remembered he was living in a trailer with no phone.

I thought of returning a few of those other calls. Then I thought better of it. I judged there was nothing that couldn't wait until the next day. So I turned out the lights and went home.

And I had barely changed from my suit to my jeans and sweatshirt when Finn called. "Gotta talk," he said.

"Good. Let's."

"Not on the phone, Mr. Coyne. I'm in these folks' kitchen."

"We can meet somewhere, I guess."

"Yeah, well I ain't got a car that works right now. So how's about you coming here?"

"Where's here?"

"Townsend."

"Christ," I muttered. I knew Townsend. The Squannacook River, a fair trout stream, ran through Townsend. Townsend was at least an hour's drive from my apartment on the harbor in Boston, assuming no road repairs, detours, or traffic. I sighed. "If necessary, all right. When?"

"What's wrong with now?"

"Only that I just got home after a long day and I haven't even had a chance to sit down, never mind have some supper."

"Well grab a bite and come on out. Listen. Here's how to find me."

He dictated directions to me. They were complicated, involving landmarks such as a lumberyard, roads without signs, fields, and a farmhouse. I wrote them down carefully, then said, "All right. Look for me around eight. And I hope this is going to be worth it."

"Well," he said, "I dunno. I sure feel I need to talk to you."

"I'll be there."

27

TOWNSEND, MASSACHUSETTS, is one of those little rural communities northwest of the Route 495 high-tech arc that continues to thrive in the same family-farm country-store way it has for the past fifty years. You don't see many cornfields being bulldozed into condominiums or office parks or shopping malls around Townsend. The barber shops, drug stores, insurance and lawyer and real estate offices, and home-cookin' restaurants that cluster around the rims of village greens in places like Groton and Townsend and Pepperell stay in the family. They get a coat of fresh paint every third summer. There's an air of tidy, modest prosperity about these towns, although it's a mystery how and where their residents make a living.

I picked up Route 119 in Littleton, as Finn had instructed, and followed it through the darkness of the October evening, past stubbled cornfields and roadside farm stands. I arrived in Townsend after driving for nearly an hour. I pulled to the side of the road to recheck the directions Finn had recited to me over the phone and decided I had already passed the country roadway just beyond the lumberyard, just as he had predicted I would. So I backtracked and found it. Four miles by my odometer and I came to the white farmhouse with the big silver silo beside the tin-roofed barn. Another right, this one unpaved gravel. It wound through woods and pasture. Past the third bungalow on the left was another roadway, this one even narrower. A hundred yards later I came to Dave Finn's trailer hunkering in a pine grove where the roadway petered out.

The trailer was a twenty-by-ten-foot rust-stained metal box. The yellow light from the two small windows bathed the pine-needled ground in front. Behind the trailer lay dark forest. A pale blue Ford Escort crouched in the yard. A clothesline drooped between two pine trees. A bird feeder and a gray blanket hung from it.

I parked my BMW beside the Escort, got out, climbed onto the pair of cinder blocks that served as a step by the door, and knocked. It took Finn several moments to come to the door.

"Ah, Mr. Coyne," he said when he opened the door, as if he had been expecting someone else. "Good. Come on in." He was holding a beer can. A half-smoked cigar was clamped in the corner of his mouth. He was wearing a gray sweatshirt and baggy jeans. There were orange stains on the front of the sweatshirt. A silvery five-day stubble bristled from his face.

He held the door for me and I stepped past him. I looked around. "Cozy," I said.

Finn took the cigar from between his teeth and laughed. Then he tilted up the beer can and took a long drink. "Cozy," he repeated, wiping his mouth on the back of his hand and grinning. "Yeah, that's it. That's good. Cozy."

Everything in the place was built in—the bunk across one end, the table that folded down from the wall, the flip-down benches along both sides of the table, and the kitchen on the other end. There was a closet with an accordion door in one corner next to the kitchen sink that I guessed would contain a shower stall and toilet—one of those arrangements where you had to stand in the shower if you wanted to urinate into the toilet.

"Fifty bucks a week, huh?" said Finn. "I was payin' nine-fifty a month back in the city. Place not much bigger than this. Not bad, huh?" He grinned lopsidedly, letting me know that he knew the place was a dump.

A radio on one of the innumerable built-in shelves played country and western music and static. A bare light bulb burned over the sink. Another swayed gently on its cord over the pull-down table. An electric space heater glowed ominously on the floor in front of the sink. The place smelled of perspiration and stale cigars and mildew. Water stains formed a wavy border halfway up the fake paneling on the walls.

Old newspapers and rumpled clothes and beer cans and whiskey bottles and Pizza Hut boxes were strewn everywhere. Finn swept one of the benches clear and gestured for me to sit. "Beer?" he said.

"Sure."

He bent to the bread-box refrigerator in the kitchen area and came up with two cans of Rolling Rock. He slid one to me and folded himself onto the bench across from me. He popped the top of his can, drank from it, wiped his mouth on his sleeve, and banged the can down onto the top of the table. He fumbled a pack of matches from his pants pocket and relit his dead cigar. It was a cheap one. Then he leaned toward me on his bulky forearms. "I been doing some thinkin'," he mumbled around the cigar.

"Some drinkin'?" I said.

He frowned for a moment, then tilted his head back and laughed. "Yeah, that too, Mr. Coyne. Some thinkin' and some drinkin'. They sorta go together, you know?"

I sipped from my beer can. "What have you been thinking and drinking about?"

His forehead furrowed. "Well, about Mary Ellen, of course. Dammit, I miss that girl. I've seen plenty of death in my job, but when it's the gal you love . . ." He shook his head quickly. "Only thing I can figure is somebody murdered her."

"Me, too," I said.

He nodded. "The other two don't make any sense. Accident or suicide."

"Sure," I said. "But who? Why?"

He smiled quickly. "Right. Exactly. Who? Why? That's what I been thinkin' and drinkin' about here. I'm circling around it, maybe. Need to try out some of it on somebody." He arched his eyebrows at me.

"Good," I said. "Try me."

"Well, don't get your hopes up, Mr. Coyne. I haven't got it figured yet. Another beer?"

"No, thanks."

Finn tilted up his own beer can, drained it, and went back to the refrigerator. He returned with another can of Rolling Rock.

"She was a good kid," he said. "But she was kinda screwed up, you know? You don't really think about it at the time. Hey, she was a lot younger than me, you figure she's just, you know, young. A little wacky. Lovable that way. She had this huge picture of her old man hanging there, with its own little special light for it, you know? Like it was a shrine or something? Like he was some kind of saint? I don't really understand how stuff like that works, but I can tell you that it was kinda screwy. The old man's been dead for quite a while. I mean, it's time she got over it."

I nodded.

"She didn't like her mother much."

"Mary Ellen told you that?"

"You betcha. Look, I don't know diddly about psychology. But I've seen it. Cops get to see weird family stuff. And, now that I think about it, this was pretty weird. It was like they were both married to him. Mary Ellen and her mom. I mean, even after the old man died it was like her and her mother were still competing for him, like he was some stud lover or something, not a dead father. In her mind, I mean. Wanna know something?"

I shrugged and smiled. He was going to tell me.

"When we made love? Afterwards, I mean? She'd kinda snuggle against me, put her pretty head on my chest and sorta pull at the hairs on it, and she'd call me Daddy. 'My nice daddy,' she'd say. Or, 'Tell me a story, Daddy.' " Finn mimicked a little girl's whine. "And, I don't wanna get personal here, Mr. Coyne, but even when we were goin' at it, she'd sometimes call me Daddy. Like, 'Oh, yes, Daddy.' Or, 'Touch me here, Daddy. Give it to me, Daddy.' At first I thought it was cute. Kind of a turn-on. But after a while it got kinda spooky. Sick, you know? Once she tried to get me to spank her, for chrissake. I mean, it was almost as if she really thought I was her father, like she forgot it was just her old Huckleberry laying there with her. Finally one time I says to her, 'Don't call me Daddy, honey. I'm not your daddy.' And she grabs a big hunk of my chest hair and yanks on it so the tears come to my eyes. And she starts yelling, 'You *are* my daddy! You *are* my daddy, Goddamn it! If I say you're my daddy, then you're my Goddamn daddy!' And after a couple minutes she calms down a little, and she starts kissing me and all, and she says, 'Please, won't you be my daddy? I want you to be my daddy.' And I told her, as soft and gentle as I could, I told her that it was just me and she better get that straight." He paused and stared up at the ceiling, chewing his dead cigar. "Now that I think of it, Mr. Coyne, that was one of the last times we were together. In bed, I mean."

Finn tilted up his beer can. It was empty. He dropped it onto the floor. "Shit," he said. "I don't know why I'm telling you all this."

I flapped my hands.

"I mean, makin' you come all the way out here . . ."

I shrugged.

"I don't want you to think . . ."

"Don't worry about it."

"It probably has nothing to do with anything."

"It's okay," I said. "We're all upset."

"You want another beer?"

I shook my head.

"I do," he said.

He got up and went into the kitchen. He seemed none too steady. He came back with another beer. I had lost count of how many he'd had since I arrived. I assumed he'd also had some before I got there.

He relit his cigar butt, of which only about an inch was left. He closed one eye and squinted and still had some trouble lining up the end of the butt with the flame.

"So whaddya make out of this, Mr. Coyne? Huh?"

"I don't know. Nothing. I don't know how it relates to her death. Her murder, if that's what it is. I can't figure out why anybody'd want to kill her, never mind who. I sort of thought you might have some insights for me here."

"Yeah," he sighed. "Yeah, I wish I did. I don't know. Maybe she did kill herself. She really was kinda fucked up."

"Depressed?"

He shrugged. "I dunno. No. She never seemed depressed. More like edgy, wound up all the time. You know. Fucked up."

"To the point of being suicidal?" I said. "Still mourning her father's death? Is that what you're saying?"

"Christ, he's been dead, what, like ten years?"

"Eleven," I said. "Maybe it was some kind of delayed reaction."

"Maybe." Finn shook his head. "I don't know. She sure talked a lot about her old man. Mostly, how she thought he loved her mother better than her. But I never really got the impression she was depressed about it. Shit, I never really thought she was depressed at all. At least not so bad that she'd do something to herself. But who'd want to kill her? I knew that sweet little girl about as good as anybody, I bet, and there was nothing about her that'd make anybody want to kill her." He shrugged. "So maybe it *was* an accident, and they just can't figure it out."

"Dave," I said gently, "why did you want to talk to me tonight? What was so urgent?"

"Urgent?" He frowned. "Did I say something was urgent?"

"I got the distinct impression . . ."

He shook his head. "Yeah, well, I been laying around with nothing to do except miss Mary Ellen and maybe play a little detective in my head. Needed to talk before I went totally batshit, you know?"

"So you don't have an idea of who might've killed her, then?"

He shook his head.

"Or even whether she really was murdered? As well as you knew her, you're still not sure that it wasn't an accident or suicide?"

"Nope." He shrugged. "I'm not sure. When I first heard it I was sure. But thinkin' about it, I don't know. It's like I don't know anything anymore. Not yet. But by Jesus, I'm gonna figure this sucker out. I got nothing else to do except drink beer and pick the lint outa my belly button and feel sorry for myself and wait for Internal Affairs to shitcan me." He burped, then yawned.

I started to slide out from the table. His hand snaked across the table and grabbed my wrist. "Hey, where you goin'?"

"Home. I've got work tomorrow."

"Don't knock it," he said. "Wish the hell I had work tomorrow. Don't know how lucky you are, you got work tomorrow. Siddown, willya?"

"I think you ought to go to bed and I should leave. You're kind of drunk."

He laughed through his nose. "Kinda drunk. Ha! You don't know drunk when you see it." He yanked on my arm. I sat down. He kept his grip on my wrist and leaned across the table toward me. "You wanna know something?"

"You can let go of me. I'm not going to run away."

He looked down to where his hand was holding me. The sight seemed to surprise him. He took his hand from my wrist and picked up his beer can with it. "Twenny-two years, pal. I been a cop twenny-two fuckin' years. Know what I got?"

"Probably not much," I said. I hate humoring drunks. Their jokes aren't funny, their self-pity is pitiful, their anger is irrational. "Why don't you go to bed, Dave?"

He narrowed his eyes. "Don't fuckin' try to be nice to me, pal. Nothin', that's what I got. I'm out on my ass is what I am. Those fuckers. Know who I feel sorry for?"

"Who?"

"Teachers, that's who. These snot-ass kids drive up in their Porsches and Bee Em fuckin' Doubleyews, cost more'n the poor bastard tryin' to teach 'em how to spell makes in a year, and they think they're so much better than Mr. English teacher. Twenny-two years and what've I got? Debts, that's what. I got a wife somewhere gets sixty percent of my paycheck before I even see it, two kids who don't even know me anymore. What'm I s'posed to do? Catch guys who've figured out how to make a livin' and turn 'em over to rich lawyers to get 'em off, and maybe if I do a helluva good job the chief says, 'Nice work, Finn.' Which don't exactly buy the groceries. So whaddya do, huh? You figure, I wanna buy *me* some groceries, and what happens? The chief says, 'Shitty piece of work, Finn, and you're fired, baby.' "

He leaned back and closed his eyes. A gurgling sound rose in his throat. It started out as if he was going to vomit. It ended as a wet belch.

I slid off the bench and went around to him. I tugged at his arm. "Come on, Dave. Let's go lie down."

"Sure," he mumbled. "Fuckin' A."

I wrestled him off the bench and half-carried him to the bunk. It was a jumble of damp sour-smelling blankets. He collapsed on the bed. I pulled a blanket over him.

"The joke's on her," he muttered.

"Who?" I said.

"Doreen. She don't get nothin' anymore. Sixty percent of nothin's nothin', right?"

"Right. I'm leaving now."

"Joke's on me, too, pal."

"Yes?"

"Yeah. They think I got something. I didn't get dollar one from those douchebags."

"Which douchebags?"

"Those bookies, supposed to be payin' me off. Shows how dumb I am, huh?"

"Maybe you'll be cleared, then."

He opened his eyes. They tried to focus on me, but failed.

Finn laughed. "Sure. Justice for all." He closed his eyes and rolled away from me. "Who'd wanna kill her, anyway, huh?" he mumbled. "Who'd wanna kill my little girl. Tell me that. Who'd kill my sweet baby? Fuckers . . ."

I turned the dial on the space heater way down, snapped off the bare light bulbs, and left. The air outside Dave Finn's trailer smelled awfully sweet.

I DIDN'T GET BACK to my apartment until nearly midnight. I found the message light on my answering machine winking at me. I pressed the button and heard a soft female voice. "It's Jill," she said. "Jill Costello, remember? It's Thursday night. Um, listen, I was hoping to talk to you. It's kind of important, I think. Give me a call? I'm home." She left her phone number.

"Too late," I mumbled to the machine. "Not tonight." I jotted down her number on the notepad beside the phone and proceeded to undress my way to my bedroom. I was tired.

I was especially tired of slumming around in the history of Mary Ellen Ames's complex love life. She had died. It was tragic but final, and there was nothing to be done about it. Whom she had chosen to sleep with, and for whatever reasons, were none of my business and apparently irrelevant. Charlie was right. Occam's razor. I found myself feeling like a Peeping Tom, and I wanted no more of the policemen or the professors or the hippies or shrinks or landladies of Mary Ellen's X-rated sex life. Susan was my client. She had asked me to find Mary Ellen. After a fashion, I had. My job was done.

So I went directly to bed, vowing to attend strictly to the boring but necessary business of making a living for a while.

There'd be no Gone Fishin' sign hanging on my door tomorrow, even if it was a Friday. Julie would be happy. My various clients would be happy. Assorted lawyers throughout the Greater Boston area would be happy.

So what if I wouldn't be particularly happy.

And on Friday that's what I did. I returned all the calls I had accumulated during the week. I read all my letters and jotted notes in the margins. Julie would magically convert those notes into lucid letters of reply. I stoically set aside all the fishing catalogs that arrived in the morning mail without opening them. When Mrs. Arthur Fortin appeared in my office at eleven for her scheduled appointment to complain about Arthur's obstinacy, I did what I did best: I reminded her that divorce, like everything else in the American legal system, is an adversarial process, which is what keeps lawyers in business, so it's best to have a competent one.

This was the same sort of reminder I found myself frequently needing. It sounded fairly convincing when I explained it to Amanda Fortin.

At noontime Julie went around the corner to the sub shop and came back with a small tuna for herself and a large ham and cheese for me. We ate at my desk while she ticked off my appointments for the following week.

I thought of returning Jill Costello's call, but figured she'd be at school. I'd try her in the evening.

After lunch I huddled with several pages of notes and began to draft a revised will for Steven and Holly Morgan. It was a complex and unpleasant task involving trust funds for the three Morgan progeny and seven grand-progeny, a horse farm in Sherborn, a string of polo ponies, a large house on Nantucket, and a collection of priceless old British and Italian shotguns.

The Morgans were typical of my clients. They were rich,

boring, and elderly. Unlike most of my clients, however, the Morgans were people I didn't like very much, and it was hard to summon great enthusiasm for my task of keeping all of their wealth safely in the family.

Hammering out a will for people like the Morgans always made me grouchy.

So when Julie buzzed me in the middle of the afternoon, I jabbed the button on my console and growled, "What?"

"Hey," she said. "Don't shoot the messenger. You got a call."

"I've probably had a dozen calls this afternoon, and you haven't interrupted me so far."

"You should take this one."

"I'm not here."

"Yes you are. It's Gloria."

"I don't care if it's Brigitte Bardot. I'm busy."

Julie giggled. "You *would* take it if it was Brigitte Bardot."

I sighed. "Okay. But only so I could practice my French. Look. I don't feel like talking to Gloria right now, okay? Tell her I'll call her back."

"Brady," she said, "really. I think you better talk to her."

"Why?"

"Please?"

"Shit," I muttered. Then I said, "Okay. All right. For you."

"Line two."

I sighed, pressed the button, and said, "*Bonjour,* hon."

"Brady, you said you'd call me today."

The usual accusation. But something else in her voice made me hesitate. Something subtle that fuzzed her anger. It sounded like fear. "Right, hon," I said. "I was going to call you. I hadn't forgotten." A lie. "But listen. I'm really busy right now. Can I get back to you?"

"About the house?"

"Yeah. We'll talk about it. Look—"

"Forget it, Brady."

"No, I promise. I'll call you."

"Forget the house, I mean."

"Well, actually, I didn't—"

"Oh, shit," she mumbled.

"Hey," I said. "Are you crying?"

"Don't worry about it, Brady."

"You *are* crying. What's the matter?"

"Nothing. It doesn't matter. The house isn't for sale, that's all. That's what I wanted to tell you."

"What happened? The condo deal fall through?"

"Yeah. That's it. The deal fell through."

"Well, too bad. But condos aren't that hard to come by. You should be able to find another one."

She laughed quickly. "There was no condo, Brady."

"But you said . . ."

"I didn't have the courage to be honest with you. There was no condo. There was a man."

"Oh, yeah, okay."

"That's the deal that fell through."

"Robert, huh? The lawyer?"

"Richard," she said quickly. Then she paused. "How did you know?"

"Billy told me."

"Well, God damn it, you could've told me you knew."

"I figured if you wanted to tell me about it you would have."

I heard her let out a long breath. "Yeah. I guess I was

embarrassed or something. I knew you wouldn't approve of him."

"What difference would that have made?"

"Jesus, Brady," said my former wife, "I wish I knew. But for some reason it mattered to me." She laughed quickly. "Isn't that something?"

"That's something, all right," I said quietly.

"Maybe we can have a drink sometime, huh?"

"Sure. I'd like that."

"I feel like I owe you an apology."

"You don't owe me anything, hon."

"You're right. So I'll let you buy. I'll call you, okay?"

"Sure."

"You didn't want the house, did you?"

"No."

"You could've told me."

"I suppose I didn't want to disappoint you."

"Well," she said, "that's nice, I guess."

"Naw," I said. "It's just cowardice."

After I hung up with Gloria I swiveled around to look out the window. It's not much of a scene—mostly concrete and steel and glass. But on a clear day there are treetops off in the distance, and when the sun is low in the afternoon I sometimes can catch a glimmer of the Charles River. Glimpsing the treetops and the water usually comforts me.

On this Friday afternoon heavy clouds hung low over the city and darkness was seeping in early. No comfort there.

With a sigh, I rotated back to the Morgan will.

Julie stayed late to reinforce my good behavior. Before she left, she loaded up my briefcase. "Hey," I said. "If we don't watch it, I'll be all caught up."

"That's the idea, buster," she said.

I watched the Celtics on TV that evening. At halftime I

tried Jill Costello's number. Her machine answered. Her message was curt and cautious—she told me that I had reached the number I had dialed, that I should leave my name and number, and she'd get back to me.

I did as instructed.

The Celtics beat the Hawks in a close one. I was in bed before midnight. Jill did not return my call.

I woke up early. A nor'easter had blown in overnight. Hard pellets of rain clattered against the glass sliders that overlooked the gray angry harbor. A good day for paperwork.

At noon Terri called me. "Still coming?" she said.

"Sure. Looking forward to it."

"Know how to get here?"

"Boy, am I dumb," I said. "No. You never told me, and I forgot to ask. I guess I would've called you."

"Well, I'm not at Susan's, and my number's unlisted, so you would've had a problem."

She lived in an apartment complex on Route 2A in Acton. It was very close to Ciao, the Italian restaurant where we had dined. I agreed to get there around six-thirty.

I fooled around with my paperwork for the afternoon, and gave myself an hour to get to Terri's. I stopped at a liquor store on her street and bought two bottles of red wine recommended by the clerk. And I was ringing Terri's buzzer at precisely six-thirty.

She buzzed me up and greeted me at the door. She was wearing jeans and a pink T-shirt. She gave me a quick, nervous smile and a perfunctory hug and took my hand. "Come on in," she said. "Let me show you around." She lived in a cramped two-bedroom apartment. Her living room was decorated with cheap museum posters and worn furniture. Houseplants were clustered at the single window. There was a circular dining room table in the end near the kitchen. A boom box on top of a bookshelf was tuned to a classical music station. It was playing a Mozart piano concerto.

Melissa had the smaller of the two bedrooms. Stuffed animals of every imaginable species slept on her bed and huddled on the floor. Colorful pictures, most of them featuring smiling people and stiff-legged horses and lollipop trees and spectacular rainbows, were tacked on her walls.

Terri's bedroom featured a king-sized water bed.

Savory aromas wafted from the narrow stand-up kitchen.

We ended up in the living room where we had started. "Pretty nice," I said.

She shook her head. "It's not nice. It's an apartment. I'd like to have a house in a neighborhood. Not for me, but for Melissa. But I had that choice." She shrugged. "Drink?"

"We can try the wine." I gave her the bag that I'd been carrying.

She took out the two bottles and looked at the labels. Then she smiled at me. "I don't know much about wine."

"Me either. The clerk recommended them. Said they'd go perfectly with gnocchi."

"We've got time for a glass. We can eat in a few minutes."

We sat side by side on the sofa sipping our wine and listening to the music and not saying much. Terri seemed preoccupied, and I didn't try to intrude on her thoughts.

Her gnocchi were light and tasty and her sauce rich and spicy. It was delicious, and I told her so repeatedly.

"My grandmother's secrets," she told me. "She came over from Calabria when she was about fourteen to marry the man her parents had decided on, a cobbler from the village who'd come over a few years earlier. She brought her recipes with her in her head and gave them to all of us. She never wrote them down, and neither have we. It's a pinch of this, a handful of that, and keep testing, make sure it feels right and tastes right, and if it doesn't, you add more of this or that until it does."

"The gnocchi I've had usually end up feeling like hunks of lead in my stomach," I said. "This is different."

"Sure. It's made from potato, the way it's supposed to be."

We sat at the table for a long time after we'd finished eating, sipping wine and exchanging family stories. Terri's father was Calabrian, her mother Irish. She'd been raised Catholic. Four years at the University of Vermont had cured her of religion. She'd majored in history, minored in math, met Cliff her senior year, worked as a secretary until Melissa was born. Since then she'd done temp work. That's how she'd got the job with Susan.

"Best job I've ever had," she said. "Susan pays the agency, which pays me. But she also pays me extra, under the table. She says I'm worth more than the agency pays me."

I smiled. "That's Susan."

After a while we cleared the table and did the dishes. When we were done, Terri said, "Do you play cribbage?"

"Sure. I'm the cribbage champion of Fort Smith, Montana. All the fishing guides play."

We played five games at the dining room table. I pegged out on the fifth game before she had a chance to count her double run. "Well," said Terri, "I guess you're the cribbage champion of Acton, Massachusetts."

"You were a worthy opponent."

She sat back and propped her feet up on the seat of her chair. She hugged her legs and gazed at me. "Well," she said.

I smiled at her and nodded.

"I think," she said quietly, "that we need to talk about something."

"Okay."

"I mean," she said, "we've had three dates now, and I invited you to my place, cooked for you, my daughter's spending the weekend with her father. So . . ." She shrugged.

"Look," I said.

"No. Please. Let me try to say it. I'd like to go to bed with you—"

"Terri—"

"Let me finish. I'm attracted to you. I like you a lot. I've got—I'm normal, okay? I don't have hang-ups." She shifted in her seat and reached for my hand. She held it in both of hers. "I haven't been with a man since Cliff, Brady. I'm not particularly happy about that, but there just hasn't been any-body I've liked enough. To me, making love is just that. It's not sex. It's—well, it's loving." She squeezed my hand and peered at me. "Am I making any sense?"

"Yes."

"Do you love me?"

"Wow," I said. "What a question."

She shrugged. "Unfair?"

"No. Fair." I smiled. "Do I love you? I'm not sure. It's been a long time. It's been a long time since I could even say I wasn't sure."

She nodded. "Me, too. It feels good. But I'm not sure what it means. So—can we wait?"

"Yes."

"Can we see each other a lot, do things together?"

"I'd like that."

She got up, came around the table, and sat in my lap. She kissed me softly on the mouth, then put her arms around my neck and rested her cheek on my shoulder. I stroked her back and kissed her hair. She undid the top few buttons on my shirt and slithered her hand onto my chest.

"Hey, Brady?" she murmured.

"Yes, General?"

"Pretty soon, I think."

I nuzzled the nape of her neck. "I certainly hope so," I said.

29

A LOUD BUZZ awakened me. I slapped at my clock radio, but the buzzing continued. I picked up the telephone and heard a dial tone. The smoke alarm? The timer on the oven?

I hauled myself out of bed and stumbled into the living room. Sunlight was streaming in through the big glass sliders that looked easterly toward the ocean, so bright that it hurt my eyes. The rays came in at a low angle. It was early.

The buzz was coming from the intercom that connected me to the security guy in the lobby. I pressed the "talk" button and said, "What is it, Eddie?"

Then I pressed the "listen" button. "Hey, Mr. Coyne. There's a guy here wants to see you."

"Jesus, what time is it?"

"It's, ah, ten after seven."

"Today's Sunday, right?"

"Yes, sir."

"Well, who's there?"

"Mr. Sylvestro."

"Jack Sylvestro?"

"Yes, sir. Right."

Jack Sylvestro was a Boston homicide detective, a rumpled Peter Falk sort of guy who had once investigated a case that I was involved in. We had become friends in the process. "Okay," I said into the intercom, "send him up."

I opened the door for him, then went back to my bedroom and slipped on sweatpants and a sweatshirt. I was loading the coffeepot when I heard him rap on the door and say, "Hey, Brady."

"Come on in," I called. "I'm in the kitchen."

Jack Sylvestro is a big, shambling, bearlike man whose diffident, almost apologetic manner belies his quick incisive mind. "Looks like I got you up, huh?" he said as we shook hands.

I nodded. "Coffee'll be ready in a minute or two."

He slouched into one of the chairs at the kitchen table. "Me," he said, "I been up all night."

I sat across from him. "I'm not that perceptive this time of day," I said, "but I'll bet this isn't a social call. And if it isn't, that means it's business. And that means bad news of some kind, because homicide cops hardly ever bring good news."

He grinned wearily. "Aw, I was just in the neighborhood, figured I might scrounge a cup of coffee."

"Sure," I said. "What's up, Jack?"

"What's always up, my line of work. Young lady got herself killed." He rolled his head on his shoulders. "How's that coffee coming?"

"It's ready." I got up and poured two mugs full. I brought them back to the table. "I hesitate to ask," I said, "but what does it have to do with me?"

He sipped some coffee and sighed. "Your business card was tacked on the wall beside her telephone. There was a message from you on her answering machine." He shrugged.

"Oh, God," I said. "Jill Costello?"

He nodded.

I blew out a long slow breath. "She's been murdered?"

"Yes."

"Jesus," I muttered. I looked up at him. "Her husband?"

"Looks that way."

"What can you tell me?"

"We got a call last night. Security guy in the building. Seems that folks were trying to get ahold of Mrs. Costello all day. She's the super in the building. Supposed to be available on Saturdays. Finally someone got worried. Security guy had a key, went in, found her, called us. This was, I don't know, maybe eleven, eleven-thirty last night. I been there ever since."

"What happened?"

Sylvestro cocked his head and looked at me. "Where were you yesterday, Brady?"

"Me? Shit, I was right here all day. Staying out of the rain, trying to catch up on my paperwork. I was visiting a friend in Acton in the evening."

"See anybody during the day? Talk to anybody?"

I shook my head. "Hey," I said. "You think . . . ?"

He smiled. "Nope. I'm just hoping to figure out when the lady was alive. When'd you talk to her last?"

"I saw her a week ago. She left a message on my machine a couple days ago. Sometime Thursday. I got her message in the evening, late. I called back Friday and left a message. Christ, Jack, what happened?"

He held his coffee mug in both hands near his mouth. "It was pretty neat and tidy, Brady. A single stab wound up under the rib cage into the heart. A filleting knife. From a set in her kitchen."

"When did it happen?"

"Hard to figure. The ME guesses she'd been dead about twenty-four hours when we found her."

"Meaning it happened Friday night?"

"Yeah, sometime Friday night, early Saturday. Look, were you her lawyer or something?"

I shrugged. "Sort of. She was in the middle of a divorce. I agreed to advise her."

"Not your usual sort of client," he said mildly.

I smiled. "You don't miss much, do you? What happened was, I ran into her, we got talking, she told me her situation, and I agreed to—"

"Were you involved with her?"

"Me?" I shook my head. "No. She was lonely, unhappy, afraid of her husband. Christ, she could've been my daughter." Anyway, I thought, I'm involved with Terri Fiori, whatever that means.

"How'd you say you ran into her?"

"I don't think I did say. I was trying to contact a person who lived in the building." I stopped. "It's a long story. You want to hear it?"

"Yes. I think I better. I also want more coffee."

I refilled our mugs and told Sylvestro all about my search for Mary Ellen Ames, her death, and my frustration with the case. I told him that Mary Ellen and Jill Costello had been "involved in a relationship." That was the euphemism I chose. Sylvestro just nodded at my clichéd word choice. I also told him that John Francis Costello had tried to beat me up one evening when I came out of Jill's apartment, that he had threatened me and, according to Jill, her, too.

Sylvestro listened without interrupting. When I finished, he said, "We're holding the husband. It's pretty clear-cut. Naturally, he says he didn't do it, and he's got a lawyer who's gonna get him bailed out. Soon as the ME can pin down the time of death, we'll have a better handle on it. The guy works at a restaurant in the evenings. But he's off around midnight and not back until four in the afternoons, so it just depends. He admits he went over there on Friday night and banged on her door. Claims she didn't answer, and he didn't get in. Could be just covering his ass in case we come up with a witness who saw him there." Sylvestro shrugged. "This fight you and him had, we'd probably want a deposition from you, okay?"

I shrugged. "Sure. It wasn't a fight, though. He attacked me. I never had a chance to get a poke at him."

"Yeah," he said abstractedly, "too bad."

"He said he'd kill both of us."

Sylvestro peered at me for a moment. "Look," he said.

"What?"

"Would you mind coming over there with me?"

"Where?"

"Her apartment."

"I guess so. Why?"

"You've been there, right?"

I nodded.

"Well, you're about the only person we can find who's been inside. Maybe you'll notice something."

"Like what?"

"Shit, Brady, I don't know. Something missing? Something out of place? Something that's there now that wasn't there before?"

"You're a thorough man, Jack."

He shrugged. "Something about this Costello guy doesn't seem right," he said quietly. "Nothing I can put my finger on."

"You don't think he did it?"

"Oh, I guess he probably did it, all right. Everything points to it. You know, when a wife dies, it's almost always the husband. Especially in this situation."

"Occam's razor," I said.

"Huh?"

I smiled. "The simple explanations are the best ones. The commonest things most commonly happen. Sure. Let me get dressed and we can go over."

"Take your time," he said. "I'm gonna have more of your coffee."

We drove to Beacon Street in Sylvestro's unmarked Ford LTD. He had a passkey, so we went directly in the front door, past the security desk, and down the stairs to Jill's little basement apartment. A uniformed policeman was standing outside her door. Sylvestro nodded to him and he stepped aside to let us in.

I stood there inside the doorway and looked around. "What am I looking for?" I said to Sylvestro.

"I don't know. Try to remember what it looked like when you were here. Try to see if anything's different. Out of place, missing, whatever. Just, anything that strikes you, don't judge it. Just tell me."

A crude outline of a human body had been chalked onto the linoleum in the kitchen. That hadn't been there before. I didn't think I needed to tell Sylvestro that. And a dark blotch the size of a bath mat stained the area around that chalked sketch, and shards of broken glass glittered in the dried puddle. A wine bottle stood beside the sink.

"The wine," I said. "The broken glass. How do you see it?"

"She was pouring them wine. The bottle was less than half full, so I'd guess she was getting them refills by the sink. When she turned to face him, that's when he stabbed her. She dropped the glasses, they shattered, and then she slumped onto the floor. She died quick, the ME figures. And there wasn't that much blood. Her heart didn't have much of a chance to pump a lot of it out."

"Looks like a lot to me," I said.

He shrugged. "You should see it sometimes."

I looked around the dining area. Her books and notebooks and yellow pads and pencils had been shoved to one side of the table, just the way she had done when I visited her, so that there'd be a place for us to put our elbows and drinks while we talked. I pointed that out to Sylvestro. He nodded.

In the corner of the living room was a small rolltop desk and beside it a two-drawer file cabinet. Neither appeared to have been rifled. Her sofa was opened into a bed and neatly made.

I stood there in the middle of the living-room area and looked around. Then I turned to Sylvestro. I shrugged. "I'm sorry, Jack."

"Take your time."

"Except for the broken glass and the—the blood . . ."

"It's hard. I want you to try to remember. I'm interested in knowing if something's missing, or out of place."

"I know. I've only been here a couple times. Always at night. We just sat in the kitchen. I haven't even really been in this part of the place."

"Go through it again."

I did. Then I shrugged again. "Nothing."

Sylvestro nodded. "Okay. Thanks for trying."

"She was really afraid of him."

"The husband?"

I nodded. "You figure he came in the private entrance?"

"Must have. There's a security guy upstairs all the time. None of them saw anybody."

"The husband knew about the side entrance," I said. "That's where he bushwhacked me."

I wandered through the place again, ending up in the kitchen staring down at Jill's outline on the floor. I looked up at Sylvestro and shrugged.

"Any thoughts at all, Brady?" he said. "I mean, aside from what you see—or don't see—here?"

"Well, the obvious one. That Mary Ellen Ames, who lived upstairs, is dead. Maybe murdered, maybe not. And Jill Costello, who lived here, got murdered. Both of them young women, attractive, living alone in the same building."

"What was the connection between them?"

"As far as I know, just what I told you."

"They were—lovers," said Sylvestro.

I nodded.

"That's something, I guess," he said. "Oh, well. I'll take you home, Brady. Give it some thought. If you don't mind, come by the station tomorrow morning so we can take a deposition, okay?"

"Sure."

"In the meantime, give it some thought."

"I will."

"We'll want to know all about your encounter with John Francis Costello, and anything the lady might've told you about him. And anything else that occurs to you. People she might've mentioned, problems in her life. You know."

I nodded. "Okay."

We left the apartment and went up to the lobby. We started for the front door. I stopped. "Jack, do me a favor."

"What?" he said.

"Let me into Mary Ellen's apartment."

"Why?"

"I don't know. I just want to see it again."

"Okay. Why not."

We took the elevator up to the fourth floor. Sylvestro

unlocked the door to 4-B. He went in first. I followed him. I
switched on the light. It was exactly as it had been when Jill
brought me there. I went over and stared at the bigger-than-
life portrait of Charles Ames that hung in its place of honor
over the piano. It showed the upper half of his body. His head
was turned in three-quarter profile. He had a noble nose,
wide-set eyes slightly downturned at the outside corners, a
firm chin, and a head of steely hair combed straight back from
a high forehead. He was wearing a brown three-piece suit.
One fist was propped on his hip. In his other hand he was
holding an open book. I put my face close to the painting. The
artist had not bothered to make any of the words on the book
legible.

I went back to where Sylvestro was standing by the doorway. "Okay," I said. "Thanks."

"That's it?"

I nodded.

He frowned, then shrugged, and we left.

Sylvestro dropped me off in front of my apartment building. It was a few minutes after nine on a sun-drenched Sunday
morning in late October.

"Have a good day," he said as I slid out of the car.

"Don't see how," I said. "It didn't start off that good."

"I'm sorry about the girl."

I nodded. "Yeah, me too. It'll hit me later, probably."

"Good idea to be with friends today, Brady."

"You're probably right. What about you?"

He smiled. "I've got a lot of work to do," he said.

MONDAY MORNING I called Sylvestro from my apartment and then went to the station to give my deposition into a tape recorder. He and a young assistant district attorney took turns asking me a lot of questions and I answered them as fully and truthfully as I could. It took about two hours.

I got to the office a little after eleven. Julie greeted me coldly—her way of commenting on the unexcused tardiness of my arrival at work—until I piled all my completed paperwork upon her desk. Then she gave me a grudging smile. I went into my office, where a day's worth of chores was waiting for me. I dug into it, grateful for it. The day passed and Julie never asked how my weekend had been, and I never told her.

On Tuesday I tried to call Susan Ames. Terri answered the phone.

"Hello, General," I said, "it's Brady."

"Well, hi." I thought I detected real warmth in her voice. "How are you?"

"All right. How's Susan doing?"

"Not good. I guess she had a bad weekend. She's staying in bed now. She's allowing the doctor to keep her medicated. There's a lot of pain. She mostly sleeps."

"I should get out there to visit her."

"She probably wouldn't know you were there."

"That bad, huh?"

"Yes. Ever since she heard about Mary Ellen it's been pretty much downhill. Downhill steep and fast."

I sighed. "She was something when she was well."

"I know. Full of energy and life."

"Damn," I muttered.

"I'll let you know if anything changes."

"Thanks."

I followed Jack Sylvestro's advice in my own way. I tried to help my clients. I tried to focus on their mundane legal problems, tried to keep in mind that, to my clients, their problems weren't mundane at all. Solving them would make them happy. That was something I could do.

When I got back to my apartment on Tuesday, it was nearly seven. The message light on my answering machine was blinking. One message. I depressed the button.

"Hey, Mr. Coyne. It's Finn, huh? Look, this time I really gotta talk to you. I think I got it. Mary Ellen, I mean. It's like, uh, five o'clock maybe. I can't keep—see, I'm here alla time, so just, if you can, come on out here. Big pain in the ass for you, I know, but—shit, anytime, really. Sooner the better. Can't say much, these nice folks' kitchen, you know. Come on. I'll give you a beer, we can talk."

I doubted that Dave Finn had anything new to tell me. He was just a lonely man in need of company. He had lost his job and the woman he loved was dead and he was living alone in a cruddy trailer in the woods.

I decided to go see him anyway.

So I changed my clothes, gobbled a peanut butter sandwich over the kitchen sink, and around seven-thirty I was in my car headed for Finn's trailer in Townsend. I hoped I'd find him reasonably sober.

There wasn't much traffic, so I got to the turnoff by the lumberyard around eight-thirty. I found the turn past the duck pond, took the left after the third bungalow, and drove up the hill. I passed only one car on the country road, that one traveling too fast in the opposite direction.

When I pulled up in front of Finn's trailer, the orange lights from the two small windows in front seemed unnaturally bright, and they appeared to be flickering strangely. When I got out of the car I smelled the smoke.

I ran to the door and ripped it open. Heat and smoke and the poisonous odor of burning plastic burst through the door at me with a force that staggered me backward. Finn's tin box was an incinerator. I dropped to my hands and knees and crept back to the doorway. The heat was a powerful, almost physical force, but I forced myself to stick my head inside. I was able to see that the flame seemed to be coming from the kitchen area. That electric space heater had evidently either overheated or ignited something. I yelled, "Dave! Are you in there?"

I had to pull back. Opening the door had fed oxygen to the fire, and even as I watched, the flames rose against the wall and rolled across the ceiling in a fiery wave. I pulled my jacket up over my face, got down onto my stomach, and crept through the doorway. Now the fire was blazing. I squinted through the smoke and looked around the inside of the trailer. And I saw his leg through the smoky haze at the opposite end of the trailer from the kitchen. He was on his cot, in a half-sitting position. His back leaned against the wall and one leg dangled over the side. He was either asleep or he had passed out. "Dave!" I screamed. "Wake up! Hey! Wake up!"

He didn't move. He was obviously unconscious. I was gagging on the smoke and vile fumes that were filling Finn's tin box, and the heat was intensifying by the second. But I had to get Dave Finn out of there. I crawled all the way into the trailer. By keeping my face close to the floor, I found enough air to breathe. Even with my jacket pulled up over my mouth, my lungs burned and I hacked and gagged on the fumes I was inhaling. My throat felt as if a Brillo pad was stuck in it. I hitched myself to the cot. My eyes were watering so badly that I could barely see. The heat burned on my back as if my clothes were aflame. I squeezed Finn's leg. "Wake up," I wheezed. He didn't stir. I yanked at his leg. "Dave," I rasped. "Hey. Come on." He didn't respond. His leg moved limply in my grasp. I didn't bother wasting any more of my precious breath yelling at him. I pulled on him until he flopped off the cot, and then I kept pulling on his leg as I crawled backward, dragging Dave Finn behind me.

I backed out of the door, then reached in and got both of his legs. I pulled him out onto the ground and dragged him away from the trailer. I crouched there on my hands and knees on the pine needles. I gasped for breath. Tears streamed down my cheeks. I coughed and gagged. Then my stomach bucked and flipped. I puked my peanut butter sandwich onto the ground and then kept trying to bring up more. It seemed as if I'd never stop retching.

The flames were now darting from every seam and orifice in the trailer. I managed to get myself under control enough to tow Finn farther away from that incinerator. It occurred to me that there was probably a propane tank mounted on the outside wall of the trailer that could explode.

I knelt beside Finn. He lay very still on the pine needles. He did not appear to have been burned. But he didn't move. I put my face close to his. He didn't seem to be breathing. I laid my ear against his chest. I detected no heartbeat. I slapped his face. "Come on!" I screamed. "Wake up! Breathe!"

I pounded on his chest, and listened again. Nothing.

I rolled him over and pressed on his back in my best imitation of CPR. After a few tries I listened again. No breathing. No heartbeat.

I wrestled him onto his back and tried mouth-to-mouth. I thumped his chest. I slapped his face. I yelled at him. I was only vaguely aware that the trailer had become a great ball of flame. The fire roared with the din of a powerful waterfall. Fireballs and embers shot into the sky. Needles on nearby pine trees burst into flame, sparked brightly, and died quickly. And I kept pounding on Dave Finn's chest and trying to blow air into his lungs.

I don't know how long I kept at it. I never heard the sirens and I didn't notice when the trucks arrived. A man came up behind me and wrapped his arms around my chest. "That's good work, buddy," he said soothingly. "Come on, now. We'll take it from here."

He helped me to stand and wrestled me away from Finn. I collapsed on the ground. Then I began to cough and gag again, and when I puked this time the EMT held me and murmured to me the way my mother used to when I was a child. When I finished heaving and spasming, the EMT wiped my face with a soft cloth. "How we doing, pal?" he said.

"I'm all right," I croaked. "How's Finn? Is he okay?"

"We're working on him. Want to try to stand up?"

"Sure." I pushed myself to my hands and knees. Another wave of nausea came over me. I tried to vomit. Nothing came up. I hacked and gasped. Then I took several deep breaths. "I think I'm okay now," I said.

He helped me onto my feet. The earth tipped and swirled under me. He guided me over to the ambulance and sat me on the ground so that my back was resting against the side of the vehicle. He reached through the open doors in back and came out with a plastic bottle. He handed it to me. "Just water. Sip it slowly."

I took small mouthfuls. It was cool and it tingled almost painfully in my mouth. I forced myself to swallow tiny amounts of it. My throat felt as if it had swollen shut. While I was drinking, my EMT wrapped a blood pressure cuff around my arm. He puffed it up and let it out, studying the dial. Then he took my pulse.

"Am I going to live?" I said.

"You're fine, pal. I'm gonna check on your friend."

He went over to where Finn was being worked on by two other EMTs. I sipped water and watched.

My EMT came back. I noticed for the first time that he was very young. It didn't look as if he had even begun shaving. "How is he?" I said.

He shook his head. "It don't look good. How're you feeling now?"

"I'm okay."

He squinted at me, then nodded. "Okay. Come on. Let's move aside, then. We gotta get your friend to the hospital."

The EMT helped me to stand up. My dizziness had passed. He looked at me. "All right?"

I nodded. "I'm fine. Really."

He went over to Finn. In a minute he and his two partners came back to the ambulance. They had Dave Finn on a stretcher. One of them was holding a plastic bottle in the air. It had a tube that was connected to Finn's arm. A plastic oxygen mask covered his mouth. They slid him into the back. One EMT climbed in behind him. The other two slammed shut the doors and went around to the front. A moment later the ambulance roared away.

A fire truck was pulled up close to the trailer. They seemed to have the fire just about extinguished. I sipped water and watched them work. A few minutes later I heard a siren, and then a police cruiser skidded to a stop in the road.

Two uniformed cops got out. One of them went over to talk with the firemen. The other approached me. "You a witness to this?" he said.

I nodded. "Sort of."

"What's your name, sir?"

I told him.

"What happened?"

I shrugged. "I came to visit my friend. Dave Finn. He was living in the trailer. When I got here, it was on fire. I dragged Dave out. I don't know. Then the fire trucks arrived . . ."

"It was on fire when you got here?"

"Yes. He had one of those electric space heaters in there. When I got here, the fire was in that end. Where the kitchen is. It looked as if that space heater overheated or something. Finn—Dave—he drank a lot. He was on his cot." I shrugged.

"Like he might've passed out before the fire started?"

I nodded.

"Kind of a warm night for a space heater," he said.

I shrugged. "He had a lot on his mind."

It sounded like a non sequitur when I said it, but the cop just nodded. He looked at me closely. "You all right?"

"I'm okay. The EMT checked me over."

"Gonna be able to drive?"

"I think so."

"You saved the guy, huh?"

"I don't know. I got him out of there and tried to revive him, but . . ."

"You tried, anyhow."

"Is he going to . . . ?"

"I don't know. You got a driver's license?"

I reached into my hip pocket and took out my wallet. I handed it to the policeman.

"Take it out for me."

I removed my license and handed it to him. He copied from it into his notebook, then gave it back to me. "Why'd you say you were here?" he said.

"I came to visit him. He lives here alone."

"And the place was burning when you got here, right?"

"Yes. It was full of smoke and fumes. When I opened the door, I think it fed the fire."

The cop nodded as if he wasn't really listening. "Right. Sure." The firemen were spraying foam inside the trailer. We watched them for a minute or two. Without turning to me, the cop said, "What can you tell me about this—Finn, that's his name?"

"Yes. Dave Finn. He's a Boston police officer. He's under suspension right now, without pay. So he's living here. I think the trailer belongs to a friend of his."

He turned to look at me. "A cop, huh?"

"Yes."

"Suspended? Why?"

"I'm really not sure."

"And you?"

"I'm a lawyer."

"Finn's lawyer, is that it?"

"No. Just a friend. An acquaintance, really."

The cop stared at me for a moment, frowned, and scribbled in his notebook. Then he slapped it shut and shoved it into his pocket. "Okay, Mr. Coyne. If you're sure you're okay, you can leave. We might want to talk to you later, okay?"

"Of course."

I retraced my route slowly, down the sloping dirt road,

past the bungalows and duck pond and barn with the silo. I turned east on Route 119 by the lumberyard. I stopped at a Dunkin' Donuts in Groton for a cup of coffee and a cigarette. I felt as if I'd been punched in the stomach, but I no longer had the urge to puke.

And all the way home I kept trying to figure it out. Mary Ellen Ames, Jill Costello, and now Dave Finn. There had to be a connection.

"**Y**OU LOOK AWFUL," Julie told me the next morning.

"Gee, thanks. You look beautiful."

"Are you sick, Brady?"

"I'm on the mend. Something I ate, I think."

I fled into my office. For some reason, I didn't want to tell Julie about my visit to Dave Finn. She'd ask a lot of questions that I was still asking myself, and I didn't have any answers. And inevitably she'd end up shaking her head and telling me what most of my friends ended up telling me—that I should stop mucking around in other people's affairs and stick to fine points of law. And she'd be right, of course. But I didn't want to hear it.

I called the Townsend police. I wanted to know whether Dave Finn had made it. They wouldn't tell me.

I tried to get some work done. It went slowly. I had trouble concentrating.

Horowitz showed up around noon. No surprise. Julie ushered him in. We shook hands and he smiled at me. "Well, well," he said.

"What the hell is 'well, well' supposed to mean?"

"You do get around, Coyne."

"Look," I said. "I really don't need a bunch of shit from you today, okay?"

"Lady X drowns up in New Hampshire," he said, holding up his right fist and prying up the forefinger with his left hand. "Lady Y gets stabbed to death by her husband in her Beacon Street basement apartment." He pulled off the adjacent finger so that two of them were extended from his fist. "And then Gentleman Z dies from inhaling noxious fumes in a trailer fire in Townsend." Now he had three fingers sticking out. It looked like he was making the Boy Scout pledge. "These items come ticking out of my computer, and each time I see something. I see Brady Coyne's name. And I say to myself, 'My goodness, that man does get around.'"

I sat down on the sofa. "Finn died, huh?"

Horowitz sat beside me. "Yeah. I heard about what you did. He was probably dead when you got there. They said you gave it a helluva try, though."

I let out a long breath. "Shit," I muttered.

"Brady," he said, "what the hell is going on?"

"I've been trying to figure that out myself."

"Hey," he said. "I'm a great believer in coincidence. Happens all the time. Most things, they don't make much sense. Things just happen. Randomness, that's the best explanation for a lot of things. That's how the world works much of the time. But, hell, we've got these three deaths. Nothing in common with each other. Different places, different causes, people from different walks of life." He tapped my leg with the tip of his forefinger. "Except you. You're the common thread. So what gives, huh?"

"I don't know. I've been trying to figure it out. Only place I can start is by thinking that Mary Ellen Ames did not die by accident. After that it gets confusing."

"You think she was murdered, right?"

"Yes. So did Finn."

"Why?"

"Why did Finn think that? I'm not sure. But I was going out there last night to find out. He called me earlier, left a message. Give me the impression he'd figured it out."

"And the young lady, Miz Costello?"

I shrugged. "Well, of course, she knew Mary Ellen Ames. Lived in the same building. But I guess her husband killed her. Just a coincidence, I suppose."

He nodded. "I talked with Jack Sylvestro. That's what he thinks, too. Look, would you mind talking about all this?"

"With you? Now?"

He nodded.

I shrugged. "No. I guess not."

So we did. He stayed for more than two hours, and we went over all of it. He shared forensic information with me—the absence of useful fingerprints in Jill Costello's apartment, medical examiner reports on both Jill and Dave Finn concluding that Jill had died instantly from a stab wound directly to the heart and Finn had died from inhaling poisonous fumes with enough alcohol already in his bloodstream to make him comatose before the fumes got him, and the Townsend fire chief's verdict that the electric space heater had ignited the fire.

I told him about the tenuous connection among Mary Ellen and Jill and Finn. It was a lovers' triangle of sorts, of course, but it was an incomplete geometric shape. Mary Ellen had many other people in her life.

I told Horowitz that both Sid Raiford and Sherif Rahmanan had inherited one hundred thousand dollars from Mary Ellen. They might've also been her lovers, although both of them denied it. Rahmanan, at least, had been at one time, and he admitted that he continued to be obsessed with her. Raiford, for his part, had supplied her with marijuana and cocaine and helped her consume it.

I told him about Willard Ellington who also, indirectly, benefited from Mary Ellen's timely death, but there was no indication that he had ever laid eyes on her.

Any of them could conceivably have been a jealous lover.

Otherwise, neither of us could invent a reason why any of these men would care whether Jill Costello or Dave Finn lived or died.

I did not tell Horowitz all that I knew about Warren McAllister. Most of it was privileged information. I was his lawyer.

And when we finished talking, both of us shook our heads. Mary Ellen had not lived a conventional life. But there was nothing unconventional about the fact that she had many varied acquaintances and friendships. Hell, so did I. And aside from the fact that all of them had a relationship of some kind with her, coincidence still seemed to account for any other connection among all of them. Each death—Mary Ellen's, Jill's, and Finn's—had its own separate logical explanation.

I walked Horowitz out of my office and past Julie's desk to the door. We shook hands. We promised to share anything else that occurred to us. I got the impression that he already had other things on his mind. A Massachusetts state homicide cop always has lots of things on his mind.

After I closed the door behind him, Julie said, "What was that all about?"

I flapped my hands. "Just the Mary Ellen Ames thing."

"Well pardon me," she said.

I went back into my office and called Warren McAllister. His machine answered and I asked him to get back to me.

Julie left at five. I stayed. I had a messy desk to clean up.

Warren called me back around seven. When I answered the phone, he said, "Wow! You attorneys put in long hours. I tried your house first."

"It's been a busy day," I said. "Hey, have you heard the forecast for the weekend?"

"No. Why?"

"Supposed to climb up into the seventies. I don't know about you, but to me that's a gift, a weekend in October in the seventies."

"I like the way you think, Counselor. God, I haven't been fishing for weeks. I need it."

"Me, too. How's Sunday for you?"

"You got it. Where do you want to go?"

"I got a place in mind," I said. "I'll pick you up around nine."

"Trout, right?"

"Right. Bring your fly rod."

"Think they'll be biting?"

"Hell," I said, "even if they're not, it'll still be worthwhile."

I GOT to the McAllisters' big Victorian in Brookline a few minutes before nine Sunday morning. As promised, the day had dawned sunny and warm. It felt and tasted more like early September than late October.

Warren already had his fly-fishing gear piled on the back porch—two aluminum fly rod rubes, a pair of waders, his fishing vest, a net, a shapeless old canvas hat studded with bedraggled flies, and a small duffel for his fly boxes, reels, spare socks, rainwear, and all the other stuff that fly fisherman cannot travel without.

I rang the bell and a moment later Robin opened it. She smiled radiantly. "Brady, hi," she said. "I'm so jealous of you guys. What a beautiful day you've got."

She was wearing a comfortable old pale blue terry-cloth robe. The hem brushed the floor, and her bare toes peeped out from underneath. Her hair hung in a ponytail down the middle of her back. She wore no makeup. She looked quite beautiful without it.

She hugged me quickly. "Thanks for doing this," she whispered. "He's really been looking forward to it."

"Hey," I said. "I like fishing."

"Well, come on in," she said, taking my arm. "Old Izaak Walton is in there making sandwiches."

She tugged me into the kitchen, where Warren was piling slabs of roast beef onto thick slices of dark bread. "Hey, partner," he said when he saw me.

"Hey, yourself."

"Grey Poupon on your roast beef, a little horseradish?"

"Terrific."

"I've got a thermos of coffee and some Coke on ice, okay?"

I smiled and nodded. "Perfect."

"I don't know about you," he said, "but I never drink beer or anything while I'm fishing."

"Me neither. Booze and fishing don't go together."

Robin handed me a mug of coffee and then went over to help Warren stuff the thick sandwiches into plastic bags. I leaned against the wall, sipping my coffee and watching them. She actually seemed happy for her husband that he could go off fishing on a Sunday in the autumn. My experience was limited, but I believed that this was a rare and wonderful thing between married people.

The two of them loaded up a wicker basket, and then Warren said to me, "Ready?"

"I'm ready."

I drained my mug and put it in the sink. Robin crossed her arms around Warren's neck and kissed him. Then she smiled at me. "Have fun, boys. Tight lines."

We went out, gathered up Warren's gear from the porch, and loaded it into my car. Then we got in.

"Where are you taking me?" he said.

"Little pond in New Hampshire. It's supposed to be full of native brook trout. They should be dressed in their spawning colors by now."

"Wonderful," he said. "Absolutely perfect."

It took about two hours to get there. Warren and I sipped

coffee from the thermos and swapped fishing stories the entire way.

We crossed the border into New Hampshire, and a half hour later, when I turned off the main road onto a narrow country lane, Warren said, "What's the name of this place?"

"Teal Pond."

"Wasn't that . . . ?"

"Yes," I said. "The place where Mary Ellen drowned. I heard the fishing was good here. Our friend Horowitz told me how to find it."

Warren said nothing. I turned down the unpaved driveway that wound for nearly a mile down a long wooded slope before the sparkle of sunshine on water appeared through the trees. The driveway ended in a thinned-out pine grove surrounding a modest shingled cottage that was perched on the rim of the pond. A pine needle path led down a gentle slope to the pond's edge where a dock extended out over the water. Two aluminum canoes rested upside down on the dock.

I turned off the ignition. "Pretty spot, huh?"

"Beautiful," said Warren.

"Come on. Let's go look at the water."

We walked down the path and onto the dock. I lit a cigarette. The two of us gazed across the pond. It nestled snugly in a bowl formed by the foothills of the White Mountains. The subdued oranges and russets of autumn oaks reflected on the water's surface. In the middle it was riffled by the soft breeze, but along the edges and in the coves the pond's skin lay as smooth and flat as glass. Off to the right I thought I saw some tiny dimples in the surface that could have been feeding trout.

After a minute or so, Warren said, "Brady, why did you bring me here?"

"What do you mean?"

"There are lots of places we could've gone fishing. Why here?"

I shrugged. "I heard it was good. It's always fun to try new places."

"Come on," he said. "This is Mary Ellen's cottage. What's on your mind?"

"I guess I was just wondering if we might talk some more about it."

"About her?"

"Yes."

He was silent for a moment. Then he said, "I've been here before."

"I thought you might've been."

"It's where we used to meet. When we . . ."

"Yes."

He touched my arm. I turned to him. His intent gaze held my eyes. "Brady, you're my lawyer, right?"

"That's right."

"I want to tell you about it."

I nodded. "Good."

He sat on the edge of the dock. I sat beside him. We dangled our legs over the edge and looked out at the pond. The sun was warm on our faces. He talked without looking at me.

"She was different from my other patients right from the beginning," he said. "The first time she came to my office it was clear that she was interviewing me, trying to determine if I was suitable to treat her. I didn't know what she was looking for, and I certainly didn't consciously try to impress her, but even before I knew anything about her I found her unusual. And—and attractive. There was something about her that made me uncomfortable. Something subtle, sexual. I even considered refusing to accept her. But I'm an experienced shrink. I know about attraction between analyst and patient. It's often present, and a skilled analyst can manage it, even use it to advantage. Anyway, the decision was hers. I guess I passed muster, because I began to see her. This was a little over four years ago. And right from the beginning there was a different agenda between us. For Mary Ellen, psychoanalysis was a long leisurely process of seduction. That's what it was. She was paying me a hundred dollars an hour, four days a week, for purposes of seducing me."

"And you didn't realize it?" I said.

"Of course I did. It was not a problem. Or it shouldn't have been. It offered a useful way of proceeding with treatment. We talked about it. I was direct with her. I asked her why she had chosen me, why she was setting about in this obviously calculated way to seduce me."

"You were her father," I said.

Warren turned to look at me. He smiled and nodded. "Sure. Your classical case of transference. I can quote you the Great Man on it. Freud said, 'The patient sees in his analyst the return—the reincarnation—of some important figure out of his childhood or past, and consequently transfers onto him feelings and reactions that undoubtedly applied to this model.' " Warren smiled at me.

"Sounds risky to me," I said.

"Yes, it can be." He nodded. "Freud went on to say, 'It soon becomes evident that this fact of transference is a factor of undreamed-of importance—on the one hand an instrument of irreplaceable value and on the other a source of serious dangers.' "

"Serious dangers," I repeated.

"Usually," said Warren, "transference happens over a long period of time. It grows and develops as a natural part of the analytic process. But with Mary Ellen, it was instantaneous. It's what she was looking for even before she became my patient. A father substitute." He paused. "How did you know about this?"

"It's common, isn't it?"

"Well, sure."

"Mary Ellen had a portrait of her father in her condo," I said. "It's very large, and it's hung prominently in her living room, and she even had a little light mounted in the ceiling to spotlight it. You resemble Charles Ames remarkably."

"I look like him?"

I nodded. "I didn't catch it at first. But I was back there a week ago and saw the painting again. After having seen you, I caught the resemblance immediately. It's almost uncanny. The eyes and the mouth especially. Even your hair."

Warren smiled. "Well, she never told me that, and of course I had no way of knowing what Charles Ames looked like. I certainly know what kind of a man he was—or at least what kind of a man lived in Mary Ellen's memory of him."

He stopped talking. I lit another cigarette. We stared at the water.

"It's about the biggest failure a psychiatrist can ever have," he began softly after several moments of silence. "Worse even than suicide."

"What is?"

"Allowing a patient to seduce you. It destroys everything. There are philistines in my profession who rationalize it otherwise, and some who have even rationalized sex with their patients into a form of treatment, who are themselves the seducers. But that's all bullshit. It was, to say the least, very humbling for me to learn how weak I was, how readily all of my training, all of my good professional judgment, all of my experience with transference could be swept away by simple lust."

"But it wasn't simple lust for her, was it?"

He shook his head. "No. That's what makes it so bad. Mary Ellen lost her father at the worst possible time, for her, in her life, and she spent the rest of it trying to find him. All of the men in her life were considerably older than she, substitute fathers for her. None of them ever quite lived up to the standards in her mind—to him, her imagined father, the Charles Ames in her head. Not Dave Finn or Sherif Rahmanan or any of the many others. We talked about all of this, of course. She claimed I was it. I was the one. Finally, her search was over. So, Brady, no, for Mary Ellen it was far more than simple undifferentiated lust. For her, it was fulfillment. I was her cure."

"And for you?"

He sighed deeply. "I love Robin. She's a perfect wife. She is my life. Mary Ellen simply taught me that I am a weak, imperfect man, a man who may understand the complexities of the human psyche, but who can still be victimized by them. Mary Ellen was a temptation that a better man should have resisted. I did not."

I touched his leg. "So . . ."

"Hell, Brady, I didn't kill her, if that's what you're thinking. I already told you that." He frowned at me. "Is it? Is that what today is all about?"

I shrugged. "I just wanted to hear the truth about it."

"I didn't kill her."

"Her death must have been a vast relief for you."

"That's very cruel of you," he said softly. "But I guess you're partly right. It saddened me profoundly. But, yes, I was relieved, too."

"What *had* you intended to do before she conveniently took you off the hook by dying?"

"Jesus, Brady," he said softly. He shook his head slowly.

"I was going to tell her I wouldn't see her anymore. She couldn't be my patient any longer. I had colleagues I was going to refer her to. Women, who could help her with a different analytic approach."

"But you hadn't actually gotten around to saying this to her?"

"I tried. She refused to hear it. She was clever that way. Controlling. Steering our sessions in the directions of her choice. But I would have done it. I hesitated being too directive with her."

"You were afraid of her reaction?"

"Yes. Well, cowardly, too, probably. But I was concerned for her. I couldn't tell how she would respond."

"But she knew where you were headed."

"She was very intelligent, very perceptive. She certainly knew."

"Would she have killed herself?"

"No. Absolutely not." He hesitated. "She wanted me to marry her. She wanted me to divorce Robin."

"Would you have done that?"

"Never."

"And Robin didn't know?"

"I could never tell Robin about Mary Ellen. My wife understands what psychiatrists do. She knows all about transference. She trusts me completely. She thinks I'm competent at what I do. Which means that I use the transference phenomenon to the advantage of the treatment. It would never occur to her that I would actually succumb to it. I couldn't risk telling Robin, as much as I might have wanted to."

I swept my hand across the pond. "And you met her here."

He nodded. "Yes, here, in her cottage. This is where I came on Sundays when Robin thought I was off fishing. See,

Brady, I didn't give in right away. We met four times weekly for a very long time, and all the while she was doing her damnedest to seduce me and I was turning it back to her, trying to deal with it the way I have so many times in my practice, the way I was taught. Then one time I allowed myself to hug her at the end of a session in my office. A meaningless gesture, I told myself. But it wasn't meaningless for her, and of course I knew that, which meant it wasn't meaningless for me, either. And a few sessions later I kissed her. On the cheek, but the next time on the mouth. And for many months, we would kiss and embrace at the end of our hour. Finally—" He looked at me, his eyes asking for understanding.

I nodded. "You fucked her."

He let out a long breath. "Okay. I guess I deserve that. I agreed to meet her here. For a picnic, we told each other."

"When was this?"

"Last spring. May."

"A picnic," I said.

"You know what happened."

"And it happened every Sunday thereafter, huh?"

"Just about. We skipped a few times. I tried to make excuses. I told her I couldn't make it. And I can't tell you how many times, when I had agreed to meet her, that I swore to myself I simply wouldn't show up. But I always did. And I'd drive down that long bumpy driveway praying that her car wouldn't be there under the pines, that she would be the one to call it off. But she was always here. We'd have a glass of wine. We'd talk. Like lovers, not like a shrink and a patient. And we always ended up in her bed. God help me."

"You must've been consumed with guilt."

"I was," he said. "I am. Actually, I thought it was over, that Mary Ellen had finally seen the light. I met her here that last time back in September, and then she missed all of her appointments the following week. After she skipped the first one, I thought of calling her. I usually do that. Check on my patients when they miss and don't call me. But I didn't call her. I didn't want to talk to her. I just wanted her to keep skipping. To be gone from my life forever. After she skipped the week, and then the following week, I believed it had been resolved. Then you called me, and I knew that it had been resolved, all right."

"So the last time you saw her was here."

He nodded. "Yes. I left her in bed. We made love, I got up and showered, dressed, went back and kissed her good-bye. She was dozing, as she always did afterwards. She'd go home later, sometime after me. It was our routine."

"Was she nude?"

"When I kissed her good-bye, you mean?" He smiled at me. "Well, hell, we'd just been making love. Why?"

"Her body was nude when they found it."

"Hey," he said. "You still think I killed her, don't you?"

"I don't know what to think," I said. "I keep remembering a conversation I had with a friend of mine a while ago. Guy named Charlie McDevitt, who I went to law school with. He's a prosecutor for the Justice Department. A very good one. He and I were talking about the possibility that somebody murdered Mary Ellen, and I told him that it seemed as if several people would gain by her death. Know what he said to me?"

"What?" said Warren.

"Charlie said I should also think about who stood to lose by her remaining alive."

Warren frowned, then nodded. "Okay. I get it. And you think I'm the one who stood to lose by her being alive, right?"

I shrugged.

"Well," he said, "I suppose I did. But I didn't kill her, I swear. I don't know what else I can tell you."

"If you did, you could tell me, you know."

"Sure, I know that. You're my lawyer. And I'm telling you I didn't do it." He touched my arm. "You had this all figured out, didn't you?"

I shrugged. "More or less. Dave Finn told me how hung up she was on her father. You look too much like Charles Ames and she was too hung up on him for it to have been a casual affair for her. And I think I know you well enough to believe that it wasn't casual for you, either."

"So you concluded that it was I who killed her?"

"No." I shook my head. "I concluded that it wasn't."

We watched the water for several minutes. Finally Warren said, "Well, should we try to catch a trout?"

"Feel like it?"

He shrugged. "Not that much. But let's do it anyway."

We found paddles in a shed beside the cottage. We launched one of the canoes. We flipped a coin and I lost, so I started out in the stern. I pushed the canoe slowly around the rim of the pond clockwise so that Warren could cast comfortably over the bow. He handled the fly rod expertly. He cast a smooth line and twitched a Woolly Bugger over sunken weed beds and along drop-offs and against the edges of the boulders that protruded from the water. We got halfway around the pond without catching a single fish. There we beached the canoe and swapped ends. And then I fished and Warren paddled. We made it all the way back to the dock in front of Mary Ellen's cottage without a strike.

It took us about three hours to complete the circuit. We scarcely exchanged a word the entire time.

"Want to quit?" said Warren.

I nodded. "The sun'll go down soon. Midday should've been best anyway."

We hauled the canoe back onto the dock, returned the paddles to the shed, and stowed our gear in the car. Then we started home.

We rode in silence for a while. Then Warren said, "Thanks, Brady."

"Sorry about the fishing. I thought we might do something."

"I didn't mean the fishing."

I shrugged.

"It felt good," he said. "Talking about it. Confessing. But tell me something."

"What?"

"You said you had concluded that it wasn't I who killed her. How did you know?"

"I assume Mary Ellen was murdered. We know Jill Costello was murdered. I also believe Dave Finn was murdered."

"Why do you think that?"

"Occam's Razor."

"Christ," he said. "What's that supposed to mean."

"Look for the simple explanation. Assume you know all there is to know. These three deaths are awfully hard to explain unless you assume all were murdered. In this case, Mr. Occam tells me that one person, impelled by one motive, killed all three of them. Mary Ellen, Jill Costello, and Dave Finn."

"What's that one motive?" said Warren.

"Finn and Jill were intimate with Mary Ellen. They figured out about the two of you. They probably thought that it was you who killed her. That made them dangerous to you, all right. Except it couldn't have been you."

"Why not?"

"You've got a seminar to teach on Tuesday, right?"

"Yes."

"Finn was killed on Tuesday. Sometime before eight. If you were at the hospital, you couldn't have been in Townsend. So you weren't the one who killed Finn. Therefore, you didn't kill any of them. QED."

He was quiet for several minutes. Then he said, "One person with one motive." Silence again, then, "Someone who had something to gain by all three deaths—or something to lose by their remaining alive." Another pause. "I'm really a logical suspect, aren't I?"

"Yes," I said. "Jill and Finn thought it was you. They both tried to call me right before they died. I think that's what they wanted to tell me. That they'd figured out it was you who killed Mary Ellen."

"But it wasn't me."

"No."

He was quiet again, and I didn't interrupt the silence.

As I turned onto his street, Warren sighed heavily and mumbled, "Ah, shit."

I glanced sideways at him. "What's the matter?"

"You *do* have it figured out, don't you?"

I nodded. "Yes, I think so."

"Me, too."

"I thought you might."

I pulled into his driveway and turned off the ignition.

"You want to come in?" he said.

"I think I better."

33

W E WENT INTO Warren's house. Robin was not in the kitchen, as she had been every other time I had been there.

"Have a seat, Brady," said Warren. "I'll be right back."

I sat at the table and lit a cigarette. Warren left the room. A moment later I heard him call, "Robin? Hey, hon. I'm home. Brady's here."

There was a pause, then, "Okay. I'll put on some tea water."

Warren came back into the kitchen. He went to the sink, filled a kettle with tap water, put it on the stove, then sat across from me. "She'll be down in a minute," he said.

I nodded.

"When did you figure it out?" he said.

I shrugged. "About the time I decided that it wasn't you."

"Well," he said, "I really appreciate this." He reached across the table and squeezed my arm.

Robin came into the room. She rumpled my hair on her way to Warren, whom she kissed wetly on the forehead. "Hi, fellas. How was the fishing?"

"The fishing was terrific," said Warren. "The catching was piss poor."

Robin went to the kitchen cabinets. "What kind of tea do you guys want?"

"Let's have that smoky Chinese stuff," said Warren.

"Lapsang souchong," said Robin.

"Come sit with us, honey," said Warren. "I want to talk to you."

"Go ahead. I can hear you." She stood by the cabinets with her back to us.

"We know," said Warren quietly.

Robin was taking teacups from the cabinet. She said nothing.

"Did you hear me?" said Warren.

"What?"

"I said, we know."

"You know what?"

"Everything."

"I don't—"

"Robin," said Warren heavily, "come here and sit down, please."

"For heaven's sake—"

"Come on, hon. Sit with us."

She turned to face us. She shrugged. "Well, okay," she said.

She came over and sat down. She lit a cigarette. I nudged the ashtray toward her so we could share it.

Warren cleared his throat. "My business phone is in the other room," he said to me, jerking his head toward the inner rooms of the big old house. "A machine answers when I'm working and my patients can leave their messages for me on it. They often call when they're feeling stressed. Family problems, health worries, whatever. Anything. I encourage them to call, and I always return my calls. The line also runs to my office upstairs, of course. But that phone doesn't have a ringer, because I can't have the telephone interrupting my work. I use it to call out." He took a deep breath, let it out, and smiled quickly at me. "Anyone who's down here when the phone rings can hear what my patients are saying to me."

I glanced at Robin. She was staring at Warren. He looked at her, too, for a moment, then returned his eyes to me. "She knew," he said to me.

I nodded. "Yes. I figured she did."

He looked at Robin. "Mary Ellen called here, didn't she?"

Robin frowned. "What are you—?"

"Come on, babe," he said. "You heard her call, didn't you?"

Robin hesitated, then nodded.

"I never knew that she called," said Warren to me. "Robin overheard the messages, then erased the tape." He turned to her. "Right?"

"Yes," whispered Robin.

"Tell us what she said."

Robin reached over and gripped my wrist. "She kept leaving long threatening messages to him," she said in a taut voice. "She was going to expose my husband." Her eyes were wide and staring into mine, and I saw the insanity in them. "She threatened to tell me about their—their activities. She threatened to tell the newspapers, to hire a lawyer, to tell the professional association. She said she'd ruin him if he didn't divorce me and marry her."

I nodded. "That's what I thought." I touched Robin's hand where her nails were digging into my arm. She looked down, frowned, then pulled her hand away. I looked at Warren. "Mary Ellen never threatened you directly, though, did she?"

He shook his head. "I told you the truth about that,

Brady. See, when we were together, I was her father. She couldn't do anything like that. She couldn't threaten her father. It would be disrespectful. But when we weren't together, I was just a man. So she could leave a threat on an answering machine." He drew his lips tightly together for a moment. "Robin heard it all."

I looked at Robin. "So you killed her."

She lifted her eyebrows. "Wouldn't you? She would've ruined everything. What else could I do? I did it for Warren. He didn't deserve that."

"Look," I said to Warren, "I need to make a phone call right now. Robin needs a lawyer. I'm not it."

"But I thought—"

"I'm your lawyer. Not hers. And I'm not a criminal lawyer anyway. I know a good one. Just sit tight."

I went to the kitchen phone and pecked out the home number of Xerxes Garrett, the young attorney who had clerked for me several years earlier. He had quickly become the best defense attorney I knew. He was young, handsome, smart, and black, and, like me, he ran a one-man law firm. He turned down clients at whim, but he usually accepted those I asked him to defend.

The phone rang a half dozen times before he answered it. "Yo," he mumbled.

"Zerk. It's Brady."

"Shit, man. This business?"

"Yes."

"Hell, it's Sunday. Call me tomorrow."

"It won't wait. I need you."

"*Who* needs me?"

"A woman. It appears she has murdered the woman her husband was having an affair with. Couple other people, too."

"Shee-it! One of them, huh?"

"It's pretty complicated, Zerk. The husband is my client. My take on it is that an insanity plea might be the way to go."

"Hey, man. Who asked you? I'll decide that for my own self."

"Good. You'll take it, then."

He sighed extravagantly. "I ever let you down yet?"

"Hardly ever."

"So where's she at?"

I gave him directions to the McAllister house. "Come now, okay?"

"Gotta get myself disentangled from these sweet arms and legs beside me here and I'll be right over."

"Sorry to interrupt."

He chuckled. "We was all done, man. Otherwise I wouldn't have answered the damn phone."

I hung up, then turned to Robin and Warren. They were sitting close beside each other, holding hands and watching me. "He'll be right over," I said. "He'll take it."

I went back and sat down. I lit a cigarette.

"I'm not insane," said Robin quietly. "I did the logical thing."

"Shh, honey," said Warren softly.

"Don't say anything else," I said to her. "Let's just wait for Zerk to get here. You should tell him everything."

34

ZERK ARRIVED an hour and a half later. Warren and Robin and I spent the time sitting at the table. We didn't say much. Robin and I smoked cigarettes and sipped tea. Warren just sipped tea. They sat close together, and now and then they would lean toward each other and exchange whispers. Once Robin tilted her face up to his and kissed him on the jaw.

When the doorbell chimed I went to the door. Zerk looked athletic in his Nike sweats and black windbreaker and high-tech red-and-white sneakers. He was carrying an incongruous attaché case. "I thought that little Karen chick was sleeping, man," he said. "But she wasn't. Otherwise I would have got here quicker."

"That's okay. I'm damn glad you could make it. Come on in."

I ushered him into the kitchen and introduced him to Robin and Warren. Warren offered a cup of tea and Zerk refused. He sat at the table. He looked directly at Robin. "If I'm going to take your case, Mrs. McAllister, you've got to tell me everything. Okay?"

She nodded.

"Start at the beginning, then," he said.

She shrugged. "I overheard her calls. You can hear them

when the machine comes on to record them. I couldn't help overhearing her. She sounded crazy. She kept saying she couldn't keep going this way, that he—Warren, my husband —he was her sweet daddy and she had to have him all for herself. She wouldn't let him leave her again. Her daddy had left her once, and she couldn't stand it if he left her again. She called him her sweet daddy, over and over. Her sweet daddy. And she talked about when they were together at the pond, how—how good it was, how she loved him, how happy he would be when they were together forever. And then she'd change. Right in the middle of a sentence, sometimes, and she'd sound angry and nasty and mean. She said if he wouldn't do what she wanted she'd tell me and she'd get a lawyer and sue him and she'd talk to the newspapers and the television and everyone would know. So I followed Warren up there one Sunday. He said he was going fishing. I drove past the driveway that went down to the pond and left the car by the road and went back and walked in. I snuck up to that little cottage and I could see them through the window." She glanced at Warren. "I'm sorry, honey."

He patted her hand and said nothing.

"Then what?" said Zerk.

"I left. I didn't know what to do. I had to think about it. After a while I knew what I had to do. So I went back the next Sunday and I waited until Warren left and then I went in there. She was in her bed all drowsy from—from what they had been doing. And I went right up to her and told her who I was. I told her she had to leave him alone, that's all. And she laughed and said she couldn't, she wouldn't, that he was hers not mine. So I did the only thing I could do." Robin glanced at Warren, then at Zerk. She shrugged.

"What?" said Zerk. "What exactly did you do?"

"I injected her," she said.

"Huh?"

"I gave her an injection."

"With what?"

"VerSed."

"What's VerSed?" said Zerk.

"Benzodiazepine," said Robin. "We use it in the emergency room. When we need to put somebody under quickly. It causes rapid sedation. I just shot it into her shoulder. Then I dragged her down to the pond. I pushed her off the end of the dock. She sank right down. She was supposed to drown. I guess she did. Then I shoved one of the canoes in and tipped it over so it filled up with water." She shrugged. "I did the same thing to that awful man. I injected him."

"What man?" said Zerk.

"Dave Finn," I said. I looked at Robin. "Right?"

She nodded. "Of course. He was an awful man."

"Why'd you kill Finn?" I said.

"He knew about her and Warren. He called here for Warren, just the way that woman did. He just said he knew about him and her and that he had to talk to him. He said he had no phone but he left directions how to find where he was living. I erased the message and went there myself. He was surprised to see me. He was pretty drunk. I made him tell me what he knew. He knew about them. He thought Warren killed her. Said he figured it out and he was going to tell you." She turned and looked at me. "You, Brady. He said you were on your way. He expected you any minute. I didn't really believe that, but I couldn't wait to see if he was lying. So I had to inject him, too."

"Then you set his place afire," I said.

She nodded. "It was easy. He had this big electric space heater."

"You killed *two* people?" said Zerk.

"Both of them were going to tell," she said with a shrug.

"Wait," I said. "What about Jill Costello?"

"That little girl?" said Robin. "She called, left her name and a number. I knew it wasn't one of Warren's patients. I returned her call, said I was his wife, could I help her. At first she said no, it was personal, just have him call her. Then she was quiet for a minute, and then she said maybe she should talk to me. She told me how to get there. So I went right over. She said she figured I deserved to know about my husband. She thought I didn't know. She'd had a bad time with her husband, and I guess she figured we were in the same boat. She didn't seem to trust men very much. That woman had told her about Warren. I told her she mustn't tell anybody else, but she said she couldn't do that. She said she'd figured out that Warren killed her, you see. She said it was her duty to tell. I think she was going to tell you, Brady, just like that man in the trailer."

I looked at Zerk. "She stabbed her to death," I said.

Zerk looked at Robin. "Is that right?"

Robin nodded. "Yes. I didn't want her to suffer. She seemed like a nice person. But I had to do something. I made sure it was quick for her."

"Up under the rib cage into the heart," I said to Zerk. "The nurse knows her anatomy."

"I hated to do it," said Robin. "But I had to. My husband is a very eminent psychiatrist. I couldn't have these people ruining him." She looked from me to Zerk to Warren. "You understand that, don't you?"

35

I MET GLORIA for lunch at a little Greek restaurant in Newton—halfway between Wellesley and Boston, what we called "neutral territory"—on the Monday before Thanksgiving. We talked about our businesses and our sons and former mutual friends who had, over the years, tended to become either mine or hers, and we carefully avoided mention of the Wellesley house or the reasons why she had wanted me to buy it and then changed her mind.

Over coffee, she said, "William will be home from college for the holiday, you know."

"Sure. I expect we'll get together, watch some football."

"It's just going to be the three of us for dinner Thursday," she said.

I nodded. "That should be nice."

"Actually," she said, "I had expected my friend would be with us. But that's changed."

"Robert," I said. "The young lawyer."

"Richard," she said quickly.

I shrugged. "Sorry."

"He wanted to have children with me. Can you imagine?"

"Sure I can. I wanted to have children with you."

"That was twenty years ago, for heaven's sake."

"You should be flattered."

"His attentions flattered me. He's only thirty-four. Never married." She shook her head slowly. "I guess I need a grown-up."

I sipped my coffee and smiled. I knew when no comment was the best comment.

"Anyway," she said after a minute, "if you want to join us you're welcome to. There'll be plenty of food, and I think your sons would like it."

I nodded. "Thanks." I paused to light a cigarette.

Gloria made a face and waved at the smoke.

I said, "But I don't think so."

"Plans, huh?"

"Right." I nodded. "I've got some plans." I planned to sleep late, get a vat of chili a-bubbling on the stove, and watch the pro game on television while I waited for Terri to arrive. Billy and Joey would drive into town with their girlfriends, and we'd all sit around and eat chili and talk and listen to music and play cards. The boys would leave late, but Terri wouldn't leave until Sunday, and it would be a day well worth giving thanks for.

I paid the bill and walked Gloria to her car. I kissed her cheek. "Happy holiday, hon," I said. And I meant it.

"You too, Brady," she said. She seemed to mean it, too.

Zerk pleaded Robin McAllister not guilty, and they were holding her at Bridgewater State Hospital for ninety days' observation. He told me that if things worked the way he hoped, the case would never go to trial.

I talked to Warren on the phone a couple of times. He said he was carrying on his practice and visiting Robin every chance he could. He said the Victorian in Brookline seemed awfully big and empty without her, and depending on how it went with her, he might sell it and buy a condo and rent an office. He just didn't know what to do and wasn't quite ready to think about it yet.

We didn't talk fishing. The trout season was a long way off. Lots of things could change between November and April.

The New Hampshire medical examiner found VerSed in Mary Ellen's body. His counterpart in Massachusetts made the same discovery in Dave Finn.

Susan finally got to say good-bye to Mary Ellen. She buried her daughter in the Sleepy Hollow Cemetery in Concord the week after Thanksgiving. It was a sharp, clear, bitterly cold morning, and Susan was in a wheelchair bundled under a blanket. Her hair looked thin and lifeless, and the flesh had melted away so that her skin stretched taut over her fine bones and her eyes seemed too big for her face. Terri and I pushed the wheelchair. A great many Concordians were present, mostly friends and admirers of Susan. I doubted if many of them had known Mary Ellen.

Susan died in late February. The First Parish Church in Concord was packed for her service. She'd had many friends, and I was honored to count myself among them.

I sat with Terri in a pew near the back. She cried a little. I put my arm around her and she pushed her face against my shoulder. And she rode with me in the long slow line of cars to Sleepy Hollow, where they buried Susan between Mary Ellen and Charles.

Afterward Terri and I went to the Ames house on Monument Street. We had coffee and tried to discuss all the business the two of us had to finish up for Susan.

She cried again when she told me that the snowdrops

Susan had planted in September had just started to poke their pale green snouts through the mulch in the sunniest parts of the gardens out back. If Susan had lived just a few days longer she might have been able to see them. Terri thought this was infinitely sad. I thought so, too.